JULIANNA KEYES

OMNIFIC PUBLISHING
LOS ANGELES

Omnific Publishing
1901 Avenue of the Stars, 2nd floor
Los Angeles, CA 90067
www.omnificpublishing.com

First Omnific eBook edition, January 2015
First Omnific trade paperback edition, January 2015

The characters and events in this book are fictitious.
Any similarity to real persons, living or dead,
is coincidental and not intended by the author.

Library of Congress Cataloguing-in-Publication Data

Keyes, Julianna.
   Going the Distance / Julianna Keyes – 1st ed.
   ISBN: 978-1-623421-66-3
   1. Contemporary Romance — Fiction. 2. China — Fiction.
   3. Expatriate — Fiction. 4. Love — Fiction. I. Title

10 9 8 7 6 5 4 3 2 1

Cover Design by Micha Stone and Amy Brokaw
Interior Book Design by Coreen Montagna

Printed in the United States of America

For Erin Riley and Wang Xian—
Great teachers, better friends.
Thank you.

Chapter One

Olivia had spent enough time in the company of casually dangerous men to know one when he walked in. She kept up her pace on the treadmill and looked past her reflection in the mirror to watch the stranger approach Dale and Ritchie at the weight bench. She couldn't hear their brief conversation over the thud of her feet hitting the spinning rubber mat, but she could look.

She'd never seen him before, which was saying something. At present there couldn't be more than a dozen foreigners in the rural Chinese town of Lazhou (pronounced La-Joe, she'd been informed when she mispronounced it upon her arrival), and in her time there, she'd pretty much encountered them all. This one was tall, with close cropped curly brown hair and a sharp, intimidating jawline. He looked like the kind of man who rarely smiled, the kind you'd see lingering by the side of an Irish mob boss, maybe, waiting for the signal to take someone out back to be kneecapped. Or maybe Olivia had been spending too much time alone, and her imagination was taking itself to new heights.

He finished his brief conversation with Dale and Ritchie, then stripped off his heavy green jacket before approaching the empty treadmill on Olivia's right. She returned his curt nod of greeting, then, with his attention fixed on the buttons on the machine, she studied him some more. He was several inches taller than her, probably six feet, with broad shoulders and slim hips like a swimmer. He wore an old white T-shirt and black track pants, and set his speed to a full mile faster than hers.

Olivia shifted her gaze to the wall of mirrors, watching her feet fall in a rhythmic pattern. When she next looked up she found him staring at her reflection, waiting. "You the teacher?" he asked when he had her attention. He had an unnerving way of looking at people—or her, at least—and Olivia got the impression he not only knew the answer to that particular question, but several others. He wasn't doing anything outwardly menacing or unkind, but he didn't seem friendly, either.

"Yes," she said, pushing a strand of sweaty blond hair off her cheek. Her long ponytail swung between her shoulder blades like a pendulum, and she had the fleeting wish that she could use it to cover her chest as it bounced beneath her fitted tank top. His eyes hadn't dropped below her chin, but he still made her feel self-conscious. When he didn't say anything else, she gathered her breath and added, "I work at the kindergarten down the street. Are you working for Brant?"

He nodded. "Yeah. About a month now."

"I haven't seen you."

Another nod. "Jarek McLean."

It took her a second to realize he was introducing himself. "Jarek?" she echoed.

A faint smile. He probably got that all the time. "Polish mother. Irish father."

"Olivia Clarke. Both parents American."

The tiniest increase in the smile. "How far are you going?" His eyes finally left her face, glancing down at the display panel on the dated treadmill. She'd covered just over two miles, almost halfway to her goal.

"Five."

He nodded, then increased the speed on his machine. "Well then. Let's see if I can't catch you."

Thirty minutes later, Olivia stepped off the treadmill as Jarek did the same. They were both shiny with sweat, but he wasn't breathing nearly as hard despite having caught up to her as promised, even with her two-mile head start.

Olivia collected the towel from the bag she'd deposited next to the machine and mopped her forehead and the back of her neck. Jarek retrieved one from his coat pocket and copied her, though this time she couldn't help but notice his gaze flicker to her chest as she raised her arms. They hadn't spoken for the rest of the run, but he'd made occasional eye contact, silently taunting her as he gained invisible ground.

"You always run indoors?" he asked eventually.

"Um," Olivia said. The simple question actually had a semi-complicated answer, but she wasn't about to get into it. "Yes."

His eyes lingered on hers for a second, then shifted to the door where Ritchie and Dale had put on their coats, workout finished. "You okay, Ritchie?" Jarek asked when the smaller of the two men, and the only one Olivia particularly liked, winced as he put pressure on his right foot.

"Fine," Ritchie replied. "Just twisted it."

"We've got ice in the other trailer," Dale said, opening the door and letting the cold night air wash in. "Wrap it up, it'll be fine."

"Yeah," Ritchie said, unconvinced. "Do you mind walking Olivia home, Jarek? It's just fifteen min —"

"Oh, that's okay," Olivia interrupted quickly. She dabbed at her throat with the towel in order to keep her chest covered; the cold air was having an undesirable effect, entirely obvious through her green tank top. "It's not far. I can go alone."

"I'll take her," Jarek said, looking down at her, amused. "Don't worry about it."

She was vaguely annoyed to be discussed as though she were a child and not a twenty-seven-year-old woman, but she wasn't going to stand there arguing.

"Good night," Ritchie said. Dale echoed the sentiment as they stepped outside and finally closed the door.

Jarek followed Olivia to the small stretching area set up in the middle of the trailer and arranged a mat next to hers. They didn't speak as they stretched, and she got the distinct impression that he was just waiting to walk her home. "It's not necessary," she said. "Walking me back. It's a straight line. It's not that late, and there are lots of people out."

"It's fine," he answered. "I could use the exercise."

Olivia started to protest, then realized he was mocking her, as though outpacing her on the treadmill had required no effort at all. She shot him a peeved look, which he studiously ignored, and finished stretching. They wiped down the mats in silence, then put on their jackets and stepped outside, shutting off the lights and locking the door.

Brant Construction had set up a temporary headquarters near the site of their current job rebuilding a travel office that catered to foreigners interested in touring the lesser known parts of China. A year prior a flash flood had washed through the small city, destroying everything on its north side, and the restoration was still underway. The workers on the project were a mix of American and Chinese, and they had a small series of trailers that housed everything from a kitchen and lounge area to the small gym and work spaces. The workers lived in a newly constructed apartment building a five minute walk in the opposite direction of Olivia's decidedly less new building.

They wove through the trailers to the busy street that edged the north side of the town, where small shops and businesses had slowly emerged from the detritus that littered the area post-flood. Both street and sidewalk were clogged with cars and bicycles, motorcycles and pedestrians, and the scents of fried food and other, less identifiable things filled the air.

They barely spoke, but Olivia paused when Jarek stopped in front of a small handmade noodle shop, half-full at eight o'clock at night. She watched him through the icy puffs of breath hovering between them, mingling with the steam from the restaurant.

"You eat yet?" he asked.

Her stomach rumbled in response to the smells wafting out the open door. "No," she said. "I could eat."

Olivia had been in the restaurant before, a small, unadorned space with square tables topped with napkin holders, hot sauce, and containers of disposable chopsticks. The open kitchen allowed diners to watch chefs in white jackets stretch and cut noodles, flinging massive lengths of stretchy dough back and forth between hands.

Jarek trailed Olivia to the counter where she ordered clumsily in Mandarin; the cashier recognized her regular, mangled order, and when Jarek said, "I'll have the same," Olivia shrugged and held up two fingers. They snagged lukewarm bottles of Sprite from the fridge on the counter, then Jarek waved away Olivia's money and paid before leading her to a seat in the corner, his back to the wall. She shivered slightly as she sat down. The air inside was almost as cold as outside; they didn't have central heat in this part of the country, and jackets indoors were the norm.

"So," he said, twisting the caps off both glass bottles and sliding one her way.

She took a long drink and watched him watch her. "So."

"Talk."

"I beg your pardon?" She raised a fine blond eyebrow, bemused.

"Make conversation."

"You first."

"I paid for dinner."

She rolled her eyes. "I'll give you your fifty cents tomorrow."

Jarek laughed and looked away, downing half his drink. "How long have you been here?"

Olivia figured he already knew the answer, but told him anyway. "Three months."

"You like it?"

"Sometimes. You?"

He shrugged and shifted back as the server arrived to drop two steaming plates of fried noodles in front of them. Olivia plucked a set of chopsticks from the canister, slid them from their paper wrapper, and rubbed them together to remove slivers.

"I'm starving," she said, when it became obvious he considered his shrug an actual reply.

Jarek said nothing as he dug into his own dish. They ate in silence for a minute, then he studied her. "Why'd you come?"

She licked sauce from the corner of her mouth. "Because you asked me."

"To China."

"Oh." Olivia shifted her gaze to the tiny window that looked onto the street, motorbikes and foot traffic still whizzing past. She lifted a shoulder. "For a change."

"From what?"

She smiled, a faintly wistful twist of the lips as she recalled her parents' shocked stares when she'd announced she was moving to

China with little warning. Or perhaps there'd been an entire year of warning, and they'd just never credited her with the courage to step out on her own. "The usual," she said finally. "I wanted things to be different."

Outside, a taxi driver laid on the horn, a cyclist furiously rang a bell, and shrill, angry voices cut through the cold night air. "This is different," Jarek said. "Isn't it?"

"Yep."

"What are you running from?"

Olivia stilled in her chair. His posture was unaffected; anyone peering in would see only a semi-bored-looking man and a startled blond woman. It didn't really matter, since she was hardly a criminal, but still she asked, "Are you a cop?" as she plucked a large piece of green pepper from the noodles and set it aside. She put an unduly large amount of food into her mouth and stared back at him.

"No," he answered.

She eventually swallowed the noodles. "Were you? At any point?"

"No."

"Hmm." She strummed her fingers on the table and looked at him thoughtfully. "Something sociable, I see. Politician? Wedding planner?"

A ghost of a smile. "You got me."

She took another bite of food and chewed slowly.

He squinted at her. "You gonna answer?"

"No."

"Left at the altar."

Olivia blinked at the abrupt guess. "No."

"No?" He glanced pointedly at her left hand, the faint pale line that lingered at the base of her ring finger.

She kept her voice level, unconcerned. She was telling the truth, anyway. "No."

"Came home early one day to find him in bed with your sister."

"I don't have a sister."

"Brother?"

"Only child."

"Neighbor, then. An older woman."

"No affairs."

"Huh." Jarek polished off his drink and eyed her pile of castaway peppers. "What's wrong with green peppers?"

She scowled. She positively loathed them. "Everything. Don't get me started."

He took one and ate it. "Were you a teacher before? Back at home?"

She nodded. "Kindergarten."

"Where?"

"Michigan. Where are you from?"

He shrugged. "Hard to say anymore."

"Say it anyway." She worked with children for a living; he might enjoy asking questions, but she knew how to get answers, too.

He watched her as he chewed. "My brother's in Virginia. That's where I go when I'm not…elsewhere."

"Elsewhere where you're not a cop."

"That's right. So where's the ring?"

Olivia smiled thinly and pushed away her half-empty plate. She was full, and the reminder of the ring wasn't doing much to increase her appetite. "At the bottom of a lake somewhere. I'm done."

He gestured at the peppers with his chopsticks and transferred them to his own clean plate. "This is wasteful."

She watched him eat, then looked at her watch. Almost nine o'clock. "I should go."

Jarek finished the peppers and zipped up his jacket. "After you."

Olivia waved good night to the cashier and stepped into the busy street. There wasn't a lot of room to walk side by side but they did it anyway, Jarek's bicep bumping against hers, transferring his body heat.

"Why kindergarten?" he asked after a couple blocks.

She glanced up at him, then narrowly missed being run down by an older woman on a scooter. "I thought it seemed nice," she admitted. "Songs and games and crafts all day. And my mother was a teacher."

"You must like it, if you traveled halfway around the world to keep doing it."

"I do like it. But 'nice' isn't the word."

"No?"

"You should try teaching a class some time. Stand in front of thirty six-year-olds and try to hold their attention."

"I'll pass."

"What is it you do, exactly, Jarek? Construction?"

"Whatever they want," he said. He put a hand on her shoulder to steer her out of the way of a bicycle towing a large wagon full of garbage before stuffing his hands back into his pockets. "Some construction. Some electric. But…carpentry, mostly."

Olivia was surprised to get an actual answer from him. "What kind of carpenter lives 'elsewhere' and asks so many questions?" She stopped when they reached the front of her unimpressive apartment building. The five-story gray concrete façade radiated cold, and the large green door was ajar, eliminating the need for the keys she held in her palm.

"What kind of kindergarten teacher throws her ring in a lake?" Jarek leaned in and Olivia had the fleeting impression he might kiss her, then an equally fleeting and curious sense of disappointment when he reached past to tug open the door.

"One whose fiancé moved in with her parents," she replied, stepping over the ledge into the building. She gripped the edge of the door to tug it closed. "Thanks for walking me home."

Jarek held the door a second longer. "What are you doing tomorrow night?"

She looked at him, but it was hard to discern intent in the darkness. She could see little more than the slant of his cheekbones and the hard slash of his unsmiling mouth. He was intimidating, cold. Not handsome, but sexy, maybe. If you liked ruthless.

"Why?"

"I'll meet you here at seven. Let's run outside. Get out of that fucking trailer."

Olivia's brows lifted in surprise, but she was happy to be invited somewhere. Anywhere. "Okay."

Jarek let go of the door. "Okay. See you."

"Good night."

He didn't say anything else as he turned and walked away, hands stuffed into his pockets. Olivia was tempted to watch him go, trying to puzzle through his motives and intentions—assuming he had any—but didn't. Without him beside her the cold crept in, and she hustled up four flights of dark stairs to her apartment, grateful for the detour that ate up an hour of her four-hundred-and-fifty-ninth lonely night.

Jarek was in no rush to get home. He kept his head down, ignored the abundant stares, and made his way through the cold night, thinking about Olivia. It went against everything in him not to pry when he knew someone was holding something back, but he knew equally well that there was a time and place for demanding answers, and tonight hadn't been it.

Before today he'd glimpsed her from afar on a couple of occasions, just the glint of that long blond hair as she came or went from the gym trailer, and of course he'd heard the men at the site talking about her. There weren't many female foreigners in town, not slim blondes in their twenties with legs that went on for miles and breasts he'd struggled not to ogle as she'd run on that damn treadmill for far too long. She was prettier than Dale's lewd descriptions had implied; he'd gotten the impression she was the kind of blonde you saw in a men's magazine, but in reality she was more of the fitness model-type. Tan skin, big blue eyes, no makeup.

Jarek had spent much of his adult life working overseas; he'd been to more places than he could count, certainly more than he'd care to remember. Unlike the Dales of the world, he didn't take advantage of being a white male in a second or third world country; he didn't take advantage of young women desperate for a chance to marry into a better life. It made things difficult, on a personal level, especially when he was abroad for months or years at a time, or when he spent half an hour running next to someone whose hair smelled like apples every time her ponytail swung his way.

Despite the fact that she was American and of age, Olivia wasn't Jarek's type. She was too…wholesome. She'd no doubt grown up surrounded by cornfields, with a family that had a flagpole in the front yard and said grace before every meal. He preferred his women a little more jaded, the kind he met in dark bars and took home to dark rooms, the kind who didn't expect him to be there in the morning, the kind he didn't disappoint. He didn't do second dates; hell, he didn't do first dates. They got everything they needed in the span of a few hours, and then everybody moved on. That was how he liked it.

If it hadn't been for that faint white line on her finger and the strange sadness in her smile, he wouldn't have asked her to meet him tomorrow night. He may have left his old line of work behind, but he couldn't shake it completely. If someone had a secret, he needed to know what it was. And Olivia Clarke had a secret.

"Back already?"

Jarek turned at the sound of Dale's faintly southern drawl. Pushing forty, he was a beefy guy with a dutiful wife and a couple of children back at home, family he promptly put out of his mind when he was out of the country. Jarek hadn't known him long, but he didn't like him. He'd already assessed that the guy was harmless, but he was an asshole — the kind of guy who used his hands instead of his words to describe women. He'd given Olivia an hourglass shape with heavy emphasis on the curves.

"Yeah."

They walked the remaining minute to the apartment building that housed the workers, a new construction that still smelled like paint and metal. They each had their own apartment, and Jarek lived across the hall from Dale. They stepped into the elevator and Dale looked over meaningfully. "Thought you'd be gone longer," he remarked, prying.

Jarek shook his head. "Nope."

"Not your type?"

"Not interested."

"Bullshit."

Jarek glanced at him as the doors opened on the fifth floor. "She your type?"

Dale laughed, cheeks red from the beer he'd chugged as soon as he finished working out. "I already tried, man."

"No luck?"

"Just takes some work, I guess."

Jarek reached his apartment and stepped inside. "See you tomorrow."

"Night."

He closed and locked the door, then kicked off his sneakers and dropped his coat on a chair before walking into the bathroom to strip out of his sticky clothes. He turned on the hot water and climbed into the shower, doing his best to keep Olivia out of his thoughts. He'd only been in China four weeks; prior to that he'd stayed with his brother in Virginia for two months. He'd hooked up twice while he was there, and this certainly wasn't the first time he'd gone more than a month without sex. But standing here now, with the hot water sluicing down his chest, he could only see Olivia on the treadmill, sweat trickling between her slightly bouncing breasts.

He washed his hair and willed away the image, but then imaginary Olivia smiled at him, and he saw her nipples harden when Dale opened the trailer door, the ones she'd tried to hide behind her towel. He smelled her hair and the faint tang of her sweat, then he gave up the fight and reached between his legs, determined to get her out of his head.

"**F**ish *likes to swim, the fish likes to swim. The fish can swim all day long, the fish likes to swim!*"

A chorus of high-pitched *swims!* rang out, and Olivia smiled at the sea of giddy six-year-old faces staring back. "Good job, everybody. Take a seat, please." Familiar with the start of class song and dance routine, the kids sat down, gazing at Olivia expectantly. "You're getting too good at that one," she said, popping the disc from the ancient CD player and sliding it into its case. "It might be time for a new song."

No response, which was expected. To date their vocabulary spanned the alphabet (sort of), the numbers one through ten, a variety of fruits and vegetables, a few methods of transportation, and classroom items.

"Liv, Liv," a little girl in the front row whispered loudly. "Okay. Okay. Me. Okay?" Her tiny hand was extended, fingers opening and closing, desperate to hold the CD.

Olivia shot her a smile. "I've got it this time, Rose. Thank you." All of the students at the school had English names, as did most of the teachers. It was common practice for people to have both a Chinese name and an English name, and the way the names were picked varied. Some parents chose the name, some asked the teachers to do the choosing. Some students were named after popular book and movie characters (Nemo, Harry Potter), but most had something simple and easy to pronounce. The school teemed with Johns and Leos and Sunnys and Judys.

Rose, understanding "thank you" and the polite rejection, sat back, dejected, with an obedient, "You're welcome." Rose had abundant amounts of energy, good intentions, and little to no self-control. After a split second to absorb the setback, she proceeded to tie her own shoelaces together.

Olivia wiped her hands on her jeans and picked up the stack of well-worn flashcards she'd inherited when she'd taken over the classroom upon her arrival in January. The only class in the school with a foreign teacher, the Australian woman who'd been teaching there since September had opted not to return after the holidays, leaving the school with a vacancy and Olivia with the opportunity to hop on a plane with little to no preparation for life abroad.

"Okay, everyone," she began. "Today we're going to learn some new words. Are you ready?"

Half the kids heartily chorused, "Ready!" as they'd purportedly learned the year prior, but half just stared back, perplexed. Though she'd turned up for every day of work since she'd started, a good number of students, teachers and parents still stared at Olivia as though it were her first day all over again. And like she had a second head.

"Good enough," she said, holding up the first flashcard. "Who knows what this is?" It was a chicken, which she had to assume was the word they all cried in Mandarin. "That's probably right. In English we say 'chicken.'" She paused, but only one kid started to try to repeat the word, and he quickly gave up when no one else moved. "Come on, guys. It's been three months. Repeat after me, please. *Chicken.*"

"Chicken," Rose parroted politely.

"Thank you, Rose," Olivia said. "That was excellent. For that you get a sticker." She approached the small box she kept on her desk, and extracted a shiny heart sticker. Immediately the students sat up and took notice. Rose beamed and held out the back of her hand so Olivia could affix her prize.

Garbled shouts that sounded vaguely like "chicken" mixed with a bunch of expletives rang out. "Too late!" Olivia interrupted, holding up a hand. "Rose repeated it first, so she's the only one getting a sticker." She wasn't above bribery, but she didn't have that many stickers left, either. "Now please repeat after me: chicken."

"Chicken!" they chorused.

"Excellent. What sound does a chicken make?"

Dead silence.

"Does a chicken meow?" Olivia meowed, and the kids cackled and cried, "No!"

"Does a chicken moo?" Olivia mooed, and they killed themselves laughing.

"No?" she asked, scratching her head. "What sound does a chicken make?"

The room filled with thirty clucking chickens, complete with arm flapping.

"Ohh!" she exclaimed. "I think you're right. Chickens cluck!" She copied the sounds and arm movements, and the kids giggled helplessly. "Well. I think you're familiar with chickens. Are you ready to learn the next word?"

"Ready!" Rose shouted.

"READY!" everyone else hollered, eyes on the sticker box.

Olivia held up the next card. "This is a gorilla…"

Two and a half hours later, Olivia was finally alone in the classroom. The kids were shuttled off to eat in the cafeteria where the school employed several older women to feed and control them. She'd made the mistake of venturing into the cafeteria during mealtime once, and the combined cries of discovery, shock, and horror had her backing out, gesturing guiltily to the women minding them. Later that night she'd found a tiny prawn in the back pocket of her jeans.

Across the courtyard Olivia could hear the Chinese teachers laughing in an empty classroom as they ate and played mah-jongg, a tile game she'd learned had nothing in common with the simple version she'd played online a couple of times. She'd been invited to play on her first day, then promptly cast out of the game when it became obvious she had no idea what she was doing.

A few of the teachers spoke a little English, but those that did were too shy to try, so Olivia was treated like a fragile princess, waved to from afar but never approached. Or, more often, ignored. As the only foreign teacher at the school, she'd been shocked to learn she made six times more than the Chinese teachers for doing half the work, and many understandably resented her for it. So while people were polite, they were distant, and in a country with a population of a billion, Olivia felt, for all intents and purposes, alone.

She sighed and continued to color in the alphabet chart she'd been making. The school had been repaired after the flood, but the classes were woefully lacking in visual aids and supplies — it had taken the full three months of her tenure to get her hands on the flashcards she'd used this morning. She lacked pretty much any artistic talent, but with time on her hands, Olivia had taken to making up her own materials. She carefully filled in the letter J with a red marker, then ate a forkful of the instant noodles she'd had for lunch forty-eight times since arriving.

Jarek had been distracted all day. He'd spent the morning working alone in the carpentry trailer, his preferred activity, but after he'd mis-measured the same piece of wood three times, he'd given up and tracked down Ritchie, helping him mix and pour concrete for two hours. Every now and then he'd glance over at the other guy, who was undoubtedly scribbling something on the notepad he kept in his coat pocket. It was uncanny how much Ritchie resembled a scrawny Clark Kent, right down to the firmly gelled dark hair and black-rimmed glasses. They didn't have much in common, but he talked less than Dale, and that was all Jarek was really looking for.

He took a break to eat one of the leftover steamed buns that had been brought in for lunch, and gave up trying to identify the mystery meat inside. He wasn't a picky eater, never had been. Unlike Olivia, with her strange aversion to the humble green pepper. Fuck. There he went again. He couldn't keep her name out of his head, her face from his thoughts. He'd woken up this morning with a hard-on that wouldn't quit, and found himself jerking off for the second time in twelve hours, like he was a teenager. And then, like a teenager, he'd been unable to focus on anything all day, thinking about tonight, when all they were going to do was bundle up in winter wear and run side by side for an hour.

"How'd you meet Olivia?" he asked Ritchie before he could stop himself. The younger man selected a bun and took a bite, brown filling dripping down his chin.

"Um…Shoot. Sorry. One second." He looked away to clean himself up, then turned back. "Olivia. I met her in town a couple months ago. You know Jolly Mart? The grocery store?"

Jarek shook his head, and Ritchie shrugged. "Well, anyway, we both happened to be there, and she said hi."

"She approached you?"

"Yeah. I'd never seen her before, which was strange, since she kind of stands out, but…Anyway, she'd been here a month and hadn't met anyone and was pretty bored, so I told her we had a gym and whatever and she could come by, and she did."

"You know much about her?"

"A bit. Like, she's a kindergarten teacher at the school down the street and isn't really sure she likes it here."

Jarek nodded and finished the bun. He had to force himself not to keep asking questions; his previous line of work wasn't a secret, but he didn't like to get into it if he could help it. Too bad he was a nosy bastard, and where Olivia was concerned, he couldn't stop the steady stream of questions running through his head. Or the lewd pictures that kept popping up at the most inconvenient moments. Like now. Which made him feel like a dick, since the woman was obviously lost and lonely, and sad, and all he could think about were the hundred and one ways he wanted to fuck her, even though she wasn't his type and would likely expect more from him than he wanted to give.

That night he was deliberately late arriving at her apartment. He wanted to see if she was the kind of woman who'd tap her watch and point out his tardiness, or the kind that would smile, just grateful that he'd turned up. Knowing what he did about her loneliness, Jarek figured Olivia would fall into the latter category. And he kind of hoped she would smile, not just so he could see it to satisfy some perverse sort of self-torture, but so he could confirm that she'd be the clingy type, and turn these lustful feelings down to a simmer instead of a rolling boil.

But when he showed up outside her seedy-looking apartment building, she wasn't waiting out front, and he didn't know her buzzer number. Not that the panel of buttons next to the now-locked green door was actually numbered. Jarek glanced at his watch and looked around: seven ten. He knew people, and he was pretty damn confident a kindergarten teacher didn't make a habit of standing up her dates.

He rubbed his hands together and peered up and down the street in case she was nearby, but there was no blond hair to be seen. He blew on his fingers, his breath coming out in thick white bursts.

Lazhou was freezing when the sun went down, and still not much warmer during the day. He was used to uncomfortable environments, but all this cold was really fucking frustrating.

"Hey."

Jarek stepped away from the green door as it swung open and Olivia emerged, clad in a red down jacket, running pants and sneakers. Her hair was hidden beneath a bright blue wool hat and her expression was neutral. He didn't bother to hide his once-over, and she didn't pretend not to notice.

"I saw you coming down the street," she said, explaining her timing. "It was too cold to wait outside. It's actually not much warmer inside, but at least I don't feel like a freak show. Sort of. Anyway, ready?"

Jarek blinked, unprepared for the sudden slew of words. He was pretty sure no one had said that much to him all day. He cleared his throat. "Yeah, this way. There's a path by the water. Should be empty now."

"Sure. I know it."

The street and sidewalk were too crowded to run, so they strode briskly through the throng of people and vehicles, Olivia standing out in her colorful gear, Jarek drawing attention because he was the man with her. If she noticed the looks it didn't show, so she didn't catch him staring at her ass and legs in the tight black pants. They crossed a second street, passed a row of tiny trees planted in large urns, and emerged onto the broad paved path that lined the murky river.

They started to run. Olivia was in shape, but Jarek still slowed his pace to match hers, catching the occasional glimpse of her face when they passed beneath a lamp post. The path was almost completely empty given the dark and the cold, and they ran quietly for almost twenty minutes, just their twin breaths and even footsteps to keep them company.

"Why'd your fiancé move in with your parents?" Jarek asked abruptly.

Olivia glanced over at him, her expression curiously bland. "He didn't want to live with me anymore."

"His own parents?"

"Dead."

"You close with your parents?"

A split second pause. "Yes."

"But?"

She shot him a small smile. "But now I live in China. How old are you?"

He wasn't prepared for the question, as simple as it was, but reasoned there was no harm in answering. He figured her for mid to late twenties if she'd gone to college, gotten a degree, and taught for a couple of years in the States. His own age shouldn't scare her off, though perhaps he should wish it would. "Thirty-four."

"You ask more questions than my students."

He smiled, hoping to lower her guard. She didn't look angry, though she didn't smile back. She might be lonely, but she wasn't clingy, either. "Guilty."

"And you're not a cop."

"You have a thing against cops?"

She turned and jogged backward so she could face him. "What are you, then?"

"A carpenter. A laborer. Whatever Brant asks."

He had to slow so he wouldn't run into her, but kept just a foot of space between them. He could tell the closeness unnerved her, but didn't let up. She could turn around if it made her too uncomfortable. He let his eyes drift down her body for a second, taking in her flushed cheeks, parted lips, torso covered by that damn quilted jacket. He wanted to run outside to get away from the trailer, like he'd said, but also to get away from Dale's knowing looks and obvious eavesdropping. He'd wanted to get her alone.

She turned around and gave him her back. "If you say so."

"You don't believe me?" He moved alongside her, adjusting his black knit hat.

"I believe you."

"So if he didn't leave you for another woman…"

She coughed out a startled laugh. "Jesus!"

"What?"

"You're a gossip, is that it? You want to take this back and tell the boys at work?"

"I have to contribute something to our quilting circle discussions."

Olivia stopped suddenly, the light from a flickering lamp casting shadows under her eyes. "Everyone talks about me at the school. They talk about me in the street and in the shops and in the restaurants. And it's one thing if I can't understand it, but it's different when I can. I don't want anything from you, Jarek. Just company on this run. And I don't want to be the subject of anybody's discussion. Is that too much to ask?"

He stepped close and she shifted back. He didn't press the issue. "There's no quilting circle, Olivia."

"He didn't like me anymore, and if I feel the sudden urge to pour out my heart, I'll call, okay?"

He held up his hands as though he were harmless, as though those hands hadn't inflicted more damage on more people than she could ever imagine. "I'll wait for your call."

She resumed running, her breath coming out erratically. She was doing a noble job of keeping her face blank, but he could tell she was upset. He wondered if the boyfriend had spread rumors about her; Jarek was a dick, but he didn't do shit like that, either.

"Tell me something about yourself," she said, eyes on the path in front of them.

Jarek ran close enough to brush their arms together. She glanced at him but didn't move away. "I like green peppers."

"That's the best you can do?"

People rarely called him on his shit, and he couldn't help but smile. A glossary of unpleasant terms could be used to describe him: daunting, menacing, asshole. He'd heard them all. His brows were always pulled together like he was unhappy, and his mouth was stuck in a perpetual scowl. It worked for him, and it kept people at bay. But she didn't seem to care. "What do you want to hear?"

She pursed her lips. "Nothing, maybe."

He nudged her again. "Nothing?"

"You could tell me why you were late on purpose."

He almost stopped in his tracks, only his forward momentum kept him moving. "Come again?"

"Don't pretend you didn't hear me. I saw you taking your time on the street, looking at your watch. What was the point? Did you change your mind?"

He appreciated honesty, even when it was entirely unexpected, so he told her the truth: "I wanted to see how you'd react."

"Yeah?"

"I wanted to see if you'd flip out."

"What would that prove?"

Well. He'd thought it would tell him something, but he was fast learning he didn't know shit about this woman. "It didn't prove anything except that your apartment faces northeast." When she didn't say anything, he continued, "Why'd you come out, then, if it bothered you?"

"Because I didn't have anybody else to run with, and it's too dark to go alone."

"Better than nothing, huh?"

Now she gave him the once-over. "I thought so."

"Ouch."

She shrugged and he touched her elbow to stop her. She turned to look at him, breath coming quickly. God help him, she might be the prettiest woman he'd ever seen.

"Okay," he heard himself say. "I'm sorry. Let's start over. I don't have anyone to run with, either."

"You don't need anyone."

That was true; he didn't. But he wanted someone. He wanted her. "I wanted the company, too."

"Then give me something better than you like green peppers."

He ran a hand across his jaw like he was thinking. "I've been look-ing at your ass in those pants all night. And I'm sorry. I'm not coming on to you, I just couldn't help it." He was a liar; he was totally com-ing on to her, with the apology bullshit and the too-close running. But he wasn't going to do anything about it, and not because she was clingy as he'd feared, but because he didn't know what the fuck she would do to him.

"All right," she said. "Let's keep going."

They started moving again. "That's it?" he asked.

"What more do you want?"

"Nothing," he said, but it was a lie.

By the time they finished the route they'd exchanged no more than six words, but Jarek had run close enough that their breath mingled, that he'd touched her arm with his, her thigh with his knuckles. He couldn't figure her out. He'd had one proper girlfriend in his entire life, and that had ended when he was twenty-one. He'd made a life out of understanding people, reading body language and nonverbal cues, but even when Olivia spelled things out, he couldn't get a handle on her. Which was precisely why, even though he wanted nothing more than to quite literally get a hand on her, he wouldn't.

They reached the end of the path and doubled back, exiting early at his urging to walk down a busy shopping street with no shortage of food vendors. Jarek bought them both lamb skewers and bottles of something that purported to be orange juice, but tasted like poison.

"You like this?" he asked, gesturing with his bottle when Olivia continued to drink hers without complaint.

She looked at him in surprise. "No," she said. "It's disgusting, I'm just really thirsty. Plus these are unexpectedly spicy." She held up a skewer and shot him a smile. She had a very wide smile, he decided. It showed too many teeth. It should have made her look really happy, but it didn't. It just looked…polite.

"You still pissed about earlier?" He bit into his last piece of lamb and looked down at her.

"No." She didn't return the look, was, instead, staring into a shop selling thousands of counterfeit DVDs.

"You need to go shopping?"

"Always with the questions, Jarek." Olivia tossed her empty wooden skewers into a trash can and he did the same, trailing her into the store. The woman standing at the ancient cash register greeted her with a smile but the look of surprise was reserved for Jarek; Olivia was a regular here, then.

He started to ask if she had a big DVD collection, then stopped himself. "You must watch a lot of movies."

"Mmhmm." She fingered through a box of colorful titles, just flimsy cardboard faces inside cellophane. He stopped her when she came to an old Julia Roberts movie, that famous smile gracing the cover.

"That's you," Jarek said.

She frowned up at him. "What?"

"The smile. The teeth. That's you."

"That's Julia Roberts."

"You've never heard that before?"

She laughed. "No. That smile makes her famous."

"I wasn't complaining."

"Well. It's nice to hear you make an assertive statement for once."

He laughed and went outside to wait for her, passing off his half-full juice bottle to a kid collecting recyclables. Olivia exited a few minutes later, toting a small green bag full of illegal materials.

"So you're a criminal," he observed, walking beside her as they headed to her apartment.

"Here to corrupt young minds."

"I don't think you could corrupt anybody." He glanced down to watch the emotions play across her face, too quick and varied to identify.

"No," she agreed. "I don't think I could."

They stopped outside her apartment, much as they had last night, only this time the green door was closed. Olivia turned to unlock it, and Jarek leaned in to pull it open, getting close enough to smell her shampoo, telling himself it was the last time. She was an anomaly, a question without answers, and he always needed answers. That was the last thought he had before she kissed him.

He kissed her back for ten seconds. He was too much of a dick-head to stop any sooner, and too self-serving to stop any later. She had a hand on his shoulder as she stood on her toes to reach him, and he took one step forward to press her into the wall as he kissed her back. And then he pulled away, breathing hard.

"I'm not what you're looking for," he said. He meant it in a nice way, but it didn't sound nice. And he knew it was too dark for her to see his face, to see that he meant it nicely, not that anyone had ever looked at his face and considered it *nice*. Then, before he could do something even nice*r*, he turned and strode off down the street without looking back.

Chapter Three

"Okay, everybody, one more time to prove to me that you really, *really* know this…" Olivia pointed to the three shapes she'd drawn on the board and mouthed the words as the kids enthusiastically screeched their names: "CIRCLE! SQUARE! TRIANGLE!"

"Excellent! I'm convinced. Does everybody understand the assignment?" They didn't understand half the words in that sentence, but they did know "understand," and they'd been staring at the crayons and blank paper on their desks for the better part of five minutes and were desperate to touch them.

"YES!" they cried.

"All right, then. You can draw any picture you want, but you need to use at least three circles, three squares, and three triangles. Begin!" Olivia realized she was still holding up three fingers, and tucked her chilly hand in her pocket to warm up. Since January, she'd become addicted to speaking with her hands, nearly poking out her eye on several occasions. The Chinese used hand signals to communicate numbers one through ten, and she'd studiously learned them in her first week, facilitating her visits to the local market where she couldn't always understand the quoted prices.

She strolled around the room to study the kids' work, expecting to see a riot of shapes and colors, but instead found almost unanimously neat rows of circles, squares and triangles. Three of each. No pictures.

"Guys!" She held up a hand to interrupt their not-so-creative processes. "I don't want you to just draw three circles. I want you to draw a *picture*." She was a terrible artist, but Olivia did her best to draw a house on the whiteboard, naming the square base, triangle roof, and circular sun as she did so. "See? Make a picture. Do you understand?"

"YES!" They got back to work, this time somewhat less certainly. Olivia wound her way through the tiny maze of tables, each holding five students, most of whom were now merely coloring in their shapes.

"Liv?" Olivia made her way over to Rose, who had drawn her best approximation of a snowman standing next to three triangular trees. She sighed. It was an imitation of the holiday picture that was taped to one of the windows, left over from the Australian teacher's stint. But at least it was a picture.

"Good job, Rose." Olivia smiled and patted her shoulder, and Rose looked relieved. Olivia paused next to Davy, a quiet, strange boy being raised by grandparents who dressed him in approximately seven layers of clothing to compensate for the chilly weather. The poor kid could barely walk, and his arms hadn't touched his sides since November.

Davy's artwork was more abstract than Olivia had intended, but he was deeply focused, for once enjoying his time in class. She didn't know a lot about art, but his piece was rather impressive for a boy who still wrote half his English name backward.

She checked on the rest of the kids, made a few suggestions and encouraging remarks, and glanced at the clock. Five minutes until the three o'clock bell rang and classes let out for the day. Olivia sat at her desk and skimmed the next day's lesson plan, just as she'd done when she'd arrived that morning, and again at lunch. She'd only brought three books with her to China, and she'd burned through them in two days. Lazhou didn't appear to have a library, though they did have a massive bookstore, and she planned to head there after work, determined to buy something to help pass the time.

It had been two days since she'd kissed Jarek, two days since he'd backed away as though she'd burned him, and said he wasn't what she was looking for. The rejection had stung, but more than anything, she was embarrassed. A tiny bit humiliated. The first man in over a year whom she'd wanted to kiss had not wanted her to kiss him. She felt like an over-aggressive man-eater, though she had little doubt he knew how to protect himself.

Just the memory of the encounter made her cheeks flame, and she waved good-bye to the kids when the bell rang, still lost in her mortifying memories. He'd kissed her back, that much she knew. The actual moment when she decided to kiss him was a blur, but the kiss itself was starkly clear, frozen in her memory the way things you'd rather forget tended to be. His cheeks had been cold but his mouth had been warm, his lips surprisingly soft given his terminally stern countenance. He'd made a quiet, pained sound as they'd kissed, and Olivia had put a hand on his shoulder to get closer, feeling his reassuring strength under her fingers. She'd been so damn lonely, and there was something about him that she wanted. Maybe it was the fact that he wasn't intimidated or cowed by her. Or maybe it was just the way he was completely different from Chris, the boyfriend — then fiancé — she'd been with for ten years.

She dropped her head into her hands and willed away the thoughts. She hadn't found the courage to return to the gym, though she desperately wanted to get back on the treadmill, get back into the company of people who at least understood what she was saying, even if they didn't like it. As it was, she'd made a fool out of herself and would wait until that shame had burned away before showing her face at the construction site again. Somehow she doubted he'd told the members of his "quilting circle" about her unrequited passion, but the possibility had her shaking her head anyway.

"O-liv-ya?"

She jerked upright to find Davy still sitting at his desk, then had the fleeting thought that he was stuck there, as round and cumbersome as the Michelin man. "Sorry, Davy!" she exclaimed, jumping to her feet. "I didn't realize you were still there. Don't you need to go home?"

He looked at her with big, solemn eyes and nodded, glancing anxiously at his paper as she approached. The abstract print was carefully colored and shaded in a riot of blues and greens and yellows. It was actually incredibly beautiful. Strange, soulful little Davy was an artist, in a roomful of kids who'd already had their creative instincts scrubbed away.

"Davy," Olivia said, taking the tiny seat next to him. "This is very, very good." He gestured at the wall and said something in Mandarin that she couldn't understand, but could guess at. "You want to hang your picture?" she guessed, taking the page and standing to hold it next to the whiteboard.

He nodded cautiously.

"What a great idea." She found one of the plastic sleeves she used to preserve her few handmade teaching materials, and tucked the paper inside, using a thumb tack to pin it to the wall next to the board. "How's that?"

Davy shot her a tentative smile, then methodically put his eight crayons back in their tiny box and tucked it into his backpack before heading for the door. He paused. "Thank you," he mumbled into one of his many sweaters.

Davy disappeared across the courtyard, trailing after a dozen other stragglers, all toting the same bright blue pack that bore the school's logo. Over the excited laughs and shouts of children she could hear Honor, the Chinese teacher the next class over, alternately calling good-bye and scolding kids for doing something or other they had been forbidden to do.

Honor was twenty-five, slim and cute, though not "beautiful" by Chinese standards—or so Olivia had been told on her first day, both by Honor and another teacher. It was her first exposure to the brutally honest assessment Chinese girls inflicted on themselves and others: too fat, too tall, too short, eyes too small, ears too big. Olivia had winced and assured Honor that she was indeed pretty, but the teacher had waved away her compliments, and Olivia wasn't sure if she didn't understand or just didn't believe her.

Now she went to the classroom door and stood just outside, a few feet away from Honor. She glanced over and smiled. Honor smiled back. "Hello, Olivia."

"Hi, Honor. How was your class?"

"Fine, thank you." She took in Olivia's hands, still jammed in her pockets. "Are you cold?"

"Yes. Pretty much always."

"It will be warm soon."

"I hope so." Even today, a bright and sunny day in mid-March, it was still cold enough to warrant a jacket, though maybe she could take off one of her underlayers.

"What will you do tonight?" Honor asked.

Olivia glance over, surprised. "I want to go to the bookstore," she said. "Then…home, I guess."

"To your apartment?"

"Yes."

"Alone?"

Ha. "Yes." *Always.* "What will you do?"

Honor picked imaginary lint off her green dress, somehow managing to look remarkably slim despite wearing a sweater and thick tights beneath it. "I will have dinner with my friends."

"That sounds nice." Olivia desperately wanted to be invited, and for a second she thought Honor might ask. Then Mary, one of the Chinese teachers who had booted Olivia out of the mah-jongg party, approached. She gave Olivia a cursory smile, then started up a loud, speedy conversation with Honor in Mandarin.

Olivia sighed and collected her things.

On Thursday she bumped into Ritchie at the outdoor market. She wasn't much of a chef, but she was getting tired of the limited number of items she could order unassisted at the noodle shop, and cooking at home helped pass the time.

"Hey, Olivia," Ritchie said, approaching from behind.

She glanced over her shoulder as she bought a plastic bag of sliced beef—she was pretty sure it was beef—and smiled. "Hey."

"Planning a feast?"

"Party of one. What are you up to?"

"Not much. Just getting some exercise."

"How's your ankle?"

"It's okay. I'll live."

"You're tough."

Ritchie scoffed and adjusted his glasses. "Yeah." They walked together as Olivia shopped, taking her time so she'd get home later. After a few minutes Ritchie interrupted her thoughts, asking, "How do you do it?"

She paused as she rifled through a box of ginger. "Do what?"

"Ignore everybody."

She gave up the hunt and looked at him, surprised. "What?"

He gestured at the openly staring fellow shoppers. They were the only two white people in the crowded market, and though several of the vendors were no longer interested in Olivia's visits, there were many people who still studied her. She felt her cheeks redden, but he would never know the real reason she had learned to ignore the stares and comments, a full year before she'd ever arrived in China.

"Practice," she said, with a shrug that belied the sadness in the word.

He seemed to buy it, because it was a few more minutes before he asked, "Why haven't you been at the gym?"

For lack of anything better to do, Olivia kept a pretty regular routine, turning up around seven o'clock in the evening on Mondays, Wednesdays and Fridays, then one afternoon on the weekend. She felt bad lying to Ritchie twice in a row, but wasn't about to tell him she'd come on to Jarek and been soundly rejected. She made up a story about feeling a cold coming on, citing it as one of the hazards of working in a school, and he didn't question her. "Do you want to come over for dinner?" she asked as penance. "I'm not much of a cook, but…"

"Sure," Ritchie said quickly. "I could use a change of scenery." They'd hung out infrequently since meeting in February; Olivia thought he was nervous around women and, being of the female persuasion, she probably set him on edge. He was good looking, if a bit on the small side, jittery and anxious in a way that made her want to reassure him the way she would a younger brother, if she had any siblings.

They stopped at a small stand so Ritchie could buy drinks for dinner, the sun rapidly setting now, turning the sky pink and orange. Olivia waited at the curb, fiddling in her pocket for her keys, and tuned out the noise pollution just as she'd become so attuned to ignoring everything else. Unfortunately this time she ignored the rapid pinging of a bell, the last warning she had before one of the large bicycle wagons used to collect trash crashed into her, sending her sprawling forward onto her hands and knees.

"Olivia!" Ritchie shouted, darting out to help her up, collecting her scattered purchases. "Are you okay?"

In the street they saw the tipped wagon, one of the back wheels spinning to a stop a few feet away. Evidently it had come loose and the worker had lost control, the heavy wooden wagon toppling onto Olivia's back. If there was any blessing to be found, it was that the thing was empty, so while she might be covered in scrapes and bruises tomorrow, she wasn't covered in garbage.

"I'm okay." She winced, waving away the onlookers. The worker gestured and rambled apologetically, and Olivia shot him a smile, assuring him she understood it was an accident. "No problem," she said in Mandarin, earning a relieved look. "Let's just go."

Ritchie carried her bag back to her apartment where she popped a few painkillers and promised him she didn't need a doctor. She'd had to go to the hospital for a physical as a part of her visa requirement, and wasn't anxious to return to the cold concrete structure with even colder nurses and doctors muttering things she couldn't understand. She'd played sports growing up and knew when she was truly hurt and when she just needed rest, ice, and anti-inflammatories.

Even still, he ordered her to sit at the tiny dining room table to wait while he made a surprisingly tasty stir-fry, then kept her company for a couple of hours, asking questions about her job. It wasn't until long after Ritchie had left and she'd eased carefully into bed that Olivia realized *his* questions hadn't bothered her in the least.

It was midafternoon when Jarek entered the gym trailer on Saturday. He shook the rain from his hair and wiped his sneakers on the mat inside the door, nodding at Ritchie, who was doing sit-ups on one of the mats. He didn't bother with stretching, just got on one of the two empty treadmills, and turned the speed up higher than was comfortable. He'd come in every night this week, and Olivia hadn't turned up. He still wasn't sure what he'd say or do if she did show, just that he wanted to see her. He'd turned down women before; some had taken it gracefully, some had been angry, but never before had he walked away from one he'd wanted. And it killed him that he'd walked away because she made him nervous. A kindergarten teacher versus a former interrogator, and he was the one on edge. Fuck.

He increased the speed so he had to focus on running and nothing but, watching his feet slam onto the racing rubber mat, the old machine shaking. Already his shirt was sticky with sweat; it trickled down his temples, plastered his hair to his head. He kept up the brutal pace for thirty minutes, until both the machine and his legs were ready to give up, and finally climbed off. He wiped his face and neck with a towel, cleaned up the treadmill, and joined Ritchie on the mats to stretch.

"Quiet in here lately," he observed, just for the hell of it.

"Yeah," Ritchie said. "Dale's been sick."

"I noticed."

"Guess it's going around."

Jarek wasn't really one for small talk, but he went with it anyway. "Yeah? I hadn't noticed."

"Plus he said he didn't really have motivation for coming in right now." The younger man looked a little perturbed.

"What does that mean?"

"You know," he said awkwardly, waving vaguely at the machines. "Because Olivia's not here. Running."

"Oh yeah," Jarek replied, as though only just noticing her absence. "Wonder why that is."

"She's hurt, probably."

He looked over sharply. She'd told Ritchie he'd turned her down? He hadn't known they were that close. "What'd she say happened?"

"She didn't have to say anything. I saw."

"You were there?"

"Yeah. We were coming home from the market, and the garbage wagon thing crashed right into her. She said she was fine and refused to see a doctor, but I'm sure she's got bruises."

Something that felt an alarming lot like relief and concern coursed through him. "When was this?"

"Couple days ago."

"You seen her since?"

"I called her. She said she was fine. She went to work. If she can make it up and down four flights of stairs, she must be okay."

"Yeah. It's probably nothing." Except Jarek had seen those wagons; their shoddy wooden walls came up to his shoulders. They weren't light, and Olivia might be fit, but she wasn't that strong. And maybe he wanted an excuse to see her.

He talked himself in and out of going until eight o'clock. By then the rain hadn't let up, he'd finished some dreadful science fiction novel abandoned by one of the other workers, read two pages of a tattered Hardy Boys book he was way too old for, and the only thing on television he understood was the occasional European pop song on MTV Asia.

He should probably call, but he didn't have her number. And if he was being honest, never in his life had he called a woman for a date. Not that this was a date. He was just being…neighborly.

He didn't do relationships. He met women in bars, and he didn't take their phone numbers, since they both knew he wouldn't be calling. Oh yeah. He was a colossal asshole, he'd heard it a thousand times. And still he stuffed a small first aid kit in his pocket and stopped at that noodle place to point at pictures of two dishes he thought Olivia might like, miming that he needed them to go. And then he bought Sprite and a box of what he believed to be chocolate covered cookies at a second shop, just in case.

A scrawny twenty-something kid was coming out of the building when Jarek approached. He caught the green door before it could latch shut and entered the dark stairwell. The concrete entrance and stairs were nothing but a patchwork of shadows, sparsely lit by the faint moonlight shining through the random window.

Jarek counted four floors, relieved when he reached the top without breaking his neck. He tried to tell himself this was stupid; if Olivia could make it up and down this treacherous thing she couldn't possibly be injured. And if she was taking such pains to avoid him—avoiding the only social situation she'd managed to find in this small, strange town—his was probably the last face she'd want to see.

Still, he took a guess at her apartment number, figuring it faced northeast, the direction of his own building, and rang the bell. There was a small barred window next to the door, and though the shades were drawn, he could see a light on inside. After a minute he saw movement, then the shade was pushed aside and Olivia's right eye came into view.

If he weren't so fucking uncomfortable, he would have laughed at the surprise, chagrin, irritation, and hesitation that played across her face. But he was too anxious waiting for the sound of the lock on the inner door to turn—and finally, thank Christ, it did—that he just stood there holding his makeshift olive branches, face blank.

The wooden door swung open, leaving them with the outer door, composed of a series of thick metal bars, between them. Olivia wore sweatpants, wool socks, and a threadbare white T-shirt with a high school logo straining across her breasts. Her blond hair was pulled up in a messy bun, and she wore no makeup. She looked him up and down, gaze lingering on his peace offering, then she took a deep breath. "What's this?" she asked.

"Let me in." Jarek tilted his head so rain water dripped off the ends of his curly hair.

"What do you want?"

"Ritchie told me about your accident."

"I'm fine."

"Just open the door."

She looked ready to argue, then her eyes flitted back to the bags in his hands and she reached gingerly for the keys on the table inside the door, selecting one and twisting it in the lock. She stepped back as he entered, closing the doors behind him, and he stepped out of his shoes and hung his wet coat on a chair.

"It's fucking pouring," he said, for lack of anything better. "Where's your bathroom?"

The apartment was small, just four rooms leading immediately off the main entrance area, and he could see into three of them from where he stood — bedroom, office, and kitchen — so he went into the fourth, found a hand towel, and dried his face and hair. When he emerged, Olivia was peeking into the bags.

"I brought you dinner, in case you hadn't eaten."

"I haven't."

"What were you doing?"

"Getting ready to watch a movie."

"Want to eat first?"

She looked him over strangely. "Sure."

There were only two chairs at the small table, so she took one and he took the other, peering around the sterile room. White tile floors, white-painted plaster walls, neon tube lights on the ceiling. A few handmade posters with English and Chinese words written on them.

"Do those help?" Jarek asked, nodding at the posters as he twisted the caps off the bottles of Sprite.

Olivia peered into both takeout containers. "As much as knowing the word for 'nose' can, I suppose. What is this?"

He leaned forward to study the contents of one container; he had ordered it based on the picture, but couldn't possibly identify it now. "I'm not sure."

The second dish was the one they'd had the first night, so Olivia took that and he ate the mystery meal, which wasn't bad. They barely spoke and she avoided his gaze, though she didn't look angry. Tired, maybe. But not angry.

When half her food was gone, Olivia polished off the Sprite and pushed her container away. "Do you want this? I'm full."

He'd finished his own meal. "No. I'm good."

She stood and took the carton to the narrow fridge that stood in the corner of the room, its only furniture apart from the table. When she closed the door, he was standing behind her. She jumped and clasped a hand to her chest. "What are you doing?"

"Don't take this the wrong way," he began, "but take off your shirt."

Her jaw dropped. "I hope you're kidding."

He held up the small first aid kit. "Ritchie told me what happened. I can see the marks through the back of your shirt. Let me look at it."

She looked mutinous. "I'm fine, Jarek. Thanks for dinner, but I don't need medical treatment." She said the words disdainfully, just like he'd say them, no matter how much pain he was in. But he'd seen and inflicted enough injuries to know when someone was hiding their discomfort, and she'd been moving like an old woman.

"You're walking like a senior citizen. Just turn around and lift it over your shoulders, then. That's more than bruises."

"They're just scrapes. I looked in the mirror."

"You can't reach them."

"I don't need to. They're not infected. I checked."

"So let me check. For my peace of mind."

"Forgive me, Jarek, but I don't give a fuck about your peace of mind."

He smiled. "Just let me look. I'll clean them up for you. Then we can watch your movie."

"I don't want your company."

"Like hell you don't. I'm bored, too, Olivia. I read a book about blue people colonizing a country populated by fish people, and their battle for oxygen."

"What on earth are you talking about?"

But she was weakening, he could see it. He glanced past her into the bedroom, sparsely furnished with a twin bed covered in a purple comforter, a laptop resting on the pillow. Jarek pushed his luck, loosely gripped one of her shoulders, and steered her into the room until she was sitting on the edge of the bed.

"Take your shirt off," he ordered, unzipping the first aid kit and fishing out the antiseptic and a cotton ball.

Olivia heaved an irritated sigh, then fumbled to lift the shirt halfway up her back. He helped her push it to her shoulders, and she folded her arms across her midsection, keeping her breasts and stomach firmly under wraps. Jarek swallowed a curse at the cuts and bruises that marred her tan skin. She looked like she had a nasty case of road rash.

But he kept his voice mild when he said, "Must have hurt," and began to carefully wipe her skin with the moistened cotton ball. Her breath hissed in at his touch, and though she had a space heater on and it wasn't particularly cold in the bedroom, goose bumps sprang up along her spine when he gently daubed the marks on her rib cage, stopping when he reached her plain cotton bra.

"Let that dry," he said, putting a hand on the shirt to stop her from rolling it back down. "I'll put some scar cream on for you."

"It's not going to scar."

He knew that, too, but he felt bad. He'd hurt her feelings and then she'd actually gotten hurt, and holed up all alone in this sterile apartment like a wounded animal. "Just let me. I brought cookies."

"What kind?"

"Fuck if I know. They looked good."

She laughed weakly. "Do you have a sweet tooth?"

He inhaled and smelled apples. "Yeah."

A few minutes later he'd covered the worst of the scrapes with cream and helped lower her shirt. He left her long enough to fetch the cookies and put the first aid kit in his coat pocket, then returned to the bedroom to frown at the bed.

"Who sleeps in a twin?" he asked rhetorically. The bed was tucked in the corner of the room, with the wall on one side and a tiny nightstand on the other. Olivia had shifted to the corner and the laptop rested on her knees. There was just enough room for him to sit beside her, and he waited for her nod of consent before joining her, his left side pressed up flush against her right.

"I hope you like awesome movies."

"What'd you pick?"

"*Love, Actually.*"

"What's that supposed to mean?"

"You'll see. Hugh Grant explains it at the beginning in his voice-over—"

"Hugh Grant? Is this a chick flick?"

"You say 'chick flick?'"

"Olivia. What is wrong with you?"

"I was going to watch this before you got here. Be quiet or leave."

"I just—"

"Have you seen it?"

"Of course not."

"Well, you're going to love it. Actually." She smiled, pleased with herself.

He grunted. "Don't make this harder than it has to be."

Two hours later, he was officially as hard as he'd ever been. He was wearing track pants, and he kept one leg up so he could adjust himself and hide the erection that would send her running for the hills. The movie wasn't the worst thing he'd ever seen, but it had been fucking difficult to keep his eyes on the screen propped on her lap when beyond that she'd nudged off her socks so he kept getting distracted by her bright pink toenails. Worse still was every time she'd laugh, or sigh, or look at him like, *Right? Best movie ever!* and he felt the soft swell of her breast shift against his arm.

His senses were in overdrive. He could feel her. See her. Hear her. Smell her. The only thing he hadn't done was taste her—except he had, for ten whole seconds a week ago, and he remembered it like it was yesterday. Shit shit shit shit shit.

"So," she said, turning off the movie and closing the laptop, leaving them in the light of the lamp on the nightstand.

He avoided her eyes. "So what?"

"What was your favorite part?"

"What?"

"Your favorite plotline. I know you have one."

He racked his brain to remember anything but the time he'd glanced down and noticed that her nipples were hard. "Ah…the one with the writer and the maid, I guess."

"Jarek! I knew you had a heart!" She elbowed him in the ribs and straightened to look at him fully. Even sitting upright she still had to tilt her head to see his face, and he had to lean back to put more than three inches between his lips and that too-big smile.

"Did you take a lot of painkillers today?"

"What? No. Just two."

"Any alcohol?"

She scowled at him. "No, Jarek. I'm in my right mind. Everyone in their right mind loves this movie. It's wonderful."

He sighed and leaned his head back against the wall, closing his eyes. "What's your favorite plot, then?"

"I was hoping you'd ask. It's the one where Keira Knightley marries the guy's friend and you think he hates her, but secretly he's in love with her. When he shows up with the cue cards and the Christmas carols…"

Jarek forced himself to take a deep breath. She was keeping her breasts to herself, but he could still feel her knee pressing into his calf. If he just got up, walked to the door, put on his coat and shoes and left, he'd be a decent human being. It was fifteen, twenty feet at best. A completely reasonable distance.

He interrupted her. "You know it's not real, right?"

"The movie? Of course I do."

He gestured at the laptop. "All that corny stuff. It's not real."

"I'm fully aware of that, Jarek." He could practically see her spine stiffening as he tried to burst her bubble. He was such an ass. For a second she'd seemed happy, no trace of the melancholy that normally lurked in her eyes. And here he was, about to take it all away.

"Olivia…" he said tersely. "I'm really straightforward."

She blinked and looked at him like he was crazy. "Great. Terrific."

"Too straightforward. People don't like it."

She blinked again, realization dawning. "Do you think I chose this movie to seduce you? Because I didn't get the message the other night? Don't worry, Jarek, you were perfectly 'straightforward.' I told you, I already planned to watch this, I wasn't expecting company. I didn't invite you—"

"So forgive me," he cut in, curling his left hand behind her head to hold her in place as he leaned over. "For sending mixed messages." And then he kissed her.

Chapter Four

Olivia was officially confused. She'd been that way since she peered through the window to see Jarek standing at her door several hours ago, and the feeling hadn't really gone away. He'd treated her exactly the way he had the past two times they'd been together, and she'd decided to take his general looming broodiness as his personality, not any sort of strange physical chemistry. The fact that he was here…Well, he'd said it himself: he was bored.

Except now he didn't *feel* bored. He was curved over her, one hand at the base of her skull, fingers threading through her hair, kneading the base of her neck with his palm. The other hand rested on the mattress next to the wall, keeping his weight off her as his mouth did positively filthy things to hers. Things he continued to do as she struggled to get her thoughts in order.

"Jarek," she said on a gasp, breaking away. She put her hands on his chest and it was absolutely, ridiculously hard. His tongue stole inside her mouth again and she met it with her own before shaking her head and reminding herself she was trying to ask a question. Except…What was the question?

She tried again. "Why…? What…?" But he kept stealing her breath like he was on some kind of mission to possess her soul and she couldn't decide if she wanted him to succeed or not. She'd kissed three boys in her life, and only Chris for the past ten years. She'd liked kissing Chris. There were times when it had been her favorite thing to do. But now she wondered if she hadn't wasted ten years with him, when there were people out there who could merely rasp her jaw with day-old stubble and make her want more.

"Jarek." She found her voice and stopped his hand with hers when she discovered he'd snuck it under her shirt and was now covering her breast through her bra. He was good. She was feeling things in places she hadn't felt them in a while. And not just the hard nipples and the growing ache between her legs; she could feel his erection pressing against her hip, and she kind of wanted to feel more of it.

"What?" he mumbled, tugging her head back and dragging his lips over her exposed throat.

"I don't…"

He paused, waiting for her to finish the thought.

"…get it." The words were breathy and unconvincing, but he didn't kiss her again.

"I know," he said.

"You know?"

"I don't get it either. You want to stop?"

Well, no one could accuse him of not getting to the point. His hand was still on her breast, her fingers still covered his, and his face was still buried in the place where her neck and shoulder met, each one of his ragged breaths sending chills up her spine. She used her free hand to nudge his face up so she could look into his eyes, not some sappy, meaningful stare, just…looking. And all she found was arousal. Intent. Promise.

Good enough.

"Don't stop," she said.

He smiled slightly and kissed her again, pushing his hand under her bra so his calloused palm chafed her skin and pulled the already tight flesh even tighter. He kissed her and stroked her for so long that she began to wonder if that was all he intended to do, when finally his hand slid down her stomach and dipped below the waistband of her pants.

"Okay?" he murmured against her ear.

"Okay." She parted her legs slightly and tried to focus on anything other than how much she wanted to feel him there, and how nervous the thought made her. It had been a year. She'd only ever done this with Chris. And Jarek had nothing in common with her ex. Chris was the town golden boy, superstar athlete and student, everybody's favorite. Olivia had a hard time imagining Jarek as anybody's favorite, but right now she'd tell him anything he wanted to hear because he'd pushed his fingers beneath her cotton panties and dragged one thick finger right through her slick folds, stopping at the place that needed it the most.

"Jarek," she groaned. One of her hands joined his over the fabric of her sweatpants, and he stilled.

"Not okay?"

"Too okay."

"Shh. Let me."

She laughed a little. He wasn't charming. He didn't spin golden words out of straw, and he didn't tell her things he thought she wanted to hear. Didn't tell her anything, really. But still she lifted her hand to stroke his hair, surprised by how soft the short curls felt when everything else about him was so frighteningly sharp and hard.

Her heart was pounding and she was sure he could feel it against his chest, even as he was careful not to put too much weight on her, no doubt thinking about her back. But Olivia wasn't thinking about the scratches; she couldn't think about anything except the hand between her legs, doing things she hadn't anticipated doing tonight. He sank one, then two fingers inside her, moaning into her mouth, and Olivia felt herself getting close.

"I'm going to come," she whispered.

"Yeah?"

"Yeah."

"Good." His thumb circled the swollen bundle of nerves at the top of her cleft and his fingers thrust deep and hard. He tried to work a third finger inside but Olivia grimaced and stopped him and he gave up, kissing her jaw, silently telling her to trust him as he rubbed his cock against her hip without thought.

She came on his hand with a quiet, shuddering groan, feeling her internal muscles squeezing him painfully tight. She felt him pull back to watch her face and turned her head away, reveling in the release she'd needed for too long. At length he removed his hand and shifted to grab tissues from the box on the nightstand, wiping his fingers before turning back.

Olivia lifted up to kiss him; his eyes were an ever-changing shade of blue, and tonight they were dark and glazed with need. "I don't have any condoms," she said softly, sliding a hand down to cup the erection straining at the front of his track pants.

He winced. "Me either." His head flopped back on the pillow and she followed him down, pressing her breasts into his chest, liking the way he dragged in a breath that sounded like it hurt. "You have two hands and a mouth, right?" he asked finally.

She burst out laughing against his lips. "That's really sweet, Jarek. Have you been working on that for a while?"

He opened his eyes, looking guilty and amused and really, really turned on. "You don't have to do anything you don't want to do."

"I know." She pushed her hand into his pants and inside his boxers and raised her eyebrows at how hot he was, searing hot against the soft skin of her palm. "You want me to?"

"You know I do."

She jerked him off like they were teenagers hiding out in the basement, fully clothed and desperate. Olivia had done this many times before; Lord knew she'd made Chris wait almost a full year before giving him her virginity, and they'd spent months doing everything but to compensate. She kissed his mouth and his jaw and his ear, trailed her wet tongue over his throat, felt his blood racing. When he was close he turned his head away and covered her hand with his own, squeezing himself harder than she ever would have dared, doing everything rougher than she would have.

"You're so hard," she murmured in his ear. "So big. I want to feel you come in my hand, Jarek."

"Fuck." He ran his free hand over his eyes, as though he could block her out.

To be honest, Olivia was surprised to hear herself say the words. She'd never talked dirty with Chris; never really wanted to. But something told her Jarek wanted to hear it, wanted the okay to sully her hand with his release, to know he hadn't talked her into doing something she didn't want to do.

She kissed the shell of his ear, bit on the lobe. "What are you waiting for?" She squeezed her hand tighter than she thought he'd like and he came, back arching, teeth gritted, a pained sound dragged from his throat. She felt him pulse beneath her fingers, bathing her hand with slick heat, then loosened her grip and stroked him until he stopped her, snatching more tissues from the nightstand and passing them over so she could clean up.

He lay flat on his back and adjusted himself as she wiped her hand, his raspy breathing slowing to a steady, even pace. "Did I hurt your back?" he asked eventually, eyes on the ceiling.

Olivia lay beside him, but when she turned her head, he didn't return the gaze. "My back's fine. That was fine."

He took a deep breath and sat up, striding out of the room and disappearing into the bathroom. She heard the water run as he washed his hands, then returned, drying them on his T-shirt. "I'm going to go," he said.

Olivia sat up, too, keeping her expression bland. She was a little surprised he was taking off so quickly, but she hadn't expected him to spend the night. She had a twin bed, for crying out loud. It was barely enough for one person to sleep in. She watched from the bedroom door as he sat at the table and tugged on his shoes and pulled on his coat, then unlocked both doors and stepped through before turning back.

"I'm going out of town with Brant for a few days," he said, looking at her shoulder. "He's got to buy some supplies, so…I won't be around."

Olivia didn't know if that was true, but suspected that it was, given how uncomfortable he seemed talking about his itinerary. "Have fun," she said mildly. "Thanks for dinner. And the company."

He looked her in the eye. "You're welcome. Lock up after me."

She came out to pick up the keys from the table. "You bet."

He smiled a little then, and nodded good-bye before turning to disappear into the dark stairwell.

Olivia locked both doors, turned off the light, and went into the bathroom to wash up and brush her teeth. She spent a minute staring at herself in the mirror, trying to decide how she felt about things. It was hard to say. She appreciated the gesture, him bringing food and first aid, and she was grateful for the company. The orgasm. It had been a while since she'd even wanted one, so that was nice. It wasn't the best orgasm she'd ever had. She hadn't seen stars or JFK's face or anything, but she'd appreciated the feeling of a big, hard body next to hers, hands and words that wanted to make her feel good, no more, no less.

If all Jarek wanted from her was sex, she could certainly handle that. She wanted a friend, and if that was too much to ask of him, he could find someone else to jerk him off. Somehow she didn't think he would. He seemed hyper paranoid that she might ask something of him, feelings or commitment or something, but she had no such plans. Her contract was over at the end of June and she'd move on with her life, and so, presumably would he. But if the intervening months were a little less lonely, she would be okay with that. She was less certain that he would, but they'd find out soon enough.

Jarek pushed away the empty beer bottle—his fourth of the night—and shook his head at the approaching server. He was done.

"Aw, come on," Dale goaded him. "It's early." It was a little after one o'clock in the morning, and they'd been on the move all day. Brant had hired a driver to take the three of them to Yangzhou, a mid-sized city on the Yangtze river, to pick up supplies. They'd spent an hour on a boat that appeared to be held up by nothing more than tires, sat in traffic for two hours because of an accident no one seemed all that inspired to clear up, and several more hours loading bags of cement mix and boxes of Chinese-labeled supplies into the truck.

All bad enough, except Dale had been there, yammering on all day like he couldn't figure out when to shut up. Brant liked Dale, had known him for twenty years, and that's why he'd been allowed to come along, even though Jarek would have much rather done the work alone if it meant a moment's reprieve from the man's incessant stories about his kids. It was hard to reconcile the guy who'd recounted in great detail his sexual exploits of the night before with the man talking about the look on his son's face when he'd gotten a signed baseball for Christmas.

Brant was single too, Jarek knew, and though he wasn't as sleazy about it as Dale, he was still scoping out the crowded, upscale room like someone might catch his eye. He was a decent-looking guy who owned his own business, swore up and down he'd never get married, and threatened to kill anyone who called him Sherman, his first name.

Yangzhou was considerably bigger than Lazhou, and had a much larger population of foreign workers, many of whom were in the bar tonight. Try as he might, however, Jarek couldn't muster up much interest in any of them, even though this was the way he preferred to pick up women. Not by showing up at their apartments uninvited with cookies, then slipping his hand in their pants and fingering them. How old was he, fifteen?

"One more beer," he said, when Dale continued to hound him. "That's it."

"Another round!" Dale shouted to no one in particular. He'd already been through six or seven bottles, and showed no signs of slowing.

Brant smiled at Jarek and Jarek forced himself to smile back, though it felt fake and probably looked worse. All day he'd been thinking of Olivia describing the night as "fine," and it made him want to pull out his hair.

Fine? *Fine?* He'd felt her come on his hand. He knew she hadn't faked it. But he knew with just as much certainty that she hadn't been messing with him when she'd said it either. She meant it. It was fine. He'd done a *fine* job.

His pride was hurt. He'd spent the morning denying it, then the afternoon telling himself it didn't matter. There were worse things than fine. Except there were better, too. And though he should march away from Olivia and her backhanded compliments and her shiny hair and find a woman in this bar who looked and smelled and tasted nothing like her, he didn't. He stared down the new bottle of beer like it owed him money, and then he drank the thing and barely tasted it.

He lacked any and all rational thought when it came to Olivia Clarke. She was like an insidious vine, winding its way through his brain, choking out all his common sense. He wasn't looking for a challenge. He couldn't even remember the last time he'd seen a woman again after sleeping with her. But they hadn't slept together, had they? They'd gotten each other off like teenagers, and he'd only done a halfway decent job, from the sound of it. And instead of wisely packing up his things and moving on, he couldn't stop wondering how great her fiancé must have been in bed, and what he could do to be even better.

"Dude!" Dale pounded the table in front of Jarek, making the bottles jump. "What the fuck have you been obsessing over all day?"

He looked up sharply. "Nothing."

"Bullshit," Brant piped up, sounding a little wasted. "It's something."

"You got in late last night," Dale said.

Brant looked intrigued. "How late?"

"Midnight."

"What are you, my mother?"

"It's Olivia, right? The kindergarten teacher?"

Brant pulled a face. "The teacher, Jarek? Really? Isn't she kind of…
sweet?"

Uh, no. She absolutely wasn't. "I didn't see her. I was just out walking."

"Until midnight? In the pouring rain?"

"Listen, Frank and Joe —"

Brant and Dale exchanged puzzled stares. "Who?"

"The Hardy Boys. Stop monitoring —"

"You were with the Hardy Boys? Who are these guys?"

"What? The Hardy…they're teen detectives, like Nancy Drew.
Friends with Nancy —" Good God, why the hell was he talking about
this? "The point is, what I do is none of your business, so stop asking."

"He was with Olivia."

"Absolutely."

"How was she?"

Jarek wasn't one to kiss and tell under the best — or most inebri-
ated — circumstances, and the only thing Olivia had really asked of
him was that he not talk about her behind her back, so he wouldn't.
But these two were drunk and gossip hungry, and he really wasn't in
the mood, so he polished off his beer and stood. "I'm going to my
room." He checked his watch. "It's one twenty-three, if you want to
make a note of it in your journal."

"Aw, sit down, Jare," Brant said, waving him back. "We're just
messing with you. If you want to date the kindergartener — oops,
the kindergarten teacher —"

"There is a huge difference," he interjected.

"Then we won't stop you."

"Just tell us one thing about her," Dale said.

"I don't know anything." He fished money out of his wallet and
dropped it on the table.

"Does she make you recite the alphabet before she goes down
on you?"

"Stop."

"Does she give you a gold star for—"

"See you tomorrow. Or not. I don't care." Jarek strode off through the crowded bar, their laughter ringing in his ears. In the past, their comments wouldn't have bothered him. He'd never cared about anything enough that he could be bothered. But even now, irritated though he was, their words weren't the ones getting his back up. Olivia's special little F-word, four letters and one syllable, was digging into his gut, making him feel all sorts of things he didn't want to feel.

Two days later, the cause of his recent frustrations strolled past the open door to the carpentry trailer at three thirty in the afternoon. Jarek was bent over a table saw, cutting a piece of wood for one of a zillion door frames, when her hair caught the sunlight and sparkled brightly enough to catch his eye. He finished the cut and placed the wood carefully on the table, watching as Ritchie walked beside her, scribbling in his notepad as Olivia chatted and gestured with her hands.

Jarek took off the safety glasses and gloves, wiping dust off his nose before striding to the door to look out. They were about twenty feet away, moving slowly, lost in their conversation. Olivia wore faded blue jeans that clung to her ass, and had traded her winter coat for something black in a lighter fabric that showed her shape. Her long hair fell halfway down her back, pin straight and gleaming, and Jarek wanted nothing more than to wrap it in his fist and drag her into the trailer.

He scuffed his foot on the top step of the makeshift staircase, and Ritchie glanced back at the sound. "Hey, Jarek."

"Hey." He was speaking to Ritchie, but his eyes were on Olivia.

"Hey," she said.

He nodded, not trusting himself. It was sunny today but there was a cool breeze, and her lips and cheeks were pink. She was the prettiest girl he'd ever been with, hands down, and he hated that he even noticed.

"We're just talking about this thing for her class," Ritchie said, when the silence stretched on too long.

"Sure."

"How was your trip?" Olivia asked. He couldn't tell if she was testing him or not; it was quite possible she suspected he'd been hiding out in this trailer for the past two days, avoiding her.

"It's over."

"He had to go with Dale," Ritchie pitched in, bailing him out. "His best friend."

She smiled. "Did you have a slumber party?"

There's only one person I want to sleep with, he thought. "No."

"What are you working on?"

He stepped away from the door and gestured inside. "Come see."

Olivia glanced at Ritchie, who fumbled to put away his notepad. He was an awkward guy, but he wasn't stupid. "I'll look at this and give you some ideas tomorrow," he said quickly. "I should probably get back to the site, anyway."

"Thanks, Ritchie."

"Any time."

She watched him hurry away before turning back to Jarek and slowly approaching. He liked watching her come to him; he liked everything about her. She climbed the four steps to the trailer and he didn't shift back to let her in, making her brush against him as she entered, squinting to let her eyes adjust.

Jarek followed her inside and closed and locked the door, letting the click hang in the air. He saw her stiffen for a second, but she didn't turn around or argue, so he figured it was okay.

"This is it, huh?"

"Some of the time."

He moved past her into the room, wiping sawdust off the table saw and into a small garbage can. The room was well organized, every inch used efficiently, and because he was the only one in here ninety percent of the time, it was exactly as he liked it. He had tools, a desk, a window — curtains drawn — and a water cooler. Everything he needed, until now.

She moved farther inside, looking at the equipment, touching the edge of the wood he'd just finished cutting. His desk was in the corner, looking out over the room, the surface bare except for a stack of notepads and an empty water glass.

"But this is what you really like, right?" she asked. "Carpentry?"

"Why would you say that?"

"When I asked you what you did here, you said it was mostly this."

He hesitated. It wasn't a big thing for her to inquire about, his hobby. His interest. "Yeah. This is what I prefer to do."

"What are you making now?"

"Nothing special. Door frames. Trim. Stuff like that."

She stroked a finger over the grooves in the wood he'd cut, decorative touches requested by the client. "It's nice."

"Is it fine?" He was surprised by the tension in his voice.

She may have been too, because she glanced over her shoulder to look at him. "I said it was nice."

He nodded and looked away, then followed her down the narrow aisle, closer to the desk. "Do you know who Frank and Joe Hardy are?"

"Boy detectives? Nancy Drew's — *Oomph!*"

He'd turned her, lifted her, seated her on the desk, and covered her mouth with his in approximately one-eighth of a second. She didn't put up a fight, didn't pretend she'd come in here to talk about his hobbies. He dragged her hips right to the edge of the desk, pressing his against hers, grinding himself between her legs. Olivia wrapped her arms around his neck and he unzipped her jacket, filling his hands with her breasts, still kicking himself for not getting her shirt off the other night. He'd touched her in a lot of places he hadn't even seen, and the thought, among others, kept him up nights.

She stopped him, however, when he tried to remove her shirt, and he realized she was worried about the trailer. "I locked the door."

"I know. Still."

"No one's going to come in."

"Still."

He made a show of sighing heavily and pulling the V-neck away from her chest to peek inside, making her laugh. "Show me yours," she ordered, sliding her hands beneath the black T-shirt he was wearing and pushing it up to reveal his tight chest and abs. He was fit, but he wasn't bulky. He had strong hands and arms, no flab. He clutched her hair when she ducked her head to lick the line dividing his pectorals, tongue circling his nipples, kissing him right over the spot where his heart was supposed to be. His dick had been waiting for this moment for two and a half days, and didn't want to wait much longer.

"That enough foreplay?" he asked, lowering his shirt and undoing the button at the top of her jeans.

She laughed again and he liked the sound, liked it even better when she made a different sound when he slipped his hand inside her pants and covered her over her panties, pressing against her folds hard enough to penetrate a little bit. He kissed her mouth, kissed her neck, even dipped his head to find her nipples through her shirt and bra, biting them harder than necessary as punishment for refusing to show him.

She pushed his face away and admonished him not to ruin her shirt, even as he felt her grow wetter and wetter on the fingers he now plunged ruthlessly inside her. "Do you have…?" Her voice trailed off as he fished the condom out of his back pocket and dropped it on the desk.

"Did the Hardy boys teach you that? To come prepared?"

"No," he said, tugging off her sneakers and dropping them on the floor before helping her out of her jeans and panties. "You did." He freed his straining cock and she dealt with the condom wrapper as he pushed her knees wide to look at the only part of her she'd let him see. She squirmed uncomfortably after a second and he shot her a look that said he was in charge—she rolled her eyes—and dropped to his knees to drag his tongue through her wet slit and tug on her clit with his teeth.

Her eyes rolled now for another reason, and after a minute he stood and sheathed himself with the condom, unable to wait another second. That's how he always seemed to feel around her. Couldn't wait to kiss her. Couldn't wait to see her breasts. Had to taste her pussy. Had to be inside her.

Olivia braced her hands on the desk and looked him in the eye as he fit the head of his cock to her and pushed. She was really fucking tight. He'd expected it, given the look on her face the other night when he'd tried to penetrate her with three fingers, but this was brutal. He didn't want to stop. Didn't want to hurt her. Didn't want to stop.

He fisted one hand in her hair like he'd fantasized about doing, and pulled her up to kiss him, pushing his tongue into her mouth. He kissed her while he nudged his way inside, and she gasped and writhed and worked to accommodate him, yanking her head away to suck in air when he was buried to the hilt. "You okay?" he asked, instantly regretting it. *Please don't say fine. Please don't say fine.*

Her head had dropped back and her eyes were on the ceiling. "Yes."

Well. Better than nothing. "You need anything special?"

Her head came up and her lips curved. "You're special."

"Knock it off."

She smiled, showing too many teeth. "Make me."

He gripped her hips, pulled out and shoved back in, too hard. Her breath hitched and she winced, and he kissed the corner of her mouth. "I'm sorry."

"Do it again."

So he did. She held onto the desk and later onto his shoulders, and he held her hips and pounded into her with all the zealousness of a man possessed, and none of the finesse she'd probably gotten from her ex. He could feel her and smell her and hear her, and in no time at all she fit him.

She fisted a hand in his T-shirt and buried her face in the fabric when she came, a whimper, not a bang, muffled by his chest. Her pussy seized him and refused to let him go, and when she was spent he drove into her a dozen more times and exploded with a shout he tried to stifle with her hair.

When he regained his senses, his heart was pounding and he was sweating, a line trickling down his back to pool at the base of his spine. At some point she'd wrapped her legs around his hips and now they fell open, giving him the cue to pull out and dispose of the condom. By the time he'd turned back she'd already stepped into her panties, bright pink with white polka dots, and all too soon she'd covered them with her jeans.

She avoided his eyes as she picked up a sneaker and untied the laces, something he hadn't bothered to do in his haste to get them off. Jarek picked up the other one and did the same, handing it to her when she was ready, refusing to let it go until she looked at him. He cocked an eyebrow and she smiled, no teeth, and he didn't know what he was hoping for.

"Why'd you ask about the Hardy Boys?" she asked, slipping into her jacket. She untucked her hair from the collar and ran a hand over her face, pink in places from his lips and stubble.

"Brant and Dale didn't know who they were."

"Do you guys normally discuss teen detectives?"

He smiled thinly. "No. It just came up."

She glanced around. "I guess I should let you get back to work. That was—"

He stepped forward and covered her mouth with a hand. "Don't fucking say *fine*, Olivia."

Her eyebrows shot up. "What?" Her lips moved against his palm.

"Don't say *nice*, either."

She swatted his hand away. "I was going to say *stupendous*." She kept a straight face for all of one second, and then he gave up and smiled, too.

"I want to make you come properly." He hadn't expected to say that, not out loud.

She squeezed his fingers as she moved past. "You did."

He stopped her at the door, pressing a hand against the wall over her head, trapping her between his body and the trailer. "I didn't."

"I don't know what—"

"Do you have a secret fetish?"

She snickered. "No."

"Then what is it?"

"Jarek, stop. That was stupendous."

"It was good, Olivia. Not stupendous. For me, anyway. You wouldn't even let me take off your shirt."

She turned to face him. "Do you know how old I am?"

He shrugged. "Approximately."

"Do you know where I'm from?"

Uh-oh.

"Do you know my birthday or my favorite food or the name of the school I teach at?" He stared at her silently, and she tapped his chin. "Then don't ask me how I come, Jarek. That's the least of the things you should be wondering about." She pulled open the door and stepped outside. "Are you going to come over tonight?"

"Do you want me to?"

"Wrong question, dumb ass." She didn't sound angry, but she didn't look back when she walked away, either.

Chapter Five

"**W**ell. Good thing we built it on a dolly."

Ritchie looked up from his spot crouched on the floor and looked doubtful. "It's bigger than we talked about."

Olivia gnawed her lower lip. "Yeah. A bit. But it looks real."

She took a step back, a wet strip of newspaper hanging from the tips of her fingers, and studied the papier mâché tree she'd roped Ritchie into helping her design and build. It was a prototype for the forest of trees she planned to create for her class's performance of *Little Red Riding Hood* at the end of the year. She wasn't in any way, shape or form qualified to stage something like this, but the school had given her an assignment and she had nothing better to do, so she'd taken it on with gusto. And papier mâché paste.

"You're making a mess." Ritchie pointed at the pool of paste on the floor for the seventeenth time.

"I'll clean it later."

He rose and came to stand beside her, peering at the monstrosity they'd spent the better part of two hours creating. Her students had music class before lunch on Tuesdays, and they'd agreed that he would come by then to help her with the trial run of the first of many trees.

"It'll look better when it's painted," Olivia said, slapping on the soggy strip of paper with no finesse whatsoever.

"You don't think it's…enormous?"

"Um, maybe." She glanced over at him and tried not to laugh. Ritchie was an architect and he was extraordinarily uncomfortable when things did not go according to plan. The original intent had been for the tree to be approximately five feet tall—including the leaves, which she'd already constructed by tying together roughly one hundred large green feathers she'd found at the crowded indoor market. This particular…thing…was all trunk, about a foot and a half in diameter, more than double the measurements he'd given her, and stood about seven feet tall. It was just a giant, lilting, soggy newspaper covered…thing.

"Let's wheel it outside to dry," she suggested. Olivia steadied the "tree" as Ritchie maneuvered the dolly through her classroom and out the door into the courtyard to sit in the sun. "I think it'll be good," she tried.

"Yeah."

She laughed and hit him in the arm with her dirty fingers. "Shut up."

He trailed her inside and they tidied up as best they could, still twenty minutes left in the lunch break. She had a tiny microwave she used to heat up Styrofoam containers of instant noodles, and they sat at the kids' tables and ate as they made small talk. Olivia knew he wanted to ask her about Jarek; it was kind of an open secret. She hadn't been back to the gym trailer in the two weeks since she'd had sex with him on his desk. She hadn't had to; he met up with her four times a week to run outside, then followed her upstairs to her apartment for an entirely different kind of workout.

"You seem…better," Ritchie offered. "Less unhappy."

"Yeah." She forked too much food into her mouth and chewed. "It's nice now that it's warming up. Thank God for spring."

"Did you figure out how you're going to make this play work?"

She snorted. "Not a clue." She'd been told two weeks earlier that she was responsible for helping her class stage an all-English performance *of Little Red Riding Hood* for their kindergarten graduation. The school was the only one in Lazhou with a foreign teacher, and the parents of Olivia's students paid extra for them to be in her class. They needed to be wowed. More important, however, was the fact that they were supposed to have performed something at the Christmas pageant, but the Australian teacher hadn't managed to cobble anything together. The kids had eventually sung an entirely garbled version of "Rudolph the Red Nose Reindeer," which no one had understood. They were incredibly excited to have a second chance in June.

The problem was, Olivia knew *Little Red Riding Hood*. It didn't have thirty characters. The school principal had chosen it because it had "red" in the title and Chinese people *loved* the color red. Beyond that, they needed some changes to the story. It couldn't be scary, grandma couldn't be kidnapped, the wolf couldn't eat anybody, couldn't, in fact, be a wolf, and everyone had to be happy and speaking English in the end. Olivia prided herself on thinking outside the box, but she hadn't quite figured out a way to make this performance anything other than a hugely embarrassing debacle. So she'd made an enormous tree instead.

"Hello, Olivia?"

She and Ritchie turned to see Honor standing in the doorway, the sunlight silhouetting her slight shape, the flare of her dress around her knees. She still wore a long sleeve shirt and thick tights, but somehow managed to look pretty and dainty at the same time.

"Hi, Honor. Come on in. We're just having lunch."

Honor took a tentative step into the room, sniffing. "What… What is that?" she asked, gesturing out the window at the trunk basking in the sunlight. A few strips of newspaper had already come free and hung off like dripping gray moss.

Olivia stood to join her to study the tree. "It's a tree. Or it will be. For my class."

"A tree?"

"It's not finished yet."

"Hmm. Yes."

A few more teachers trailed out of the mah-jongg room and studied the tree, looking dubious, amused, and alarmed. More than a few snickered, though not all maliciously. Olivia pursed her lips. They'd see. It wasn't finished yet.

"This is Ritchie," she said, gesturing between Honor and the architect. "He helped design it. He knows what he's doing."

"Ritchie?" Honor echoed, looking at him for the first time.

Ritchie cleared his throat and stuck out a hand. "Nice to meet you."

Honor hesitated, then grasped his fingers. "Nice to meet you, too."

Olivia tried not to laugh. She'd taught her students how to introduce themselves in January, and their practice dialogues had gone a lot like this. Only…not quite like this. Because Ritchie and Honor were gazing at each other with more than the strained discomfort and amusement her students had displayed. They looked…interested.

"Ritchie is an architect," she said. "He works at the project down the road."

"Yes," Honor said, nodding. "I know it." It was the only project in this part of Lazhou that had foreign workers; everybody knew it.

"You're a teacher here, Honor?" Ritchie asked, though that was obvious, too.

"Yes. I teach the same year as Olivia. She is a good teacher."

Olivia glanced up, surprised. No one here had ever complimented her on anything other than her looks. *Your hair, so yellow! Your eyes, so big! Very pretty! Maybe a little fat.*

"Thanks, Honor."

"You are welcome." She and Ritchie were still flicking shy glances at each other, and now a few of the braver teachers meandered closer, studying both the tree and the strange man. Olivia had a fleeting image of Jarek standing here, towering over everybody, intimidating them with his stern glare. He'd never been to the school but he had learned its name, and her middle name, and a few other things that said he wasn't *trying* to be an uncaring asshole all the time, it was just his nature. But he staunchly refused to talk much about himself, so she'd settled for him being a decent person who made an effort, and chosen not to dwell on the fact that she regularly slept with a man whose middle name she did not know. Well, *slept* wasn't the word for it. They didn't sleep, and he didn't sleep over. Ever. And he never invited her to his apartment, either, not once. She rather suspected he just didn't want to schlep her back to her place in the middle of the night, since he remained convinced that she'd fall in love with him and beg to have his babies if they ate breakfast together.

What he did obsess over, however, was how to make her orgasms better, constantly grilling her about what she wanted him to do. He swore up and down that he'd do anything, there was nothing she could ask outside of having him piss on her that he wouldn't at least consider. She was both flattered and unnerved by his focus, but she didn't know what the problem was. She liked sex in general, and sex with him in particular. She didn't have any secret wants or desires she was afraid to express. There were times the build up to orgasm was promising, that she was sure it was leading up to the "big one" Jarek seemed intent to find. And then it didn't work out. She still came; she wasn't unsatisfied. But he was. And no matter how many questions he asked, she honestly didn't have the answer to this one.

She shook her head and tuned back into the conversation. The teachers were asking Honor questions for Ritchie, and she was shyly translating the responses. *How old are you? Twenty-nine. Are you married? No. Where do you live? Down the street. Do you like China? Yes, I do.*

Olivia smiled as she watched the interrogation, and thought she'd rather like to bring Jarek here one day, see him fend for himself against these women, and learn a little bit about the man who'd become her second friend in over a year.

There wasn't time to dwell on this thought, however, because right then the bell rang and seconds later came the telltale roar of the kids racing out of the cafeteria and back to their classes. Ritchie paled and took off, absorbed into the incoming swarm, and everyone returned to their regular routines. Olivia waited at the door to welcome the kids back, explaining patiently that *"what is that thing?"* was a tree, or at least it would be, exhausted by the time Davy trailed in after the others.

"Tree?" he echoed thoughtfully, staring at it.

"It will be," Olivia told him. "When I'm done."

"Yes," he said with a nod. "Okay. Very good."

She smothered a laugh and followed him into the room, ordering everyone into their seats. "How was lunch?" she asked, as she did every day.

She was answered with varied shouts in English and Mandarin, punctuated by Rose's insistent "Liv! Liv!" Olivia silenced them and fixed Rose with a stare that said she'd heard her, and now she must wait to be called on. The little girl with perpetual grass stains on her pants and tangles in her hair folded her hands and stared straight ahead obediently.

"Okay, Rose," Olivia said, trying not to smile. "Please put in the CD. We're going to play song number four today."

Rose leapt from her seat like a firecracker, and scurried over to the CD player to fumble with the CD she'd been allowed to touch for exactly seven days. Olivia had finally managed to control Rose's impulses with a tentative reward system—don't be bad, and you can put in and take out the CD when we sing songs. At six years old, this was the epitome of Rose's ambition, and she struggled mightily to maintain the privilege.

"Everybody stand up, please," Olivia called as the now-familiar opening notes of "The Hokey Pokey" rang out. The class absolutely loved this song, particularly because the last verse allowed the participants to choose the action, and they were delighted to stick their heads "in," or their tongues, or, on several occasions, their butts. More than once Olivia had been shaking her ass "in" and then "out," only to spot a fellow teacher peering through the window, bewildered.

"Alan!" she shouted, when the last verse was about to begin. "What should we do?" The kids absolutely died to be the one to pick the movement, and Alan, who had studiously hated Olivia and refused to speak to her from the second she'd set foot in the classroom, loved to dance. She'd been trying to get him to participate in this part of the song since they'd first begun learning it, and could see the urge to suggest something warring with his reluctance to speak to her. Again today, as he had for weeks, he folded his arms and shook his head stubbornly.

"Who else?" she tried. Every other hand in the room went up.

Three hours later she waved good-bye, another day over. Alan, of course, ignored her, but everyone else shouted, "See you tomorrow," before darting out of the room. Olivia waited until the courtyard was clear, then gathered the feather "treetop" she'd made at lunch the day before, and shuffled out to the trunk that had been drying all afternoon. She set down the bundle of feathers and stared at the monstrosity. It would look better with paint, definitely. She returned to the class to fetch a chair and the length of rope she'd gotten from Ritchie, and was working hard at fixing the treetop to the tree when she heard a tiny voice.

"O-liv-ya?"

She glanced down to see Davy standing a few feet away, watching. "Hey, buddy. What are you doing here?"

He replied in Mandarin and she didn't understand a word. Davy thought for a second, then put his hands on his hips and said, "The tree is green and brown." He pointed accusingly at the trunk. "No brown."

"I know," Olivia replied. "I'm going to paint it now." The newspaper felt dry to the touch, and she'd fastened it around a tall metal post Ritchie had rescued from the trash pile at the site, then covered in cardboard. She ducked into the class and returned with a bottle of brown paint, a paper plate, and two brushes. "Want to help?"

Davy nodded and they got to work. It took nearly an hour to get the trunk painted, and when they were done they stepped back—then farther back—to truly appreciate it. It looked like a tree. Like a tree from a Dr. Seuss book that had been in a storm and barely made it out the other side. But Davy was beaming.

"Very good, Davy."

A voice called out in Mandarin and they both turned as one of the older Chinese teachers entered the courtyard. She addressed Davy and snapped her fingers, and Davy handed her the brush and waved good-bye before running off. Olivia tidied up and collected her things, then contemplated rolling the tree into her classroom for the night before deciding against it. The sky was clear blue, not a cloud in sight, and she didn't want the paint and paste fumes to permeate the room.

"Hello, Olivia."

For the second time that day, she turned to see Honor watching from the doorway. "Hi, Honor." Three other Chinese teachers hovered behind their friend, looking on. "Is everything okay?" She didn't want to hear another word about the tree. Really. She could see it.

"Yes, everything is fine. Do you want to have dinner together tonight?"

Olivia's mouth opened and closed soundlessly, like a startled fish. "Yes," she said finally. "Okay. Thank you."

"Let's go."

She trailed the four girls out of the school and down the busy road, turning down one narrow street and then another before emerging in a crowded alley. "Is here okay?" Honor asked, as though Olivia might have a clue one way or the other.

"We'll see," she said.

They went inside what turned out to be a bustling hot pot restaurant. Olivia had had hot pot once before in Lazhou, at another, somewhat nicer place. During her first week at the school she learned that different teachers had been instructed to hang out with her in the evenings and show her around, and they'd half-heartedly done so, though Honor hadn't been among them. She'd eaten strange foods, been taken to McDonald's and KFC — twice — and guided around the large supermarket. Almost immediately after her initiation week, she'd been completely and unceremoniously abandoned. If she wasn't mistaken, this was the first time anyone from the school had opted to hang out with her when they weren't being ordered to do so.

The restaurant was large and crowded with tables and people and carts full of raw food. The basic premise was that each table came with its own pot of boiling broth and a sprawling order form with every possible kind of food listed — in Chinese, of course. Diners checked off which food they would like, it arrived at the table raw — beef; quail eggs; mushrooms; potatoes; pig brains; stomach lining; meatballs; live, crawling shrimp — absolutely everything — and patrons cooked it at their leisure, fishing out various items when they decided they were ready.

Olivia hadn't known what the hell was happening the first time she'd come, and though she wasn't a picky eater, she really hadn't enjoyed herself. Things went into the broth looking one way, and came out completely unidentifiable. She didn't recognize seventy percent of the food she'd put in her mouth. Diners at another table had tipped over their covered container of live shrimp, squealing with laughter when they scrambled over the table, trying to escape. Tonight, at least, Honor and Sunny, one of the other teachers, made an effort to help her find things she might like, and spoke English even though it appeared to pain them to do so.

A tray of small puffed pastries arrived, filled with an unrecognizable purplish-gray paste. They urged her to take one, then took one themselves, biting in. The pastry was light and flaky, the filling a strange texture, both sweet and salty. "Do you like it?" Sunny asked.

Olivia nodded around a mouthful. "It's different. What is it?"

"A snack," Sunny answered.

"Snack?" Honor echoed, frowning. "Or snake?"

"Hmm," Sunny mused thoughtfully.

Olivia stopped chewing, horrified. "*Which is it?*" Tiny bits of pastry stuck to her lip and she wiggled her arm like a serpent. "Snake?"

"Oh," Honor said. "No. Not a snake. A snack."

Olivia finished the pastry but declined a second one, and eventually they were eating a variety of boiled foods and Olivia was spending her first night in the company of someone who wasn't Jarek, and having a pretty decent time. What she couldn't figure out was why, until the teachers exchanged sly looks and asked her how well she knew Ritchie.

"I think I may have to pimp him out," she told Jarek the next evening on their run. "If it makes me friends at school, I'm going to do it."

"He could use a bit of pimping," Jarek agreed, running a circle around her. "He's kind of twitchy."

"I know. And Honor's so cute. They'll make a good couple."

"That important to you?"

"That Ritchie and Honor get together?" She laughed and tightened her ponytail. It was warm enough now that she could run in shorts and a long sleeve top and not freeze her ass off. "Not really. But today four people talked to me—four. That's…four more than normal."

"That's not what I meant."

"What did you mean?" She looked at him and he jogged ahead so he could turn around and run backward, watching her as they talked. They'd been running for close to an hour and his cheeks were flushed and his hairline was damp with sweat, his blue T-shirt sticking to his chest. She'd thought he was intimidating when they'd met, with his perma-scowl and fixed stares, but now she just thought he was hot. Moody. Closed off. But still hot. Hotter for trying to be a decent guy when they were together.

"You were popular in high school, right?"

"I guess."

"You guess?" He mock-punched her in the shoulder, some weird boxing thing.

"Okay, fine. I was popular."

"Beauty pageants?"

"God, no." She'd begged, but her mother said she'd rather die than see her smart, athletic daughter parade around in a bathing suit.

"Homecoming queen?"

"Maybe."

"Student council president?"

"Treasurer."

"Valedictorian?"

"So?"

"So you've never been a normal person. Not everybody gets fawned over every day."

"I know that." She certainly did know that. She'd spent the first twenty-five years of her life in a bubble, and then it had burst. "Were you a loner?"

"What do you think?"

"I don't think you had any friends at all."

He laughed. "I had friends."

"Your brother doesn't count." She'd gotten that much out of him, at least. One sibling.

"Okay, fine. I had *friend*."

She laughed, too. "What was his name?"

"Stacey."

"Girl Stacey or boy Stacey?"

"There's such a thing as boy Stacey?"

"Was she your girlfriend?" Olivia wasn't jealous; she was intrigued. A second detail about Jarek's deeply mysterious life? Color her invested.

"Yes. That's enough. I'm the one who asks questions."

"So if you weren't a cop and you weren't a journalist or a private investigator or a psychologist…"

"I was…"

"You were…"

He arched a brow and waited for her next guess.

"Just tell me."

He lifted his knees and jogged in place, the action strangely familiar.

"You were in the army?"

He nodded and turned to face forward, running beside her again.

"Why didn't I guess that before?"

"Because you're obsessed with being popular. You're obsessed with yourself."

She tossed back her head and laughed. "Am not."

He was looking down at her, smiling slightly. "Nah. You're not."

"What'd you do in the army?"

"Whatever they told me to do."

"Did it involve asking questions?"

A muscle in his jaw ticked, and she knew, without him confirming it. The scary face, the questions. How they'd felt like interrogations.

"When did you get out?"

"A long time ago."

"What'd you do after?"

"The same thing, but with a private contractor."

"Did you like it?"

He met her eyes. "Yes."

She flinched inwardly, but knew she wasn't wrong. She'd seen movies where men with exactly Jarek's countenance had strung up other men, tortured them until they got the answers they were looking for. And then.

"When'd you stop?"

"Two years ago."

"Why?"

"Time for a change. Why'd you come to China?"

"Because I wasn't popular anymore."

"Come on, Olivia. The truth."

She looked at him now, eyes serious. "That is the truth."

Jarek dropped it, but he didn't want to. They grabbed dinner at McDonald's and took it back to her place where he ate his burger while she took a shower, and then she ate hers while he washed up. They'd developed a bit of a routine, which didn't bother him. It had only been a few weeks, but everything intensified when you were in a foreign environment, the strangeness of things throwing people together in ways they wouldn't normally be. That's what he attributed it to, anyway. This…relationship he was falling into. The pattern.

Even as he'd told her about the interrogation work, he'd lied to himself, saying he didn't know why the words were coming out as cryptic as they'd been. Except he did know why. He told her because she'd started looking at him like he was a good guy, a decent guy, and he wanted to remind her that he wasn't. That he wasn't her boyfriend and he wasn't going to be, that if she got too close she'd get hurt in the end because he hadn't loved anybody outside of his family in a really long time, and that wasn't going to change.

She was lying in that damn twin bed, reading one of the *Chicken Soup for the Soul* books she'd found at the bookstore—this one for the Pet Lover's Soul—when he came out of the bathroom. The books were half English and half Chinese, and always made her cry, which he hated, because he was the one who inflicted pain, not the one who cleaned up afterward. And then, as though she recognized his discomfort, she'd put the books away and laugh and wipe her eyes, calling herself stupid when she was the furthest thing from it.

"C'mere," he murmured, taking the book from her hands and tossing it to the floor. She was wearing a different pair of shorts and a T-shirt, and he tugged off her shorts and crawled between her legs and went down on her until she came. Then he continued until she begged him to stop, and he told her he'd stop when he felt like it. Eventually she pulled on his hair so hard he had to climb up her body and kiss her, making her taste herself. He pushed her hair away from her face and worked himself inside her swollen folds, looking into her eyes. They were shiny with arousal, cheeks pink, lips swollen, and something in her face told him that this time was different. He wanted to fuck her really hard, but held back like he always did, not wanting to scare her. Instead he let it build, and when she came again she made a strangled, pleased sound, eyes fluttering.

After a minute he realized she was pushing against his chest, pushing him off, and he rolled to the side and watched as she slid down his body and pulled off the condom and took him in her mouth. It was different when she did this, different from all the other nameless, faceless women who had gone down on him. It was the way she looked up at him from time to time, the way she didn't have a game plan, the way she just wanted to make him feel good.

It didn't take long. He came in her mouth and she swallowed everything, stroking his thighs, making it last. She eventually straightened so she was kneeling between his calves and he opened his eyes to look at her. "Thanks."

"You're welcome. Maybe I should kiss you now, so you know how it feels."

He ran a hand across his mouth absently. "You taste good; there's nothing wrong with it."

"Oh yeah?" She clambered up and made like she was going to kiss him, and he held her back, laughing.

"Get away, barracuda."

She bit his fingers and flopped down beside him. "Did the new people show up today?"

"Yeah. It's a long way to come for five days."

"No kidding."

The guy commissioning the work wanted his own people to do the inspection, in addition to the Chinese workers who would make sure the building was up to country code. He'd flown six people over for the week, and they were all going out for drinks tomorrow night once they'd had time to rest.

Jarek reached down to stroke his fingers through her wetness, and she covered his hand. "Don't. I'm done."

"That second one was better, right?"

"They're all good. But yeah. That was…different."

"Good different?"

"Come on, don't obsess."

"Just tell me."

"Yes. Good different. Stronger. Okay?"

"How'd you come with Chris?"

She sat up straight and slapped his hands away when he tried to push her back down. "Don't ask me about him."

"Why not?"

"Because I don't have any pants on. Because it's none of your business."

"Is there something wrong with trying to knock your socks off?"

She kicked him in the shin with her bare foot. "I'm not wearing any socks. Mission accomplished."

She got off the bed and put her clothes back on, disappearing into the other room where he heard the fridge door opening, saw the light spill across the dark floor. He sighed and got dressed, then went after her. "Hey," he began, but never got to finish.

Lightning flashed outside and her head whipped around to the kitchen window that looked over the city. It was streaky with rain, and outside the streets and rooftops were gleaming. Her hand covered her mouth. "No!"

"What's wrong?"

She put on her sneakers and grabbed her jacket and keys from the dining room table, unlocking the door.

"Fuck, Olivia. What's wrong?" He hopped on one foot as he put on his shoe and tried to keep up with her.

"My tree!" she called, dashing down the stairs.

"Your what?"

Ten minutes later they stood in the dark courtyard outside Olivia's classroom, the melted, soggy mass of her tree now puddled around the metal post it had once covered. She had keys to the room and went inside to turn on the lights, then returned to pick up the sodden pile of green algae—feathers, apparently—that sat on the ground, cradling it like a sick child.

She got a big black garbage bag from her desk and he helped her scoop up the slimy newspaper, her face streaked with water, hair plastered to her skull. Her bare legs were shiny and he felt bad for not being able to keep his eyes off them when she was obviously distraught. "I know it's stupid," she kept muttering as she cleaned, her hands stained brown from the wet paint. "But I liked this tree, even if only one other person knew what it was supposed to be."

"Yeah? Who's that?" He followed her into the room, away from the metal post sitting on the metal dolly, and closed the door.

"Davy."

"He your friend?"

"My student." She tapped a seat next to a table at the front of the class. "He sits right here. He drew that picture." She waved in the general direction of an abstract drawing stuck to the wall, then wiped her hands on her yellow shorts, staining the fabric. "Shit."

Jarek leaned against her desk and looked at the classroom, the walls covered in various bits of artwork and streamers, the whiteboard holding the remnants of a game of Snakes & Ladders she'd drawn and only partially wiped off. "What was the tree for?"

"*Little Red Riding Hood.* I'm supposed to have the kids perform it at the end of the year. Thirty children in *Little Red Riding Hood.*" She came to stand beside him at the desk.

"How's that going to work?"

"Beats the hell out of me, Jarek."

"Sorry about your tree."

She rested her head against his shoulder and he put his arm around her, wishing he hadn't had the impulse. Consoling somebody, caring when they were hurt—that wasn't his thing. He didn't want it to be. So he took his arm back and she took the hint and walked to the door.

"Let's go back. Thanks for helping me clean up."

He exited ahead of her as she locked up, and he said good-bye when they got to her building, but he didn't walk her up, and he didn't kiss her good night. He made his way back to his cold, empty apartment alone, feet squishing in his shoes, contemplating the weather and a whole host of other things. He didn't understand the news so he didn't watch it, didn't know that the blue skies had planned to open up and rain down tonight. He didn't know about her tree. Didn't want to know.

He took a second shower to clean the paint off his hands and the mud off his ankles, and grabbed a beer and sat on the couch in the dark, thinking about her orgasm and wondering what had happened to make it different. He'd done all that stuff to her before, but this time something had changed.

And then it hit him. He knew what had been different. He knew absolutely, positively what it would take to make her come so hard she forgot the name of every other man. And he knew with terrifyingly equal certainty that he couldn't do it.

Chapter Six

The next day Olivia and Ritchie ate lunch in her classroom, and when they finished they were invited over to the mah-jongg room. Of course Ritchie wouldn't know what that meant, but Olivia accepted immediately, dragging him across the courtyard where they sat side-by-side and watched four of the older teachers play a game they couldn't understand.

Olivia was happy to be there because she'd finally been included in something, and Ritchie was happy because Honor was there. The two of them whispered quietly as Olivia watched the game, hopelessly confused. Her mind drifted and she told herself not to dwell on Jarek's sudden coldness the night before. The way he'd gone from soft and supportive to hard and remote in the span of a single second. She told herself she was just being emotional because of the tree thing, and last night she'd lain in bed and tried to imagine new ways to make trees until she'd fallen asleep.

Apparently Jarek had told Ritchie about the tree snafu, because Ritchie had called her today and invited himself over for lunch under the pretense of discussing new trees, but Olivia knew better. He was there for Honor. And she didn't mind. At least she got to participate in something, even if it was only as a spectator.

A couple of the older teachers sat at another table, where they folded the origami cranes that hung in strings from the ceiling in several of the classrooms. They noticed Olivia watching and awkwardly invited her over, showing her with painstaking care and slowness how to fold the paper. Olivia knew how to say "I'm sorry" in Mandarin and that's really all she said, repeating the words for every wrong fold and accidental crease, until someone told her to shut up.

At the end of the lunch hour she had a misshapen paper bird that everyone laughed at, and Ritchie had Honor's phone number. He'd invited her to the bar tonight to welcome the visiting workers, but she'd declined, blaming her poor English, though it was perfectly fine.

"They think you're so dreamy," Olivia teased as she walked him to the school gates that opened onto the street. "They tell me all the time."

He blushed. "Shut up."

"They like your glasses. They think you look like Superman."

"You're coming tonight, right?"

"Yeah. I'm supposed to be."

"Cool. Oh, hey, look."

She followed his gaze over her shoulder to see Jarek and Dale headed their way carrying bottles of iced tea, likely the remnants of their lunch. They exchanged greetings and Olivia wished Jarek weren't wearing sunglasses because his face was stony and impassive again, and she didn't have a clue what he was thinking.

"Long time, Olivia," Dale said.

"How are you, Dale?"

"Good. Living the life. You coming tonight?"

"I think so."

"It's a nice bar. You been?" He drank his iced tea and watched her.

"No. It's across from that electronics store, right?"

"That's the one. Jarek will show you."

"I'll meet you there," Jarek interjected.

The obvious brush-off stung, but she just shrugged. "Fine." She used the word on purpose, and was rewarded when the muscle in his jaw ticked.

"Meet her?" Dale scoffed. "Walk her over, idiot. We're not heading out until nine."

"It's okay," she said. "I can find it." She was grateful when the lunch bell rang. "Time for phonics. See you later."

She started to duck back through the gates but Jarek snagged the sleeve of her T-shirt. "I'll walk you," he said, voice flat. "Nine o'clock, okay?"

She looked up into the cold, reflective stare of his glasses. "Fine."

Olivia didn't really know if Jarek did jealous, but she dressed up all the same, in tight dark jeans, boots with heels, and a top cut low enough to show some cleavage. It was hidden beneath her black leather jacket, and if he noticed anything different about her, he didn't say so when she met him downstairs at nine o'clock on the dot. Since that first night when he'd been deliberately late, he'd been on time for everything. Just as well, since as far as she knew he didn't have her phone number and couldn't call to say he'd been delayed.

He jerked his chin in some asshole-ish way of greeting, and she said hey and looked past him, like she couldn't care less. The bar was close to the city center, which wasn't far since Lazhou wasn't big. They walked in silence for a few minutes, until Jarek sighed and gripped her shoulder, pushing her to the inside of the sidewalk so he was closer to the curb.

"Everyone asked what happened to my tree," Olivia volunteered when she started feeling awkward.

There was a second where she didn't think he'd respond, then he looked down at her. "Oh yeah? What'd you say?"

"That I sold it."

He smiled in spite of himself. "Well done."

More silence.

"Are these new people nice?"

"Yeah, nice enough. I only met a couple."

"Did they approve your work?"

They waited for a light to change and a group of young men passed by, looking Olivia from head to toe appreciatively. Jarek noticed and clenched his fist, but didn't touch her. "It's not really mine to approve." They started walking again. "They're looking at structural stuff, electrical. The door frames aren't as important."

"But you make furniture too, right?"

"Some. I'll make more later, when it's ready to go in."

"Does it take a long time?"

"Depends on what I'm making."

"Thanks for being specific."

He sighed and tugged open the door to the bar so she could step through. Smoking indoors was permitted, and the room was hot and dim. She shrugged out of her jacket and easily spotted the table of white men, one middle-aged woman looking out of place among them, Ritchie, Dale and Brant seated on one side.

"Hey!" the men called as she and Jarek approached.

She bent down to hug Ritchie and was pretty certain Dale looked down her shirt. "Hey," she said. She smiled at the newcomers. "I'm Olivia."

"Olivia," Brant said, and went around the table making introductions as she dutifully shook hands and said hello. He did the same for Jarek, identifying him as the carpenter for the few people he hadn't already met.

"What do you do, Olivia?" Carolyn, the electrical inspector, asked.

Dale spoke up before she could answer. "She's Jarek's girlfriend."

"She's not my girlfriend," Jarek said coldly, voice raised over the noise of the bar. Of course the room chose that moment to take a collective breath, and the words rang out, a humiliating denial that hung in the air for what felt like an eternity.

Then Olivia pasted on a smile and aimed it at the newcomers. "That's right," she said, pulling out her seat and sitting down. "I'm not. So feel free to hit on me."

Everybody laughed, the uncomfortable spell broken, and Jarek looked at her oddly when he sat down beside her. She kept the smile in place and struck up a conversation with Marcus, the geologist or geographer or something, and let herself enjoy the company of people who didn't hate her, and didn't resent her, and weren't afraid to talk to her.

Jarek saw Olivia put on her coat at twelve twenty. She'd had two beers and had started to yawn thirty minutes ago. He glanced around the table; everyone else seemed perfectly content to drink until closing, but he knew she had class at nine o'clock the next morning, and entertaining six-year-olds was a lot harder than pouring concrete.

She stood up and they booed her, but she just laughed good-naturedly and waved good night, telling him he didn't have to leave early, she'd get a cab. Jarek ignored her and pulled on his own jacket, pretending not to notice Dale's appraising stare. Olivia hadn't said a word to him in three hours, conversing with every single other person like a normal human being, like the woman she'd probably been before she came to China.

He followed her through the bar and outside into the clean, cool night air. "That's a fucking relief," he said, pulling in a deep breath. "I can't get used to the smoke."

"Yeah." She was looking down the street for a cab, but Lazhou shops closed early, and traffic was sparse.

"Let's just walk," he said, reaching for her wrist.

She pulled her hand away. "Let's not."

"What's going on?"

She waved at a cab, but it drove by, occupied. She muttered something under her breath that Jarek didn't catch. "Let's just walk," he repeated.

"I don't want to walk with you." She had her back to him, ramrod straight, as she waited for another cab.

He sighed. "Oliv—"

"Just go back inside, Jarek."

"I don't want to go back inside."

"Then do something else. But don't talk to me and don't touch me and don't get in this cab when it stops."

A cab had approached, blinker flashing, and was now stopped on the other side of the intersection as the driver waited for the light to change.

"Tell me what's bothering you, please." He jammed his hands in his pockets and tried to keep his voice neutral. He had a pretty damn good idea what was bothering her, but she'd seemed in good spirits in the bar, even if she had given him the cold shoulder. He'd almost started to believe he'd imagined the hurt look on her face when he shouted to the whole world that she wasn't his girlfriend. Which she wasn't.

"I know I'm not your girlfriend," she said, turning to look at him. Psychically sucker punching him when he saw the tears in her eyes.

"And I *know* I've never done anything to suggest I thought I was. But it was really fucking humiliating to have you announce it to the bar, when everyone at the site knows we're sleeping together. And it was really fucking humiliating to sit there for three hours and see them exchange little looks, like how I'm desperate or stupid or something, following you around when you don't fucking want me."

"I didn't—"

The cab rolled up and he reached for the door, but she slapped his hand away, hard. "Don't get in this cab, Jarek. Don't come over. Don't call me—Oh wait, you can't, right? Because you've never bothered to ask for my number. Just as well."

She got in and slammed the door, keeping her eyes averted as she gave the driver her address and they pulled away.

He cursed and ran a hand through his hair, flagging down the cab that trailed the first, giving the driver a hundred *kuai* extra if he drove fast, which the guy was more than happy to do. Jarek spoke approximately nine words of Mandarin, none of which were Olivia's address, which he didn't even know, if he were being honest, instead of the dick he usually was. He gave the guy directions and they got to the cold, concrete building a minute ahead of her.

He leaned against the green door and watched Olivia pay her driver, saying good night in Mandarin before climbing out and waving. She turned and froze when she saw him.

He held up his hands in surrender before she could curse at him some more. "I'm sorry," he said. "I'm sorry."

She fumbled in her purse for her keys, avoiding his gaze. "I don't care."

"I'm really sorry, Olivia. I didn't mean to embarrass you."

"Well, you did."

"I know. I'm sorry. I regretted it as soon as I said it. I didn't know it bothered you so much or I would have taken it back right away."

She found the keys and elbowed her way past him, unlocking the door. "There's nothing to take back. You're right. I'm not your girlfriend. I don't know anything about you, and tonight I realized I don't want to."

He could see tear tracks on her cheeks, shimmering in the moonlight. He had hurt a lot of people in his life, but he'd never felt bad about it. Until now. "Let me up." He ignored her efforts to close the door in his face and followed her up the stairs, keeping his hands to himself. He waited while she unlocked both doors, knowing it was pretty much impossible for her to close them if he wouldn't let her, which he wouldn't. She must have recognized the futility, too, because she didn't try. She stalked into her room and hurled her purse on the bed, partially unzipping her jacket before remembering how low cut that damn shirt was and deciding to keep it on.

He locked both doors behind him and gave her a challenging look, but she just stared back, stone-faced. She might be kind and pretty, but she was really fucking hurt and angry, and he deserved all of it. All because she'd put her head on his shoulder and he'd put his arm around her, even though they'd done far more intimate things. She was just the only woman he'd put his arm around in a really long time, and he was a really shitty person.

"I'm sorry," he repeated.

"I heard you. It doesn't matter."

"I'll go back to the bar and tell them, if it'll make you feel better."

"It won't. But you should go back anyway."

She was standing stiffly against the wall between the bedroom and the office, and he saw the moment she rested against it, tired and sad, even though she tried not to let it show.

"I'll do whatever you ask. Just don't tell me to go."

She laughed humorlessly. "I don't know what to ask you, Jarek. Every time I ask you something, you refuse to answer."

He swallowed thickly. He was afraid of this. "Ask me anything."

"What's your middle name?"

"Andrew."

She looked at him sharply, surprised. "When's your birthday?"

"January thirty-first."

"Have you ever been married?"

"No." He approached her and she watched warily, not moving. He unzipped her jacket the rest of the way and pushed it down her shoulders, then tossed it behind him toward the table.

"Don't," she whispered, with no real venom.

"Ask me something else."

"What's your favorite food?"

"Lasagna." He kissed her, softly, lingering.

"When'd you lose your virginity?"

"Sixteen. With Stacey."

"Why'd you break up?"

He traced her lower lip with his tongue, felt her breath on his cheek, smelling faintly of beer. "I enlisted. Moved away."

"Where'd you go?"

He knelt at her feet and slipped off the boots with the pointy heels that had made his dick take notice when she'd exited the building earlier that night. The ones he'd wanted to haul off and hurl at the kids who'd ogled her at the intersection. "Lots of places. Iraq. Afghanistan. Angola. More."

He unzipped her pants and pulled them down, his heart in his throat, desperate for her to let him. He kissed her knee and her thigh, massaged her foot in his big, hurtful hands.

"Have you ever killed anybody?"

He treated the other leg the same way, kissing a little bit higher, smelling her arousal, feeling so fucking exposed. "Probably. I can't talk about it."

"Why don't you feel bad?"

"Because it was my job."

He pressed a kiss to her clit and heard her sharp intake of breath. He licked her and answered her questions, easy ones, hard ones, until she was trembling. For once he didn't try to make her come, just stood up and took off all his clothes, removed the last of hers, and kissed her really, really hard.

"Are you close with your parents?"

"My mother's dead. My dad's dying; we don't talk."

"Why not?"

"Shh. Ask me another time."

He squeezed a hand between her legs and pushed three fingers into her pussy, forcing her to part her thighs to accept him.

"What's your favorite movie?"

"*Alien.*"

"Ugh." Then, "*Jarek.*" Not a sigh. An order.

"I'm going to fuck you, Olivia."

"Good."

"Hard."

"Good."

"Harder than before. As hard as I want to."

She gripped his hair and pulled his face away, looking at him. "You'd better make me come this time, Jarek. Properly."

He dug a shoulder into her stomach and hoisted her up, carting her into the bedroom and dropping her on her hands and knees on the bed. She shrieked in surprise but he just held her down, one hand splayed between her shoulder blades, keeping her ass in the air as he rolled on a condom. He kicked her knees apart and held her in place as he fitted his cock to her glistening folds, then rammed inside, deep and hard, making her cry out.

He didn't ease up. He didn't take it easy. He *fucked* her, like he hadn't really done before. He gave her everything, rough and hard, like he'd been wanting to and worried she couldn't handle. She groaned and moaned and clawed the mattress, writhing like she was trying to get away and get closer, but he didn't let her go anywhere. He held her down with one hand and gripped her hip hard with the other, knowing he'd leave marks on her tan skin and not giving a fuck.

He pounded into her until she came, a wet, noisy mess, wailing into the mattress. He slapped her ass and exploded, watching his cock disappear into her, watching her accept everything he had to give.

He knew how to manipulate her body, knew the biology. But she'd wanted to know *him*. She'd known Chris for ten years, dated him for a year before she slept with him. She knew his favorite color and his recurring nightmares and what cereal he liked to eat. Jarek had kept her locked out of the most basic, simple places because the physical had always been enough for him. But it wasn't enough for her, and when it dawned on him last night, it had scared the shit out of him.

He curled over her body, feeling her shudder as he stroked her spine, feeling the fragile, tender bumps beneath his fingers. "You okay?" he asked softly. He thought she would be; she was really fucking strong.

"I'm fine."

He stiffened and started to pull away, but she reached back and dug her nails into his ass, holding him in place. She was laughing.

"This really isn't a time for jokes, Olivia."

She snorted into the mattress. "You like my jokes."

He pried her nails out of his flesh, stripped off the condom, and lay back on the mattress. She stayed at the far end, curled on her side, eyes closed. He prodded her with his feet until she looked at him.

"Tell me if you're okay. For real. With everything."

"Don't touch me with your feet, Jarek. It's disgusting."

"Tell me."

"You'll flip out and think I'm being emotional."

He stared at the ceiling, knowing she was right. She'd convinced him to open up, but instead of crawling in like he'd feared, she was giving him his space. Showing him that just because he'd opened the door didn't mean she'd slip in and try to take over.

"I might," he answered eventually.

She moved up to lay beside him, touching only because the bed was so ridiculously small they had no choice. "That was the best orgasm I've ever had," she admitted.

He couldn't help but grin, smug. "Really?"

"Thanks."

"Ha. Thanks for letting me."

"I really didn't think you'd follow me."

"I've never followed anybody before."

"I can imagine."

"You can see my apartment if I want to."

"Do you need time to hide all your porn?"

"Nah. It's on my computer. Just don't look in the folder called 'Work Information.'"

"Okay."

He waited another minute, then couldn't take it any longer. He was getting antsy. His skin itched. "I'm going to go back to my place now." She didn't say anything as he left the room to pick up his clothes and get dressed. He reappeared fully clothed and holding up her shirt. "You know Dale was looking at your tits all night, right?"

"Were you watching Dale the whole time?"

"No. I was watching you. And your tits."

"Don't get sentimental, Jarek. It's just sex."

"Come lock up after me."

She wrapped the comforter around herself and followed him out. He unlocked both doors and stood on the threshold as she held the keys.

"Good night, Olivia."

She tilted her head. "Good night, Jarek."

He hooked a finger in the blanket and tugged her forward to kiss her. "I'll see you tomorrow," he said. It was the only thing he had to offer, but it was the truth.

Chapter Seven

"**D**o you know what time it is?"

"Six thirty-five," Jane Clarke answered.

"Mom."

"What time do you get up for school?"

"Eight. I don't have to be there until just before nine."

"Well, now you have time to talk."

Olivia groaned and rolled over, burying her face in the pillow. She winced a little bit, sore between her legs after Jarek's enthusiastic "apology" the night before. His refusal to spend the night sometimes bothered her, but she was grateful for his absence now. "What's going on?" she mumbled.

"Oh, not much. The marching band's fundraiser is going well, and Jim Carnegie plans to retire at the end of the year."

"Mr. Carnegie? He's not that old, is he?"

"Not really, no. He's got it in his head that he'd like to travel the world. I think you influenced him, Olivia."

"The blind leading the blind," she said dryly.

Her mother laughed. "How are you liking it there? Is it warming up? We haven't gotten any e-mails from you lately."

She rolled onto her back and stared at the plain white ceiling. Early morning rays of sunshine were slanting through the thin, flower-patterned curtains that came with the apartment, and for the first time since she'd arrived on a blustery January night, it occurred to her that she *was* liking it there, and she told her mother as much. "It's warmer now. No more electric blanket. The kids are just wearing one or two shirts."

"You should send some pictures."

Olivia yawned. "I'll try. I told you before, it's next to impossible to access the Internet from my apartment, and the Internet café is scary." The closest place was dank and smoky and crowded with young men hunched over keyboards, muttering into headsets. She'd ventured in a couple of times, but always rushed out before her hour was up.

"Have you done any traveling? Gotten out of, what's it called again? La-joo?"

"Lazhou," she corrected. "And I haven't been anywhere. It's surprisingly difficult to get around. I mean, I'm sure it's better in the bigger cities, but here hardly anyone speaks English, and I kept getting lost. I've been exploring Lazhou a bit, and it's better than I thought." She felt braver with Jarek at her side, ducking into shops and side streets she'd have otherwise avoided. He'd lead her on random routes for their runs, finding parks and statues and pagodas whose names they couldn't read, but which she'd liked all the same.

"Well, that's nice."

"How's dad? How's the practice?"

"He's great. You know him. Always working. There's no shortage of sick children to see."

"Sounds about right."

Jane Clarke tended to sound like a doting housewife and mother, but in fact was the iron-fisted principal of the middle school Olivia had once attended. Jane and Dr. Thomas Clarke were well-respected in the small town of Candor, Michigan, and Olivia had been their glowing, beautiful daughter, popular and adored. Until she wasn't anymore.

She tried to swallow her resentment, but it wasn't easy, so instead she climbed out of bed and grabbed a carton of orange juice from the fridge, pouring herself a glass as she looked out the kitchen window at the already-busy street below.

"Olivia? Are you listening?"

"I'm listening." She wasn't, though. Jane was talking about how she and Thomas had come to the sad conclusion that the ancient oak tree in the front yard had to come down since the roots were getting too hard to control. All Olivia could picture were the signs that had been nailed to that tree in the middle of the night, the word "BITCH" spray painted across the broad trunk in neon pink, even though she hadn't lived in her parents' house for years.

She thought of the way everyone in town had turned on her, how her parents had been torn between loving and supporting their daughter and not wanting to upset the status quo. How they'd called her instead of visited, how they'd cleaned out the spare room so Chris could move in. How they'd chosen him.

She didn't hate her parents, but something in their relationship was broken, no matter how carefully they tried to repair it. They'd turned from being the two people who loved and supported her most in the world into the two who'd had to hide their disappointment and their embarrassment. They'd both devoted their lives to helping children, but when Olivia did the right thing—the only thing—she could have done in her situation, they hadn't understood. Not really.

"Oh, Olivia, you had no choice," her mother had assured her, patting her hand awkwardly. "But we really feel that Chris would have done the same thing, had you given him the chance."

Olivia wasn't so sure. It's why she'd done what she had done. And why her picture perfect world had come crashing down around her.

"Mom?" she interrupted. "Sorry to cut you off. I have to go, okay? I'll try and send pictures."

"We'll send you some, too, honey."

She couldn't imagine what pictures they'd send since she'd seen everything Candor, Michigan had to offer a thousand times in her life, but she nodded absently. "Okay, great. Bye."

"I love you."

Olivia hung up and got in the shower, letting the hot water clear her head. She'd traveled seven thousand miles to escape these memories; she wouldn't let them catch up now.

Alan was dressed like Spiderman.

"What's happening?" Olivia whispered to Honor. Technically there was always a Chinese teacher lurking in her classroom, ready to help out whenever she needed it, but it was almost always one who didn't speak English and didn't really want to participate. Olivia was more than willing to fumble through on her own, but there were some things she couldn't decipher.

Alan said something animated, hands waving.

"It's his favorite movie," Honor translated. "And now he is Spiderman."

"I see."

"Also, his mother would like him to be Spiderman."

"What?"

"At the…How do you say? The…graduation. Your performance. *Little Red Riding*…"

"*Hood. Little Red Riding Hood.* And Spiderman."

Honor was trying not to laugh. "Yes."

"Okay. Awesome." Olivia gave Alan the thumbs up and he gave her a flicker of acknowledgement before crossing his arms and turning away. Some of the girls in the class were laughing at his costume, but most of the boys looked envious.

The next day, four boys came in dressed as Spiderman. "We can't have four Spidermen in the play," Olivia told the class, trying not to look desperate. She still didn't know how she'd fill out the cast of thirty, but she couldn't picture Spiderman — times four — carrying a picnic basket to grandma, who hadn't been eaten by a wolf, because there were no wolves in the forest that was not scary.

"Spider*mans*," Rose corrected.

"I beg your pardon?"

"*Spidermans!*" the kids cried.

Olivia opened her mouth to correct them, then promptly shut it. On her fifth day at the school, she'd learned that the parents had been invited to sit in on her afternoon class. She'd barely recognized the kids at that point, didn't know their names, and was entirely unfamiliar with the lessons. Plus, she didn't have any materials, as no one had bothered to share their flashcards with her. So she'd plowed on desperately, reviewing the vocabulary they were supposed to have learned the previous semester, until one of the parents, a man who spoke English, stood up and yelled at her because the kids weren't pronouncing the words properly. He was particularly upset that they weren't pluralizing things. Embarrassed and annoyed but unable to do much about either, Olivia had dedicated herself to getting the kids to add S when pluralizing words. And now it was coming back to haunt her. She wasn't about to get into a grammar debate with a bunch of six-year-olds, so she just gave in.

"Okay, fine. Spidermans," she said. "We have four Spidermans. Does anybody else have a costume they'd like to wear in the play?"

They gazed at her blankly.

"You are Spiderman," she said, pointing at Alan. "And you are Spiderman." She repeated it for the remaining webbed crime fighters, then pointed at Davy, who was wearing three shirts. "Who are you?"

Davy blinked up at her. "My name is Davy."

"Are you Spiderman?"

Realization dawned on his tiny, sweet face. "No. I am a butterfly."

"I am a bird!" a little girl shouted from the back.

"I am a monkey!" someone else cried.

"Okay, okay," Olivia said, waving her hands to silence them. "Let's make a list of who everybody wants to be. Then…we'll go from there."

If only to say that she had tried, Olivia detoured to walk past the Internet café on her way home that day and the next, dragging herself inside the dim interior and paying the fee to use a computer for an hour. There were approximately sixty computers in the cramped space, lined up in rows of eight, and Olivia found a free one next to the window. The guy beside her was wearing a headset and muttering furiously as he glowered at the screen where a car was careening through town, gunfire exploding out the windows.

She waited for the computer to start up and pretended to ignore the curious stares, eventually logging in to her e-mail and finding three new messages and two hundred junk e-mails. It had been weeks since she'd last come in here; she remembered the days when not an hour would pass without a text or an e-mail or some social media update. Now she had two messages from her parents—the last from a week before—and one from Willa Jetz, her college roommate, who now taught kindergarten outside of Boston.

She clicked on Willa's message and read through, feeling guilty that she wasn't keeping in touch more frequently. Willa was one of the few people who hadn't shied away from her in the past year—perhaps due to the fact that she lived in another state, but maybe not—and she'd faced her own difficulties recently, though the e-mail said she was doing better.

Olivia typed out a reply, apologizing for being an absentee friend, recounting the tale of the four Spidermans and a few other events, but omitting any mention of Jarek. What would she say, exactly? *He gave me the best orgasm of my life yesterday, just hours after humiliating me in front of all the people he works with? Please tell me I'm not desperate and pathetic for letting him in, even though he refuses to spend the night?*

She hit send, then skimmed the messages from her parents. The usual inquiries, updates about things Olivia no longer cared about. She signed out and sighed, strumming her fingers on the desktop. Back when she'd been popular, her days had been jam-packed with things to do, people to see, and she'd liked it. She liked having friends. She liked going out and meeting new people. She'd been upset at the bar, but it was nice talking to the newcomers. Marcus, the geologist or geographer or something, had been really funny. She wanted that again. She wanted to go places and do things. She had a trip to Thailand booked for early June that she both anticipated and dreaded in equal measures. She'd bought a ticket for the week of her birthday, naïvely believing she would overcome her fear of the unknown by moving to China, then spend a week in Thailand, confident and carefree.

As she had so many times before, Olivia looked up pictures of Thailand and tried to imagine herself wandering around happily, but couldn't. She could barely envision herself in China, and she'd been there for months. She had to get out more, learn how to get around strange places, gain confidence. A surge of inspiration hit and she typed "Shanghai" into the search engine. She hadn't been back since her plane had landed and she'd taken the bus to the train station. She'd conquered Lazhou, surely now she was ready for a day trip to Shanghai.

"Do you want to come with me to Shanghai this weekend?"

"No." Normally Jarek would have let the conversation end there, but Olivia looked so surprised—and so stung—that he gave in and explained. "I've traveled a lot. I'm over it. Too many people. Too much hassle. It's not for me."

"Then why'd you come to China?"

"To get my brother off my back." At her perplexed look, he elaborated again. Too much of this and he'd become a proper conversationalist. "He's friends with Brant, and I've done work for him before. Brant needed a carpenter because his usual guy couldn't come for some reason or another, so here I am."

Olivia shrugged and snagged a piece of shrimp from the plate between them. "Okay."

Jarek watched her across the small table as he finished his beer. She didn't seem upset, which was a relief. He didn't want to go to Shanghai, but if she'd pushed him he'd have agreed. Lately he'd started feeling like she was getting him to do a lot of things he didn't want to do, and making it seem like his idea. Apologizing when he was an asshole. Inviting her over to his apartment. She was coming over tonight for the first time, and he was dreading it. He never brought women home, no matter where home was at the time. He always went to their place, that way he could leave when he was ready, no awkward small talk, no strained excuses as to why they couldn't spend the night.

Still, Olivia had seemed different this evening, reserved, telling him stories about her students without her usual dry humor. "Something else bothering you?" he asked. Shit. He hated being this guy. If she poured out her heart about something, he wouldn't know what to say. He'd never been a caretaker. Jonah was the nice brother, everybody knew it.

"Not really."

He relaxed an iota, relieved, then ate the green peppers she'd shunted to the side of the plate. "Did you accidentally eat a green pepper?" *Where had that come from?* She'd said she was fine and he was still prying? He didn't. Want. To know.

"I talked to my mom yesterday."

"She all right?"

"Yeah, she's fine. Everybody's fine."

"Then what's the problem?"

"Nothing."

"Homesick?"

Her smile was sad. "No."

"You want to tell me why you left Michigan? Beyond not being popular anymore?"

She shrugged and poked her bowl of steamed rice with her chopsticks. "I did something a lot of people didn't like. It was the right thing to do, but…they didn't think so."

"You going to tell me what it is?"

She straightened in her seat and shook her head as though clearing it. "No. It's in the past. I don't want to talk about it."

"You look like you need to." He gave himself a mental kick. *Shut up, ass hat.*

"Thanks, Jarek. You don't have to do this."

He frowned. "Do what?"

"This." She gestured between them. "Be nice, or whatever."

"I can be nice."

She patted his hand. "I know you can. What'd you do today?"

Relieved, he let her change the subject. "Worked. Same as always." He decided not to tell her he'd spent the better part of an hour drawing trees, trying to figure out how much wood he'd need to make her a little forest for her class play. He couldn't decide if he was doing it because he wanted to, or because he still felt bad about what had happened at the bar. And he *really* couldn't decide which reason was worse.

The server came by and dropped the bill on the table without pausing. They watched her stroll off, bemused. "Guess we're done," Olivia said.

"You go now!" Jarek whispered in a high-pitched voice. "You stay long enough!"

She giggled. No one had ever actually said those words, but the service at the delicious-but-unwelcoming hole-in-the-wall restaurant was never exactly friendly. They'd take it personally, but everyone seemed to receive the same level of disinterested service, Chinese or otherwise.

Something in his chest loosened up when she laughed, showing all those white teeth. "You actually ready to go?" Jarek asked.

"Yeah. I'm ready."

He put his hand on her back when they left the restaurant, the closest he'd ever managed to come to holding her hand. Stacey had always insisted on holding hands but Jarek hated it, and after they broke up he'd never done it again.

It was only seven o'clock, so they stopped in a couple of stores on the way back. Olivia bought more DVDs, including the fourth season of *Parenthood*, which she'd forced him to start watching, and now they were both hooked.

He was worried his feet would start to drag when they approached his building, or that his hands would tremble when he unlocked the door, but the worst thing that happened was running into Dale in the hallway when they stepped out of the elevator.

"Hey," Dale said, looking between the two of them. He was wearing a red muscle shirt and looked ridiculous.

Jarek felt the irrational urge to explain the situation. *I'm just going to show her something. She's not staying. She's not my girlfriend, except she is.*

"Hey, Dale. Working out?" Olivia nodded at the towel in his meaty hand.

"Yeah. Training Ritchie. He wants to be in shape for that teacher friend of yours."

"Be nice to him."

"Me? Always." Dale got into the elevator and Jarek took the keys out of his pocket.

"You ready for this?" he asked.

"I don't know. Am I?"

He opened the door and she gasped as though he'd revealed a treasure trove of gold. Olivia braced a hand on the wall for support. "Is this really happening?" she breathed.

"Shut up and get in before I change my mind." He swatted her ass as she sauntered past. The place didn't look too bad with the light from the setting sun coming in. It was minimally furnished, but what was there was nice, modern. Better than everything she had.

"I like it," she said, peeking into the bathroom. "Do you ever use the kitchen?"

"Not really."

"Ooh. A television." She stroked her fingers along the top of the screen reverently. "Imagine watching *Parenthood* on this." To date they'd watched everything on her laptop, since her apartment had come with neither a television nor a DVD player. It was cramped in her twin bed, but he'd gotten used to sitting close beside her, the computer balanced on her knees as they watched.

"I got you something," Jarek said, feeling a pang of discomfort.

She looked at him with interest. "Yeah? What?"

He plucked a DVD from behind his back. He'd bought it at the store when she wasn't looking. "Your favorite movie star."

Olivia wrinkled her nose, but not in distaste. "Julia Roberts? She's not my favorite."

"Look at that smile. Those teeth. It's you."

She laughed. "I like Julia Roberts, I don't *look* like Julia Roberts. Also, she's playing a prostitute here."

"What about those boots you wore the other night? You could clomp around in nothing but those, smiling, and you'd be a dead ringer."

"Good to know you fantasize about prostitutes, Jarek."

"You want to watch it?"

She looked at him. "Do *you* want to watch it? You always complain about my movies."

He shrugged. "I've never seen it. Whatever. It's your call. We can watch something else."

"No." She squeezed his fingers and took the DVD, plucking it from its sleeve. "Let's watch. I like this one. Thank you."

For some reason he didn't know how to respond. She wasn't making a big deal about it—and it wasn't a big deal, the thing had cost, like, a dollar—but he'd done it to cheer her up, and thought maybe he had. And there she went again, making him do things he wouldn't normally do, without asking him to do anything at all.

"You want a beer?"

"Sure."

He grabbed two bottles from the fridge and joined her on the couch. They sat a full two feet apart as the movie started. "This is kind of a novelty," Olivia remarked.

"What?"

"Not sitting in your armpit. Having an actual couch, and a television."

"It's a palace."

She had a bed, a wardrobe, and a nightstand in one room, a desk and chair in the other, and the dining room table in the third. They spent a lot of time in bed, not all of it fooling around.

"It's kind of a luxury." She stretched out, crossing her feet on his table, then glanced at him. "Do you mind if I look in your bedroom?"

"Ah, sure." He paused the movie, but didn't move as she headed toward the closed door.

"This is it?"

"Yeah."

"Why's the door closed?"

"No reason." He'd left the window open, and it must have blown shut. No doubt she thought he'd done it to keep her out, which, four weeks ago, he probably would have.

She turned the knob and pushed open the door. If she was expecting something awful, she wouldn't find it. He had a king size bed covered in a black comforter with some sort of abstract silver print on the bottom, a basic bedroom set, and a picture of the ocean hanging on the wall over the headboard. The place had come furnished, and he'd never given much thought to how it looked until now.

Olivia disappeared into the room for a minute, then came back out, beer bottle dangling from her fingertips. "Pretty harmless," she said, rejoining him on the couch.

"Get over here." He patted the cushion next to him.

"What about all the space this couch affords us?"

"You think I watch these movies for fun?"

"I thought they were teaching you how to be romantic."

She scooted closer and he put his arm around her shoulders, dropping his hand onto her breast. "I'm trying."

By the time the movie ended, they were both breathing hard. She liked to torment him sometimes, insisting he not disturb her while she was watching, demanding that he rewind if he made her miss a part. Today had been no exception, but her damn hands had been wandering pretty freely, and when Julia Roberts informed the snooty saleswoman that she'd lost a big commission, Jarek started repaying the favor.

As the credits scrolled down the screen and the familiar theme song played, he pinned Olivia against the cushions and yanked off her pants. She straddled him as he freed his cock and rolled on a condom, then dragged her down where he needed her most. Her eyes sank shut and she bit her bottom lip, taking him deep. He watched her face, stroking her neck and her back, eyes settling on their joining bodies. He heard her breath hitch and looked up to see her flushed cheeks as she watched him watch them. She smiled and he kissed her, thinking that he'd been doing a lot of kissing this past month. Maybe more than he'd ever done in his whole life, all combined.

It didn't take long before they were both groaning, Olivia's hands tangled in his hair, pulling so hard his scalp ached. Jarek didn't complain as the orgasm was wrenched from him, hips pistoning upward as he held her in place. She came then, too, muttering incoherently into his ear, some strange combination of his name and God's that made him feel fucking amazing. Since the night at the bar, he'd been making her come the way he'd tried so hard to do for the first month. He'd had to open up to get the results he wanted, but it hadn't killed him. The trade-off had been worth it. The harder she came the harder he came; quid pro quo. Or something like that.

She made a silly, strangled sound as she eased off and stood, and he held her still for a second so he could look at her intimately. She squirmed and pried at his fingers but he didn't let her go, giving her a filthy look as he leaned in and swiped his tongue through her swollen folds. She shuddered and pushed him away, picking up her panties and quickly dressing.

"You in a rush to be somewhere?" he asked when she glanced at her watch.

"I have to make some signs for tomorrow," she said, sitting down on the edge of the coffee table as she laced up her sneakers. "I'm going to turn my desk into a store, and let the kids come shopping."

"Yeah?" Jarek found his own shoes and put them on. "What are you selling?"

"Oh, the usual. Toothpaste, tissues. Bananas and pencils. Whatever previously learned vocabulary items I can find." She straightened and picked up her purse, noticing that he was waiting for her. "What are you doing?"

He walked to the door and held it open, avoiding her eyes. "I have to go get something. You reminded me."

"Get what?"

He hesitated. "Milk."

She folded her arms under her breasts as they waited for the elevator. "You have to get milk at ten o'clock at night?"

"So? I drink it at breakfast."

"Ah. Another piece of the puzzle."

"Just get in, Olivia." He shoved her into the elevator and she elbowed him in the stomach, laughing when he subdued her easily.

"You don't have to walk me home, Jarek."

"I'm not."

"You are too."

"Am not." He absolutely was. But he knew what she was doing, too. He didn't want her to stay, and she was making up a reason to go so he didn't have to. And now that the situation had been reversed and she was the one bolting after sex, preparing to leave him alone in that big, empty apartment, he didn't like it one bit. What kind of immature asshole did that? He did, obviously.

So he did the only thing he could think of to appease the guilt, and walked her back to her door, bypassing all the stores on the way, insisting he needed milk from the place at the far end of the street. He walked her upstairs and kissed her good night and waited until both doors were locked before going home. He bought milk in case she was watching, though he already had some in the fridge. Then he stripped down and lay in his king size bed and asked himself what the fuck he was doing.

Chapter Eight

Jarek's phone rang at ten o'clock the following night. He usually saw Olivia on alternating days, so tonight he'd spent the rainy evening alone indoors, watching television and reading. He'd found a show hosted by a tall Canadian man who promised that learning Mandarin was fun and easy, but it had turned out to be neither of those things.

He gave up on languages and tried to read one of Olivia's sappy *Chicken Soup* books, but he wasn't in the mood to have his heart strings tugged. He was pretty sure those grasping fingers would find nothing to hold onto, anyway. He was so bored he was almost ready to cross the hall to knock on Dale's door — the guy talked a big game, but every time Jarek saw him he was in the gym or at home, not out banging "hot Asian chicks," as he liked to boast. Then his phone rang.

He stared across the room for a second, half-hoping it was Olivia. After their fight he'd given her his number and punched hers into his contacts, though he'd never once called her. And, because she knew he was an emotionally destitute moron, she never called him either. There was pretty much only one person on the planet who chose to call Jarek, and he knew what he'd hear when he answered. Still, he picked up.

"Hello." Not a question.

"Oh my God, he's alive! Honey, I still have a brother!"

Jarek could hear Katrine, Jonah's wife, shout back. "Hallelujah!"

He rolled his eyes. "Is it comedy hour already?"

"We're just getting started, my friend. I've got weeks of material stored up."

Jonah waited for Jarek to speak, but Jarek knew how to wait him out, and that's what he did. He knew what he was supposed to do here—apologize. He was supposed to say he was sorry for being a lousy brother, for not calling or e-mailing or sending postcards, but that was Jonah's burden to bear. Jonah was the good son; Jarek was the other one.

"That's it?" Jonah asked. "You're not going to say anything?"

Jarek opened a bottle of beer and drank half. "How are the kids?"

"They're great." He lowered his voice, and Jarek could picture him ducking into the bedroom and closing the door. "They're terrible, Jare. They're monsters."

He laughed. "They are not." His four-year-old nieces were twin angels, with Katrine's red curls and gap-toothed grins. He wasn't much for kids, but they were hilarious and impetuous, and he appreciated them all the more from across the ocean.

"What are you doing?" Jonah asked. "Drinking a beer? Describe it to me, please. Katrine has us on a diet where I'm not supposed to have wheat for some godforsaken reason."

"It's delicious," Jarek answered truthfully. "I'm sitting around in my underwear, watching porn and drinking amazing beer. Life is great."

"You're an asshole."

"Spare me. You love your life. You rub it in all the time."

"You're right. I do love my life. And I'd love it even more if my brother called to say he was alive from time to time."

"I'm building furniture in China, Jonah. There's nothing to worry about."

They were fraternal twins with nothing else in common. When Jarek enlisted, Jonah had gone to college and gotten a degree in horticultural science, then started a successful landscaping business. He'd been carefully cultivating new life while Jarek had methodically wrung it out of people. Jonah had married Katrine and started a family; Jarek remained very much a loner. Jonah was a volunteer firefighter; Jarek couldn't remember the last time he'd helped somebody on purpose.

"Tell me something else then."

He took another swig of beer. "I lied about the underwear."

Jonah was silent for so long Jarek thought the connection had cut out. Then his brother spoke. "Tell me about Olivia."

The bottle slipped through his fingers and bounced on the couch cushion. He snatched it up before it could spill, and gripped the phone tight as he fought to keep his voice level. His brother and his boss were fucking gossips. "What'd Brant tell you?"

"That you've been seeing her for a while. That she's a kindergarten teacher."

"Sounds like you know everything already."

"You like her, Jare?"

"She's fine." He smirked. Jonah would think he was being stubborn, but Olivia would appreciate the humor.

"Is she there now?"

He studied his feet, crossed at the ankle on the coffee table. "No."

"Then tell me about her."

Jarek rarely talked to his brother about women, in large part because he didn't know enough about the women he slept with to relay the information, and partly because Jonah was a decent guy who loved family life and didn't really want to live vicariously through his brother. "She's just a girl. We hang out sometimes. Run together. Get something to eat. She's got terrible taste in movies."

"Is she pretty?"

He finished the beer and got another one. "Yeah. She's pretty." It was the understatement of the year, but he wasn't going to gush like some stupid sap.

There was a flurry of high-pitched squealing in the background, muffled when Jonah covered the receiver with his hand. After a second he was back. "The girls say hi and that they miss you."

"Tell them I say hi."

"They also want to know if you can send them presents."

"Sure."

"And they want to see you on the computer."

Jarek blew out a breath. "I told you, and I'm sure your gossipy friend Brant told you, the Internet here is spotty. I can't connect in my apartment."

"So? Go to the one of those Internet cafés you mentioned."

"I—"

"If you don't want to Skype, send an e-mail at least. Send some pictures. Keep in touch."

"We're in touch right now, and it's going really great."

"Seriously, Jare—"

"Okay, okay. Stop." There weren't a lot of things Jarek felt bad about, but Jonah had been his best friend growing up, and was one of the few people who'd never given up on him, no matter how hard he pushed him away. "I'll send some presents, okay? And a letter or something." He really didn't want to go into the Internet café again. Truth be told, the place was grimy, and he just didn't like it. Plus he couldn't type, and sending e-mails took forever. Especially when you had nothing to say.

This time Jonah waited him out, knowing he'd gotten the knife in and telepathically twisting it. "How's the landscaping going?" he asked lamely.

"It's going all right. Keeping busy."

"Good."

"Dad's been asking about you."

"Don't."

"When the meds are working, that is."

"I said don't."

"He hasn't got a lot of time left, Jarek. A couple of months, maybe."

"Good."

"Shit. Don't say that."

"Then don't bring it up. I'm not coming back. Drop it."

"What about the funeral? Will you come for that?"

"What do you need, money? I'll pay for it. Will that shut you up?"

Jonah was quiet for a long time. Jarek felt like a dick, but he wasn't going back to Virginia to say good-bye to his father. He was as good as dead, as far as Jarek was concerned. He was a shitty father who'd loved the wrong woman, and he'd taken it out on his kids.

How the hell Jonah managed to look past that — fuck, *move* past it — he'd never know. And he didn't care. Two more months and the man would be out of his life permanently, and they could stop these rote conversations where Jonah reminded him he was a bad son and Jarek reminded him that Aidan McLean was a bad father.

"You want to talk about anything else?" he asked.

"What's Olivia's last name?"

He sighed. Jonah was a manipulative bastard when he wanted to be: make him refuse to talk about their father, then give him a chance to redeem himself by discussing Olivia. "What are you doing, Googling her?"

"So what if I am?"

Jarek sat up a little bit straighter. He didn't appreciate Jonah's methods — he was supposed to be the one who knew how to get information out of reluctant people, after all, but…He'd told himself he wouldn't investigate Olivia, even though he desperately wanted to. He'd alternately promised himself that he didn't care what her little secret was, then switched to reminding himself that he respected her privacy. But if Jonah did it…

He was going to hell. "Her last name is Clarke," he said, gnawing on a knuckle. "With an e. She's from Michigan. Candor, Michigan."

"Candor…Michigan…"

"And she went to John Millford East High —" That's what was printed on the T-shirt she slept in.

"Yeah, here she is."

"That quickly?"

Jonah was silent, and Jarek knew something was wrong. "Spit it out, asshole," he said, more harshly than he'd intended. Or perhaps just as harshly. "What are you looking at?"

"Um…some photos. Newspaper articles."

"Dude."

"It's nothing…bad. I mean, she didn't do anything. It just looks like maybe…"

"Jonah!" Jarek had been in a lot of rough situations in his life. There'd been several occasions when he'd been pretty certain he was going to die. And yet somehow, he couldn't remember a time when his heart had pounded in his chest so hard he thought it might burst out.

"Okay, man, okay. Well, she *is* pretty."

"Fuck you."

"I'm just reading the article, hang on. I'm trying to understand."

He was the slowest reader in the entire world. Jarek was looking around for his shoes, ready to storm the nearest Internet café to Google Olivia Clarke, Candor, Michigan, himself, when Jonah spoke. "How much do you know?" he asked.

"Nothing. She said she did something that people didn't like."

"Yeah. Basically it looks like this town is crazy about baseball. In the past twelve years, eight kids from that high school you named went on to play in the major leagues."

"Okay…"

"And apparently there was some sort of scandal, where half the team was accused of gang raping a drunk girl on New Year's."

His heart stopped. He thought of Olivia, the way he'd fought to make her come the way he thought she should—

"It wasn't Olivia," Jonah added.

"Motherfucker!"

"Sorry, sorry. This was a year ago. The girl was in high school. And I guess somebody filmed it with their cell phone and a video got passed around, and somehow Olivia was the one that turned it in to the police."

Jarek pinched his brow. This was a sad story, but it didn't explain shit. He waited for Jonah to continue, and in the background he could hear clicking as his brother scrolled through web pages.

"Okay," he said. "It looks like the video was e-mailed between guys on the team, and the coach was on that e-mail list. And Olivia found it on his computer and that's how she turned it in. Turned them in. The team."

He knew the answer, but he asked anyway. "What was the coach's name?"

"Um…" More clicking. "Chris Masterson."

Her fiancé. The golden boy. "Was he in the video?"

"No, not according to this. He just knew it existed, but before he could turn it over to the authorities, Olivia did. Nine members of the team were arrested and charged, suspended…Okay, here's where it gets weird."

"What?"

"When you read the bigger papers, the national stuff, it's pretty cut and dry. They raped this girl, got caught, reputations ruined, scholarships lost, blah blah blah. People are saying that's the least that should have happened to them."

"Okay. Right."

"But then when you look at the smaller stuff, just Googling Olivia's name and the town and stuff, it paints a different picture."

"Like what?"

"Like, these people fucking hate her, Jare. They think she stuck her nose in, ruined those boys' lives, took away their futures. She had to close her Facebook account, quit her job…Seven police incidents at her apartment in three months…Hey, did you know she was engaged?"

He ran a hand over his face. "Yeah."

"Well, that ended. Wow. Shit."

Jarek groaned. "What?" This was exactly why he wasn't going to pry. He didn't want to care, and now that he knew, there was no way he'd be able to keep himself from asking her about it. Plus she could see right through him; she'd know something was up the second she set eyes on him.

"There are some web sites about her. Like, hate sites. It looks like they haven't been updated in a few months, but it posts her address and phone number, her schedule, pictures of a car with stuff spray painted on it…Vandalism, mostly. Threats."

For some reason he remembered that first night when he'd asked her if she always ran indoors and she said yes. How there'd been something off about the way she'd answered. And now he knew. She had to run indoors. She'd had to stay inside to avoid everyone. For a full year.

"What about the case?"

"Um…Didn't go to trial. The girl dropped the charges. But the damage had been done, according to this article. The boys' reputations had been ruined. And the team had to cancel the season, since they'd lost half their players."

Jarek finished his second beer and spun the bottle across the coffee table, catching it before it toppled over the edge. "Well."

"She didn't tell you any of this?"

"We're not that close."

"Must have been pretty bad if she fled the country to escape it."

"Yeah." She must be pretty fucking desperate for friends if she was willing to let him into her bed four nights a week. Let him walk out when he was finished, never asking him to stay, never asking him to call her. She'd been so damn lonely when they'd met, she'd been willing to accept anything, just so she wouldn't be alone. And he'd sensed it and taken advantage.

"Do you—"

"It's late, Jonah. We've got a thirteen-hour time difference, remember?"

"It's only eleven o'clock your time."

"I've gotta go." He had nowhere to be, but he couldn't keep talking about this. He'd spent his life demanding the truth, and now that he had it, he didn't fucking want it.

The line to get a cab was about seven miles long, but moved quickly. When Olivia touched down at Pudong airport, she'd been greeted by an American representative for the chain of schools, handed a few pamphlets about China and the company, escorted to the train station, and promptly abandoned. It had been dark and cold, and apart from the bright lights, it had been impossible to get a feel for Shanghai, other than that it was big and very densely populated.

That initial impression had been a massive understatement. Just looking around the swarming throng coming and going from the train station, she was pretty sure she'd seen more people today than she had in her whole life. It was eleven thirty in the morning on a sunny spring day, and the entire vicinity of the train station was one giant, writhing mass of bodies. Marcus gripped her fingers and tugged her along the line of people waiting for taxis so they wouldn't get separated, and she felt both relief and guilt at the comfort of his firm grip.

She'd run into Marcus—the geologist or geographer, she was incapable of remembering which, it seemed—when she'd headed out to buy her train ticket two nights ago. When he'd heard of her plans he'd invited himself along, and Olivia had accepted.

She'd been disappointed when Jarek turned her down, but some part of her knew it was for the best. She'd grown up in a bubble and when that bubble burst, she'd been smacked in the face with the fact that she didn't know how to be on her own. She'd lived with her parents, then in dorms at college, and then she'd moved in with Chris. Part of the motivation for coming to China was to escape the never-ending vitriol that awaited her in Candor; the other part had been to learn how to be alone—and survive.

And she'd struggled mightily. It was too different here. It had been too dark and too cold and too lonely. And then she'd met Jarek, and she'd let him make her brave. He led her through the city, explored new streets and strange shops, a shield against anything that made her uncertain. She'd invited him to Shanghai because she liked him, not because she wanted him to guide her, but when he'd declined she admitted there was an upside to the rejection: for once she'd be forced to do something on her own. Except now she wasn't, and she was really grateful. Coming to Shanghai alone on your first-ever solo excursion was like deciding to learn to swim by jumping out of an airplane into the sea—beyond dumb. She'd brought Marcus along as a parachute or a life vest or whatever would best fit the analogy.

They climbed into a cab and asked to be taken to an area called Shanghai Old Town, according to the web site she'd studied. Marcus had never been to Shanghai, either, and was eager to explore. They'd hit it off at the bar the other night, and had talked non-stop on the two-hour train ride from Lazhou. He was different from Jarek in every way: outgoing, big easy smile, shamelessly flirtatious. He was just an inch or two taller than her, with the broad build of a rugby player, and while it had been jarring to suddenly have someone so open and willing to talk to her, it was nice. Marcus was fun and easy. Jarek was fun in his own way, but nothing about the man was easy.

"Okay," the driver said, pulling up alongside a bustling sidewalk. Olivia peered around at the long string of old-looking buildings, ornate wooden trim and red lanterns everywhere. It was beautiful and traditional, spliced with very modern neon signs and familiar fast food logos.

They paid and exited the cab as people hurried to clamber in, grinning at one another as they set out to explore. They hit every place on the list, touring the busy marketplace and buying souvenirs, stopping at a famed shop with a cardboard cutout of Bill Clinton, who had eaten there on one of his visits. In the middle of the hectic city they found a classical Chinese garden, a hidden sanctuary with still water and stone bridges, beautiful pagodas and buildings filled with artwork and ancient furniture and pottery.

More than once Marcus touched her back or her hand to get her attention, laughing every time she tried to take a picture and someone strolled in front of the camera, which was every time. She found some familiar Western stores that carried clothing in her size and bought a few new things, then they got on the subway — the first subway she'd ever been on, she admitted, feeling like a rube — and got off near an outdoor market much less refined than the first.

It was jam-packed with vendors selling all manner of things, toys and clothing and, of course, DVDs. There were knock-off watches, purses, and jewelry, some better than others, and Marcus made her laugh when he asked if he should get the Gucki belt or the Wersace.

Olivia spent a lot of time on her feet on a regular basis, but by the time they collapsed in their seats on the train at ten o'clock that night, she was exhausted and her toes hurt. They had bags of souvenirs and tons of photos, but she was a little relieved to be going home. The sheer size and volume of the city was mentally and physically draining. Having grown up in a small town, the brief experience had been awe-inspiring and jaw-dropping, but more than a little overwhelming.

"Favorite part?" Marcus asked, interrupting her thoughts.

"Hmm?" She turned to look at him, his handsome face way too close in the crowded seats. They'd been unable to get spots in the nicer car with plush, comfortable chairs, and now sat on hard blue seats with worn foam cushions. They were the only foreigners in the car and garnered more than a few stares. Olivia was used to blocking them out, but every now and then she'd catch Marcus looking perturbed.

"What was your favorite part?" he repeated.

"Oh. Um…" She strummed her fingers on her denim-clad thigh as she pondered the question, unable to stop the sudden rush of heat that pulsed through her when she remembered how she'd asked Jarek something very similar after watching *Love, Actually*. And the very vivid memories of what had happened next. "My favorite part," she echoed, mind racing. "The garden, maybe? I'm not sure how *feng shui* works, exactly, but it was amazing how peaceful it felt."

"Agreed." Marcus nodded. "Definitely beautiful."

"Or maybe the stall at the market selling the silk paintings." They were "paintings" done in tiny silk stitches depicting various scenes of day-to-day life in China. After some bartering, Olivia had managed to walk away with two. "Ooh, or the guy selling the Tony Hilfiger shirts." When she'd stopped to browse he'd quickly pounced, assuring Olivia her "husband" would love the clothing made by the "very famous designer" himself.

"Tony Hilfiger…" Marcus mused. "I'm going to wow all the ladies with my fashion sense." He'd bought one of the shirts just for laughs, and to help get the guy off Olivia's back.

"Yep," she agreed. "Paired with your Gucki belt, you'll be the talk of the town."

"Who's the watch for, Jarek?" Marcus inquired after a moment. Olivia glanced down at the bag holding a black box with a silver men's watch "guaranteed" to be a real Rolex. Not for a second did she think it was, but her dad wouldn't care. He was forever taking off his watches to distract kids with the ticking sounds, and somehow losing them.

"My father," she replied. "He can't seem to keep one for more than a few months." She'd gotten her mother a tiny vase painted with red flowers. There had been so many interesting and lovely items — fans, silk purses, tiny stamps. But she had no other friends to shop for.

"I see." A pause. "Did you get Jarek anything?"

Olivia glanced over at Marcus. "A shirt."

He returned the stare, pale eyes steady on hers. "Are you two serious?"

She shrugged, uncomfortable. "I don't know. Not really."

"So, not exclusive?"

She forced a smile. "You're leaving in three days, right?" The rest of his group had left the night before, but Marcus had been asked to stay longer to help survey another piece of property for the builder.

"Yep. Three…whole…days." He looked at her so innocently she laughed, and then so did he.

"I'm seeing someone," she said. She hated that even she could hear the tiny note of doubt in her voice; she'd never felt that way with Chris. She'd grown up surrounded by so much support and praise that she'd never experienced any real uncertainty in her life, until Jarek. Did he like her? Did she like him?

"Does he know I came with you today?"

Olivia swallowed. "No. We don't run everything by each other." Plus he'd canceled their plans for the day before, texting her for the first time ever. *Can't make it tonight,* was all he'd said. He'd offered no explanation and she hadn't asked for one. Jarek was her closest friend in town and she didn't want to push, even if she had been disappointed. Instead she'd watched a movie and gone to bed early, telling herself she'd need her energy for today anyway, and it was best he hadn't come.

"So," Marcus said. "What does he do when you're not around?"

Olivia folded her arms and turned to look out the window at the dark landscape rolling past. She had no idea what Jarek did when they weren't together. He'd begun opening up a little bit about his life, but the things he told her were mostly just broad strokes that left gaping holes that begged to be filled in, and she'd made the decision to accept it. He hadn't pressed her about her secrets, and fair was fair, even when it wasn't.

The next day was a drizzly, dreary mess. Olivia was cramped and achy from the long day in Shanghai, and a hot shower had minimal impact on her sore muscles. She watched a movie and got some groceries, then came home and tried to work on the "script" for *Little Red Riding Hood,* which was not going well. Davy had volunteered his services as both a butterfly and a painter, Rose had insisted she be the one to cue the music — music that didn't actually exist yet, but Olivia hadn't told her that — and the four Spidermans were still wearing their costumes each day in an effort to appear better and more dedicated than the others. If she wasn't mistaken, her classroom had an increased number of people walking past the window and peering inside, wondering what the hell she was doing. She had been teaching kindergarten for four years now, and often asked herself the same thing.

At five o'clock she put on her gym clothes, tossed a towel and some water in her bag, and walked down to the Brant Construction site. She hadn't used the gym in weeks since she'd been running outside with Jarek, and while she now felt comfortable enough in Lazhou to run alone, she'd avoid the rain if she could help it.

There was a young man in a rain coat watching the entrance to the site. He recognized Olivia and waved her inside, otherwise the place appeared deserted. The doors to the other trailers were closed, and no lights blazed inside. She glanced in the direction of the apartment building that housed the workers, but its gleaming façade told her nothing.

The gym trailer was predictably empty, so she switched on the lights, turned up the volume on her mp3 player, and climbed on the treadmill. She was just passing mile three of five when the door opened and Dale entered. Their eyes met in the mirror and they exchanged hellos. Dale didn't unnerve her so much as he irritated her; after they met he'd spent the first week hitting on her, then appeared mildly disdainful each time after that. She was aware of his occasional glances her way, the way his eyes rarely lifted from her chest, and she wished she'd worn a baggy T-shirt instead of the fitted black tank top and capris.

He was doing bench presses when she climbed off the treadmill and toweled off. After yesterday's excursion and today's run, she had to stretch, even if it meant moving to the middle of the trailer, closer to Dale. She sat down on a mat and reached forward to grip her toes.

"How're things?" he asked casually.

"Good," she replied. "Busy. The kids are a handful."

"I bet."

"How old are yours again?" She didn't know why she felt the urge to make polite small talk with him; blame her decent upbringing.

"Five and seven," he answered. "Boy and girl."

"Those are fun ages."

"Yep." He grunted as he pushed the loaded bar over his head, lowered it one last time, then returned it to the bench. "How about otherwise?" he asked, getting to the point. "How's Jarek?"

Olivia switched legs and avoided his stare. "I assume he's fine. You see him more than I do."

"You see him today?"

"No. Why?"

Dale chugged half a bottle of something brown and chunky, likely a protein shake. He was big but not defined; she wasn't sure the stuff was having its desired effect. "No reason."

He moved away to do leg presses, and Olivia let out breath she hadn't known she'd been holding. She crossed her legs and leaned forward, biting her lip as tight muscles continued to loosen.

A few minutes passed before Dale spoke again. "He doesn't have much to say about you."

She didn't look up. "So?"

"So if he was into you, he'd say so, right? Mention you now and then?"

What was it with guys she barely knew prying into her relationship — for lack of a better term — with Jarek? "You're the relationship expert. You tell me. Or don't."

He snorted. "I'm just saying. If I fuck someone, it's not a secret."

"Just from your wife, right?"

He shot her a dirty look. "I don't bag chicks I'm ashamed of."

Olivia stood and put the mat away. "This has been fun, Dale."

He might have said more, but the twist of the doorknob interrupted. They both looked up as Jarek pushed open the door and stepped through. The first thing Olivia noticed was that he wasn't dressed to work out. He wore dark jeans and a black waterproof jacket with the hood up, rain water sluicing down the shiny fabric. He nodded at Dale, then turned to her, face impassive, though his eyes blazed with something she didn't recognize. For a second she wondered if he'd heard Dale's comments and had come to defend her, but then all he said was "hey," and her hope deflated.

"Hey." She jammed the damp towel into her bag and slipped into her coat.

Jarek looked at Dale. "How long do you think you'll be?"

Dale was doing extensions with massive dumbbells, shoulder muscles bulging. "A while. Sorry."

Olivia frowned and looked between them. Something was going on. She had no idea what, but she wasn't really in the mood to sit around guessing. She strode past Jarek and stepped outside. The rain was coming down hard now, but she hadn't heard it over her mp3 player and the unpleasant conversation with Dale. She tugged up the hood on her jacket just as she heard her name, and turned to see Jarek descend. He loomed over her the way he normally did, but there was something off about him this time. Something more ominous, more serious. In the past she'd attributed his general air of menace as a leftover from his previous line of work, nothing particularly deliberate about it, like how she was always talking with her hands. But now it felt intentional, like he was trying to warn her away from him even as he told her to follow.

"Where?" she asked, her feet ignoring her brain and trailing him to the locked carpentry trailer.

"In here's fine." He pulled a set of keys from his pocket and opened the door, gesturing for her to enter first.

She glanced at his face as she slid past, and flashed back to the first time she'd seen him, when her instincts told her he was dangerous. She'd tried hard to dismiss the impression, attributing it to the events of the past year, when everyone was the enemy. Even in the time since, the times he'd hurt her feelings or gotten under her skin, she'd ignored the feeling, recognizing that he didn't relate well to people, apologizing for him when he should have been apologizing himself. And then sometimes he did apologize, and it carried more weight than a normal apology, because she knew how hard the words were. She was always making excuses for him; she wondered what the excuse would be today.

"What's going on?" she asked when he followed her inside. The trailer was dim, even with the blinds raised on its two small windows. The rain drummed on the roof, a steady, dull roar that slowly worked its way under her skin and made her antsy. The room smelled like sawdust, the way the kitchen had when her parents renovated it years earlier. She felt a sudden pang of yearning then, for the company of people who loved her unconditionally. In theory.

Jarek didn't speak for a while. He turned on the lights, then locked the door, then unlocked it again and put his hands in his pockets. Olivia shivered; her skin was clammy from the workout, and the air was damp and chilled. She watched him pace, his eyes on the tabletops, scanning the walls of tools, the neatly ordered desk she'd let him fuck her on. That day suddenly felt like a long time ago; it had been different then, she'd known what she was coming in here for. Now she didn't.

"Jarek," she said, finally. "What is it?"

He paused mid-step, as though he'd forgotten she was there. Emotions warred in his eyes, and she could see him fighting to keep them in check. It was the way his shoulders never relaxed, the way he kept stuffing his hands in his pockets so his fingers didn't curl into fists. "What'd you do yesterday?" he asked quietly. He was about seven feet away, and somehow the words cut through the pounding of the rain on the roof, clear as a bell.

Olivia watched him as he waited for her response, gaze trained on her face. He was waiting for her to lie, she realized. This whole thing was some sort of creepy interrogation dance, the only difference being that he'd left the door unlocked. As an afterthought. "I went to Shanghai with Marcus," she said, keeping her voice level. "I told you that."

"I don't think you mentioned Marcus, Liv." He stepped close so suddenly she barely saw him move. Instinct had her shifting away, but the tabletop bumped her lower back and kept her in place. Jarek didn't touch her, just stood there, too close, waiting for something.

"It was last minute."

"How was it?"

"It was great. Lots of fun." A muscle ticked in his jaw and he studied her shoulder, her chest, her hip, looking anywhere but at her face. "I invited you, remember? You said no."

"I remember."

"So what's the problem?"

He let out a slow breath and raised his eyes to hers. "What do you think the problem is?"

She arched a brow. He might have been an interrogator at one point, but she taught kindergarten. She knew how to handle a hissy fit. "You're the one with the problem, evidently. You tell me."

"All right. How about you spent the day on a date with Marcus, while I spent it here with my dick in my hand while everybody asked how I felt about my *girlfriend* going on a date with Marcus."

She rolled her eyes. "It wasn't a date."

"Then what was it?"

"A trip!" She put her hands on his chest and pushed him away, tired of being loomed over, as though that were somehow going to help him ascertain the truth. She had nothing to lie about; hell, her life had fallen apart because she'd refused to do precisely that.

"With fucking Marcus!" He grabbed her elbow and yanked her back, spinning her up against the table again. She'd stiffened in surprise when he yelled, and winced as her tailbone hit the wooden edge.

"Back up, Jarek," she hissed on pained breath.

He didn't budge. "You know how you asked me not to talk about you, Olivia?"

Goose bumps broke out on her skin. "What did you do?"

He gripped her chin and tilted her face to look at him. "Nothing. I gave you what you wanted, and I didn't ask you for anything in return, because I thought it was implied."

"What are you talking about?"

"Don't fuck around. That's the only rule."

"Rule? I — Jarek. First of all, there are no rules, and you have no business trying to make them; you're the one who's terrified I'll start to expect something from you at any second. And I already told you, it was just a trip. You think we screwed on the train? Get away from me. This is none of your business." She shoved him again but he still didn't move, and she saw that her hands were shaking. She was upset, not afraid. She was almost positive.

"Nothing's my business with you, is it?"

She glared up at him. "What?"

"Not the shit that happened in Michigan, how they chased you out of your own home?"

She wasn't all that surprised, but she wasn't happy either. "You looked into me?"

"Sure. Why not? I had some time on my hands." She could picture him now, hunched over a computer for hours, scouring the articles and the web sites, equally divided between praising and flaying her.

"I told you I didn't want to discuss it."

"And we didn't, did we?"

"Is this what you're really upset about? I didn't tell you about Chris and the video, so you accuse me of screwing around with Marcus?"

His face was so, so cold. She shivered. "No, this is definitely about Marcus. The other stuff is shit you should have told me."

"You're such a fucking hypocrite, Jarek. I didn't go online to find out what you used to do."

He laughed. "What'd you think a search would turn up, Olivia? I don't exist. The shit I did doesn't exist. There's nothing to find."

"Okay. Great. You're a real man of mystery. It doesn't mean you get to drag me in here and accuse me of something I didn't do. As you'll have noticed in your research, I have plenty of experience being harassed by assholes. I'm not looking for more."

"What'd you two talk about?"

She heaved an exasperated sigh. She wanted to leave but he had one hand braced on the table between her and the door, and she knew it was a losing battle. "Everything. Our lives. Being here. People we were buying gifts for. He knows how to have a proper conversation. Not everything is a secret or a scandal." She raised her brows meaningfully.

"Did you tell him about what happened at home?"

"No! Why are you stuck on Marcus?"

"Because you spent all night talking to him at the bar last week, then you snuck off to go out with him all day!"

"I invited you! You said no. And I would have told you Friday, but you blew me off with a text message!"

He ran a hand through his hair, obviously trying to get a grip on things. She wasn't sure she wanted him to control himself. He so rarely showed any emotion, this was a novel experience. A little nerve-racking, sure, but…insightful.

"Is your temper tantrum over?" she asked.

He shot her a patronizing look. "Tell me about it."

"I already told you. We went shopping. I bought you something, but I'm keeping it for myself now."

"Not about that. About Michigan."

She pinched the bridge of her nose, suddenly tired. She wondered if this was an interrogation tactic: keep people off balance so they never knew what the real issue was. But Olivia thought she knew; she dealt with children every day, after all. He was jealous. Michigan was just a diversion.

She sighed. "What do you know?"

"I read everything I could online."

"Then it paints a pretty good picture." But she summed it up for him anyway. How she'd been in the kitchen when she heard Chris at the computer, watching some kind of movie. There were screams and cheers, then the mistakable sound of flesh smacking flesh and grunting, and she'd figured he was watching porn. It had been unusual, no question; she suspected he watched when she wasn't around, but this had been pretty damn blatant. She'd peered into the room but had been too far away to see much more than a few bodies shifting around. Too far to discern faces.

Then two days later a rumor started to spread, and something in her stomach grew cold and heavy. She hadn't wanted to know. That was still the truth. She hadn't wanted to know and she hadn't wanted to look and she hadn't wanted to be right. But she did know and she did look and when she searched through his e-mail one night when he was at practice, she found what she hadn't wanted to find: an e-mail containing a link to a video that showed half the high school baseball team gang banging a teenage girl who was obviously too drunk or high to make the decision herself.

She'd saved the file to the hard drive and that night when Chris returned home she'd asked him about the rumors, if he really thought someone had been raped, if any of his athletes had been involved. He'd been the star pitcher at the high school growing up, and when injuries ended his dream of a career in the majors, he'd simply smiled and gone to college and later gotten a job as a PE teacher, soon taking over for the outgoing coach of the baseball team. The video had been sent to everyone on the team e-mail list, and Chris had been among them. He wasn't in the video — she'd checked, as hard as it had been — but she knew he'd seen it, knew he'd been acting different. And then he denied it.

"Nah," he'd said, kissing her cheek before turning off the light to go to sleep. "Those guys would never do anything like that." If she hadn't seen it herself, she would have believed him. Chris was dangerously persuasive, wielding his charm so casually he had people convinced before he even started speaking.

The next time she checked his e-mail — something she'd never done before — the message was gone. But she still had the video. A week later the girl went to the police. The boys were arrested, and though half the people involved were seventeen, the town was small enough that everyone knew their names, even though they hadn't been released.

And then the denials started. The boys were athletes. Strong students. Upstanding young men with bright futures. Look at that girl. She had a reputation. If she'd had sex with any of them — and she couldn't prove it, not a week after the event — if she had sex with them, she'd been completely willing. It had probably been her idea.

Olivia hated the fact that she had hesitated. She was a woman. She was a teacher. She'd dedicated her life to helping shape children into good people with bright futures. And still it was another three days before she saved the video to a flash drive and drove it to the police station.

It was five days before news of the video leaked, and approximately one day before her name was connected to it. Before everyone knew the boys were fucked and she was the one responsible. As though she herself had somehow lurked in a corner of the room and recorded the whole thing on her phone, then e-mailed it to the entire team as a joke.

Chris tried not to hate her. He'd cried when he asked if it was true, and she'd cried when she asked what he'd planned to do with the tape. "The right thing," he'd assured her, but she knew better. They could barely stomach each other after a month, though his presence was probably the only thing that saved her in those first weeks.

His parents had died in a car crash shortly after their high school graduation, and her parents had pretty much adopted him. When he left her they cleared out the spare bedroom and he moved in, and they'd all praised her bold independence as they left her out to hang. The first night alone in the apartment—her first night alone anywhere, ever, really—someone had thrown a brick through the front window. Without saying a word Chris's move made a very clear statement: if Olivia's parents were on his side, surely that made Olivia the villain. She would never know if the manipulation was intentional, but it was certainly effective.

Over the next month she'd paid to have her crappy car repainted twice to cover the slurs, and after she'd woken to find it tagged again—*TRAITOR, LIAR, BITCH, WHORE*, and, for some reason, *COCKHOLDER*—she'd given up. Work was getting tough. She'd been a popular teacher at the elementary school and suddenly people couldn't look her in the eye. Four parents removed their kids from the class, and she began to hear rumors that enrollment was down because people didn't want their children being taught by a traitor.

Olivia tried to be strong. She believed it would blow over. She loved her town and many of its people. She'd been popular; she'd been loved. And just like that they'd turned. Friends were too busy to hang out or call, people whispered under their breath when they passed her in the street or in the aisle at the grocery store. She used to run outside three nights a week, and suddenly she'd been afraid, hearing things, seeing things, coming home once to find her front door broken open, though nothing inside had been disturbed. She bought a treadmill and started running inside, away from the window.

And her parents. They assured her they understood what she had done, that it had unquestionably been the right thing to do. They still invited her to dinner on Wednesdays, still made her favorite foods and acted like they loved and cared for her. But how could she go home when she knew Chris lived upstairs? He'd go out on the nights she was scheduled to come over, but it was beyond weird to know he was sleeping down the hall from her parents while she'd had to install a second deadbolt on the apartment door.

By the end of June she knew she couldn't keep working at the elementary school. They couldn't actually fire her for what she'd done, but they'd made it pretty unbearable for her to continue. She didn't want to run away, didn't want people to have the satisfaction of thinking they'd chased her off, so she drove her slur-covered car and tried to keep her head up, even as she wanted to cry every time she approached it.

Willa Jetz, her closest friend from college, taught kindergarten at a school outside of Boston, and read about the story in the news. She called in July with Olivia's first real spark of hope: Willa and her husband were expecting their first child, and she'd be going on maternity leave. Olivia could fill in for Willa beginning in November, and escape Candor. Assuming she could survive that long.

She quit her job and lived off her savings, spending months researching things to do in Boston and looking at apartment listings online. She hadn't told anyone but her parents of her plans, and they'd been supportive. Maybe a little too relieved. And then, on October first, Willa called in tears. She'd lost the baby. They'd been trying for a while and she was devastated. She wouldn't be going on maternity leave. She was sorry.

Olivia said all the right things — no, she was the one who was sorry, was there anything she could do, don't worry, she'd find something else, take care of herself, they could try again. And then she'd hung up the phone and sobbed, harder than she had in ten months, as hard as she'd wanted to. She looked for jobs but it was a weird time of year to be hired as a teacher, and no one wanted her as a substitute. Her money was running out, and she'd become a friendless hermit, leaving the apartment only as necessary.

And then one day she'd been looking around online and seen an ad for a certificate program to teach English as a second language. She had nothing better to do so she clicked on it, read the testimonials, and started looking at web sites that offered job listings for ESL teachers. She was already a teacher, which qualified her for pretty much everything, and while she wasn't really considering moving abroad, it was a nice way to kill the time. To fantasize. She would never actually do it.

Then she went to her parents' house for Wednesday dinner, and there were two additional place settings at the table. Chris was there with his new girlfriend, and they were very happy. Chris, who had seen the video and not reported it, Chris who was still the coach of the baseball team, who was still the fucking town hero, was very happy. The girl had dropped the charges, the boys who hadn't graduated were back on the team, their lives would go on.

The food tasted like chalk. She couldn't look her parents in the eye. At ten o'clock she'd returned to her dark, lonely apartment and applied for a job in some town in China called Lazhou. Two weeks later she bought a plane ticket. And the day before she left, she called her parents and told them she was going.

Jarek didn't think she knew she was crying until the story was over. Her cheeks were wet with tears, eyes huge and glossy, and suddenly Olivia, the strongest, most self-possessed woman he'd ever known, looked fragile. And he'd been the one to shake the box until the pieces rattled.

"Satisfied?" she asked, swiping at her cheeks.

He felt like shit. "Of course not." He'd done far worse to a lot of people and couldn't have cared less. And now he did. And it was awful.

"Anything else you simply need to know?" The words were angry but her voice was empty of any real vitriol.

He hadn't actually intended to ask her about Michigan. After talking to Jonah on Thursday, he'd bailed on her on Friday, choosing instead to spend the night in that grimy Internet café, reading everything he could about the case. He'd felt alternately sad and angry, and hated that he felt anything at all. That he couldn't turn it off, no matter how hard he tried. And then on Saturday morning Ritchie mentioned that Marcus had gone to Shanghai with Olivia and he'd felt a whole host of things he hadn't felt before, jealousy chief among them. And he was fucking furious — with himself, for feeling that way, with her, for making him. With Marcus, for being a geologist or a geographer or something equally smug, and with Olivia, for going off with him.

He'd stewed all day Saturday, drowned his sorrows at the bar with Brant and Dale in the evening, reluctantly admitting his irritation with the news but downplaying his jealousy. They saw right through it, but pretended not to. He used to be a wall no one could penetrate, now people were walking through left, right, and center, and there wasn't a damn thing he could do about it.

He didn't know what time she was getting back from Shanghai, or he'd have been waiting at her apartment when she pulled up in the cab. He spent Sunday morning taking out his frustration on the punching bag in the gym trailer, then at home, staring blankly at the television as the Canadian guy failed to teach him Mandarin. He'd been on his way to the dining trailer when he passed the gym and heard Dale needling her. His first instinct had been to storm inside and tell the other man to back off, but he knew firsthand that Olivia was perfectly capable of standing up for herself.

His heart kicked up a notch when he went inside and saw her, cheeks flushed, the overhead light catching on the beads of sweat that dotted her chest and throat. He couldn't decide if he wanted to throttle her or fuck her, so he'd settled for the least mature option and gotten her alone in the carpentry trailer so he could make her cry.

"Fuck," he muttered, running a hand over the back of his neck. "I'm sorry about all the stuff that happened to you. You did the right thing."

Her jaw set. "I know that." But it was obvious she resented it.

"And I'm sorry about hauling you in here."

That blond eyebrow arched. "That's it?"

"What else should I say?"

"That you realize it's none of your business where I go or with whom, and then tell me why you felt like any of this was appropriate."

Oh God. She was so fucking difficult when she was in teacher mode. He loved it and hated it in equal measure. He opened his mouth to repeat the part about it being none of his business, but instead what came out was, "It's my business if my girlf—you go out with another guy. Deal with it."

Her jaw dropped and she kicked him in the shin, but not hard. "Deal with it?"

"Yeah. Deal with it."

She studied him for a few seconds, then asked, "What's a *girlf*?"

"*Shit*. Olivia."

"Yes?"

"Don't."

"Don't what?"

"You remember what I said to you that first night when you kissed me?"

"If I'm not mistaken, you squealed like a pig and ran away crying, 'I hate girls!'"

"Christ. Don't take this the wrong way, but I hate *you* sometimes."

She folded her arms, pushing up her breasts so he could see a hint of cleavage where her zipper was undone. "I'm not offended."

"I told you I'm not what you're looking for."

"Trust me, I know."

"I don't know how to—I can't be—"

"I know." Her eyes were dry now, and steady on his. Like she saw right through him, and didn't care that there were pieces missing.

"You're leaving in June."

"That's right."

"So if you want to…Until then…"

"Just say it, please."

"You know what I'm getting at."

"Do I?" She tilted her head and stared at him quizzically. He knew she knew. This was punishment for the most failed interrogation he'd ever conducted. He'd come in here expecting to get answers from her, and instead somehow heard himself putting the painful truth on the line, hoping it wouldn't hurt him.

He wiped a hand across his mouth, his tongue suddenly dry. "You're my girlfriend, so don't fucking hang out with Marcus."

She burst out laughing, surprised and unimpressed. "It looks like you've been learning something from those romantic movies after all."

"Yes or no?"

"He's leaving in two days anyway. I wasn't going to see him."

"Don't fuck around on me. I have issues."

"No kidding."

He stepped close enough that their thighs pressed together, and caught her ponytail in his hand. He didn't kiss her or grope her, just held her like that, resting his chin on top of her head, letting his thumb brush her neck so he could feel her pulse, steady and reassuring. His heart was racing, and he imagined it doing drills, back and forth, one side thrilled, the other horrified. She was his first girlfriend in thirteen years. He didn't know how to do this. But he hadn't figured out how to walk away, either.

"Say yes," he said softly.

"Yes," she replied.

Chapter Ten

"Remind me again why we're doing this?"

"Just shut up and push."

A faint thud, then a muffled curse. "I think I got hit by a car."

"*Clipped.* You got clipped. You'll live."

Jarek turned to look over his shoulder at Brant, Ritchie, and Dale, sweating as they slogged along behind him. He and Ritchie had one dolly, Brant and Dale had the other, and each was laden with a dozen unpainted wooden tree cutouts, each about five feet tall. The company trucks were still full of work supplies, so they'd had to use dollies to wheel the fake trees the twenty-minute walk to Olivia's school, and the men had been complaining the entire time. In exchange for their blood, sweat, and tears, Jarek had had to promise to buy them beer and admit that Olivia was his girlfriend.

He had never known grown men could gossip this much. After he'd left the gym with Olivia yesterday, Dale promptly spread the word that Jarek had confronted her, and this morning they'd all been waiting for him in the lobby, demanding details. The acknowledgment that she was his girlfriend had felt stiff and awkward coming from his lips, but there'd been a sense of satisfaction there, too. Like he'd accomplished something. He'd been demanding the truth from other people for so long that he'd almost forgotten what it was like to admit it himself.

They arrived at the front gates to the kindergarten, locked during the day to keep strangers out and kids in. The older woman manning the booth inside peered at them strangely, then smiled as she recognized Ritchie. She said something in rapid fire Mandarin then picked up the phone. Two minutes later Olivia and Honor emerged from the hallway that divided the front two buildings, shielding their eyes from the sun so they could see the unexpected visitors.

Jarek's heart threatened to leap out of his chest at the sight of her, and his palms grew damp on the dolly handle. He wiped them on his pants and was glad he'd chosen to wear sunglasses so she couldn't see the rising panic in his eyes.

"What *is* this?" Olivia asked as the gates slid open and they wheeled the dollies through. The trees were unpainted, just flat wooden cutouts that suddenly felt really fucking stupid. *What had he been thinking?*

Then she gasped. "Wait—are these trees? For my play?"

Everyone was staring at him. He couldn't seem to take his eyes off the trees. It had taken him days to cut them all out, using scraps of wood from the site and pieces he'd purchased from a local supplier. They were a variety of shapes, some rounded, some pointed, some abstract, as the shape of the wood he'd used had dictated. Eventually he realized everyone was waiting for his response. "Ah, yeah. We had some extra wood and you needed trees, so I just figured…we could get rid of the wood."

Brant looked at him and shook his head, disappointed at the lame response. He couldn't perform with these guys watching him. He didn't know how to be her boyfriend while they were ogling him like this.

"Well, thank you. I love them." She patted his arm appreciatively as she circled the dollies, taking it all in. "Can you help bring them to the classroom?"

"Yeah. Sure. Of course." He avoided looking at Dale; the man's shit-eating grin made him want to break something. They were loving this, the jerks.

"We've gotta get going," Brant said, nodding at Dale and Ritchie. "You bring the trees to the classroom, say good-bye to your *girlfriend,* and head back after, okay?"

He'd kill them all in their sleep and love every second of it. "Yeah."

"Good-bye, Olivia."

"Bye, Brant. Dale. Ritchie."

The men nodded, Ritchie squeezed Honor's hand, and they left. Olivia and Honor took one dolly and led the way, Jarek trailing after. He tried not to stare at her ass, but the jeans she wore fit her perfectly, and it was hard to stay focused.

"Nice shirt," she said over her shoulder, shooting him a smug smile.

His lips twitched. He'd been razzed about the shirt all morning. She'd given it to him last night after he'd spent a good hour apologizing wordlessly in bed, showing her how good a boyfriend he could be if he put his mind—and hands, and tongue, and a few other things—to it. Her gift from Shanghai was a white T-shirt covered almost entirely in bright tattoo-inspired artwork. He'd held it between two fingertips like it was radioactive before squinting at the name scrawled across the chest and getting the joke. She'd looked rueful as she recounted her fruitless search for Hardy Boys merchandise, ultimately settling on the Ed Hardy T-shirt.

Said shirt clung to the sweat on his back as they crossed the courtyard and stopped in front of her classroom. Honor said good-bye and went back to work next door, and Olivia turned. "This is really nice of you," she said, studying him thoughtfully.

He shrugged like it had been no big deal. "You gave me something," he said, fingering the shirt. "Figured I'd repay the favor."

"So we're even now? One knock-off T-shirt for two dozen beautiful trees?"

"This is a knock-off?" He tried to look offended. "I'm taking some trees back."

She laughed, then turned when a raised voice came from inside her classroom. The Chinese teacher was yelling at the kids to get away from the windows where they stood with noses pressed to the glass, taking in the scene outside.

"I think you have to come in now," Olivia said.

"No," he said firmly. "I've got to get back."

"Just for a minute."

"No."

She pushed out her bottom lip and gazed at him woefully. "Jarek."

"Don't do that."

She trailed her fingers down his forearm, her touch cool on his heated skin. Then she gripped his hand and yanked him after her into the room. "Back to your seats," she ordered. The kids scurried away, as though racing there might mean she'd never seen them at the window in the first place.

Tiny voices murmured curiously as they took in the tall stranger standing in front of the whiteboard. He took off his sunglasses and waited stiffly as they gazed up at him in awe. Olivia let go of his hand and he felt untethered.

"Don't just stare at him," she admonished the room. "What do we say when we meet somebody new?"

"NICE TO MEET YOU!" the class screamed.

Jarek flinched.

Olivia was trying not to laugh. "That's true," she conceded. "But what do we say first?" She waved and mouthed the words, "*Hi, how are you?*"

"HI, HOW ARE YOU?"

Then they all looked at him expectantly. "Uh, fine," Jarek replied.

Olivia raised an eyebrow. "Ask how they're doing."

"How are you?" he echoed weakly.

At least this time he was ready for the volume. "I'M FINE, THANK YOU! HOW ARE YOU?"

"You already asked that," Olivia pointed out. "He's doing *fine*, obviously." Her lips curled in a knowing smirk. He scowled at her and the class giggled, even though they weren't in on the joke. "This is my friend Jarek," she told the kids. "He came to give us some trees for our play. Isn't that nice?"

"YES!"

"What do we say when someone helps us?"

"THANK YOU!"

A long pause.

"Uh-oh," Olivia said, eyes wide. "What do we say when someone says thank you?"

"YOU'RE WELCOME!"

He stared daggers at her, but she just smiled politely. "You're welcome," he said through his teeth.

"THANK YOU!"

"I have to get going," he said under his breath.

One of the kids, a little girl in the front row, stuck her hand in the air and asked something in Mandarin, then pointed at the CD player sitting on a desk.

"Hmm," Olivia said. "I'll ask." She turned to him formally. "Jarek, we were just about to sing a song. Would you like to sing with us?"

The kids squirmed in their seats like live wires, unable to contain their glee at the prospect of a new participant.

"I really wouldn't," he said.

"He said yes!" Olivia exclaimed.

The room exploded in cheers.

"Okay, Rose. Start the song, please. Number four."

The little girl who had started this trouble in the first place darted to the front, punched a few buttons, and a song he hadn't heard in thirty years started playing. The kids jumped to their feet, shuffled in place, and started singing along as best they could when they were merely emulating sounds and not words. And damn Olivia, singing and dancing along with them as he stood there wishing he were dead.

"Put your right hand in," she sang loudly, snatching up his right wrist and putting it "in" something invisible in front of him.

"I'm breaking up with you," he whispered.

She was laughing too hard to answer. Her lips shaped the words to the song, but all that really came out was "ha ha ha."

The kids were ecstatic, putting their hands in and then both their feet, then, when prompted to choose an action, Olivia looked at a little boy wearing a Spiderman costume—in fact, four boys were wearing Spiderman outfits—and held up her hands as though looking for an answer. "What do you think, Alan?" she asked. "What should we do now?"

The kid stared at her as though looking over a precipice and trying to decide if he should jump off or run away. Jarek knew the feeling. She made him feel that way every time she looked at him. And like an idiot he'd been leaping over the edge, with no clue what might be waiting for him.

Alan, however, chose the sane option, and folded his arms, refusing to speak.

"Okay," she called brightly, as though he hadn't turned her down. "Who else?"

The kids unanimously agreed to stick their butts in, and Jarek staunchly refused, even as he watched Olivia bob up and down, ass sticking out, making him think very inappropriate things. The song ended and he made a mental note to pass its name along to the agency he'd worked with in his previous career. This was torture in its purest, most melodic form.

The kids clapped and giggled as they sat down, and Rose turned off the CD player.

"I've really got to go," Jarek said, and Olivia relented.

"Okay, everybody. Jarek has to go now. What do we say?"

"GOOD-BYE!" Some of them may have said his name, but it was hard to tell.

"Bye." He waved abruptly and started for the door. He could hear Olivia's sneakers behind him and turned when they were outside, far enough away that they couldn't be overheard—even if they couldn't be understood—but still well within view. He put his sunglasses back on and looked down at her.

"Did you have fun?" she asked. She was a master interrogator, smiling as she cut off fingers and pulled teeth.

"No."

"Not even a little bit?"

"You do this every day?"

"All day, every day."

"You're a sadist. And a masochist."

She laughed. "Do you still want to run later?"

"With you? Absolutely not."

She batted her eyes and, like a pussy, he caved.

"I'll see you at seven." He kissed her on the forehead and strode back across the courtyard, determinedly ignoring the snickers and whispers that emanated from every classroom.

They ran along the path by the water. Spring was in full bloom and the sky was full of fuzzy white cottonwood seeds, blown free from the trees and filling the air like warm snow. Jarek plucked several out of Olivia's hair as they ran, admiring the way her ass twitched in her shorts, and the bounce of her breasts with each step. He was sufficiently distracted that she had to swat him on the arm to get his attention.

"Are you listening to me?" she demanded.

"I—" He was going to lie, but she had a built-in bullshit detector. Plus he was pretty sure she'd seen him ogling her tits. "No."

She huffed and shook her head, but he knew she wasn't mad. "What were you saying?" he asked.

"I was telling you how excited the kids were about the trees you made. Davy—I don't know if you saw him in the front row?—he's already talking about what colors they should be. And I can't be sure, but I think the Spidermans are trying to come up with ways to climb them."

"The kids seemed to like you," he offered as penance for not listening.

"Some do. Some don't. You saw Alan, right? The Spiderman who wouldn't pick a dance move? That kid loves to dance, but he hates me. Won't say a word."

Jarek thought back to the boy who'd dismissed Olivia's offer during the song. "That kid doesn't hate you," he said seriously. "He just doesn't know what to make of you."

She shot him a baleful look. "I've been his teacher for four months. He knows what to make of me."

He shrugged and jogged a circle around her, knowing it drove her nuts. "I'm just telling you. He's intimidated. He wants you to like him."

"How do you figure?"

"I know how to read people." Plus, he knew exactly how it felt when Olivia offered you an opportunity you didn't know what to do with.

"So what do I do?"

He circled her again, tugging her ponytail until she tried to elbow him in the stomach. "Just keep trying."

She stomped on his foot and nearly tripped them both. He caught her around the waist with one hand and braced the other on the low wall before they could topple into the water. "That was a freebie," he murmured in her ear, righting them. "Do it again and I'll let you fall."

She tipped back her head to look him in the eye. "I don't believe you."

"I'm still going to make you pay for today's little stunt."

She was the picture of innocence. "What are you talking about?"

"You know exactly what I mean. Did you really think I was going to dance in front of a room full of children? Stick my ass out?"

"I saw you tapping your feet to the beat. Don't be an Alan, Jarek. You can dance if you want to."

He smacked her ass, hard. "We'll see about that."

They jogged in silence for a minute, then Olivia spoke. "Was it just me, or were Brant and Dale acting stranger than usual today?"

"They're just dickheads."

"Did you tell them anything?"

"Anything like what?"

"Like that I was your girlfriend." She was watching the pavement at their feet, not looking at him. She looked…shy. For once.

"Ah…yeah. I mentioned it."

"You did? Why?"

He cleared his throat. "They made me."

"What?"

"They're huge gossips, Olivia. They have nothing to do with their time, so they spy on me. Brant even called Jonah and told him."

"Who's Jonah?"

"My brother."

"Oh, right. Your brother."

He glanced down at her. She was still watching the path. He'd pried into the most painful part of her past, and had never offered her more than the most basic facts about himself. He sighed inwardly. "We're twins."

She looked up in surprise. "Twins?"

"Yeah. Fraternal. He's six minutes older."

"Wow." She was quiet for a few minutes.

He nudged her. "What's wrong?"

She scratched her cheek. "Have you ever slept with someone and then realized that you didn't really know anything about them?"

Ah…He was definitely not going to answer that question. He'd slept with tons of women he knew nothing about, but he preferred it that way. Olivia made a scoffing sound and he risked a look down at her. She'd obviously read the answer on his face. "Never mind, Jarek."

"You knew I had a brother."

"That's all I knew. Are you a lot alike? Was he in the army as well?"

"No. He's a gardener. A 'landscape architect,' if you believe his business card."

"A landscape architect?"

He pursed his lips. "A gardener."

"Is he married?"

"Yeah. They have twins. Girls. Picket fence, the works. They go to church, he volunteers, she's a ballet teacher."

"Wow. That's so…perfect."

"Yep. He's perfect. Everyone says so."

Another quarter mile in silence. "What about your parents? How long ago did your mom…pass?"

He cleared his throat awkwardly, swatting cottonwood seeds out of the air, the fluffy pods clinging to his dark shirt. His life before the army wasn't really a secret, he just never talked about it. It felt strange and foreign, but he tried anyway. "She died when I was six. Pancreatic cancer."

"I'm sorry."

"Sure. Thanks."

"What was she like? Were you close?"

"Yeah. I mean, the way any kid is close with their mom. She was really beautiful. I remember she always wore dresses and lipstick. She liked to go out a lot, dancing, restaurants, stuff like that."

"Were they really in love?"

"My parents?"

"Yeah."

Now it was his turn to be quiet. "My dad was in love with her," he said finally. "And I guess she loved him. But he wasn't really… enough for a woman like that, I don't think."

"What do you mean?"

"He never went out with her."

"So?"

He shot her a meaningful look. "So I didn't know it because I was six, but she wasn't going out alone. There were other men. A lot of them. I mean, she was beautiful and alive, and he just wasn't." He tried to keep his voice level and his face blank, not letting her see how difficult this was. How alike he and Aidan McLean were, no matter how many times he'd sworn he wouldn't be his father.

"And he didn't mind?"

"He didn't do anything about it. Then one day she didn't feel well and she went to the hospital, and a month later she was dead. And my dad never really got over it."

She heard something in his voice then, because she stopped running and waited for him to stop too, turning to face her. "Did you? Get over it?"

"Yeah. Let's keep going."

"Jarek—"

"Let's keep moving if you want to talk about this. I don't want to have a fucking heart to heart in the middle of town, okay?"

She pulled her lower lip between her teeth. "Okay."

They ran another quarter mile before he spoke again. "He was different after she died. Worse. Like he didn't know how to be a real person, or be around other people. He was angry."

"Did he take it out on you guys?"

"Yeah."

"Was it worse for you than your brother?"

He used the hem of his shirt to wipe sweat from his brow. "No. It was the same for both of us. We processed it differently, obviously. He became a gardener and I beat the shit out of people for a living." That was over-simplifying things, but she was smart enough to see it. He'd spent his entire life vowing to be nothing like his father, then he'd enlisted and they'd done an aptitude test and lo and behold, he was best suited to hurting people. Jonah, for whatever fucking reason, was destined to plant flowers.

"How long has he been sick?"

"Awhile now. Something to do with his liver. Jonah tells me about it, even though I asked him not to." He hadn't spoken to his father in four years. What did he say to the man who'd helped turn him into some soulless asshole? He hadn't beaten his kids for fun or sport, the way some abusers did. He'd just punished them severely for every little thing; forgetting to make your bed merited the same beating as a suspension from school. Somewhere along the way he and Jonah had diverged. Jonah took the beatings personally and tried to be better, but Jarek started to feel nothing. He recognized the pain, but on the emotional front, he was a blank slate. And that was how it had been when he was working: doing whatever it took to get results, then going home and sleeping with a clear conscience. He'd never had so much as a bad dream. He was the perfect asshole.

"That's enough, all right?" he said when she opened her mouth to speak. He didn't know what she was going to say, another question or some sympathetic remark, but he didn't want to stay on this train of thought. He wasn't even sure what had prompted the sudden sharing, except that he didn't want to keep shutting her out in case she finally gave up and walked away. They had until her contract was up at the end of June; he'd just let the pieces fall where they would and pick them up when she was gone.

"Sure." She didn't do anything to make him feel worse, didn't look at him with pity or try to hold his hand. She just ran beside him, her breathing even, footsteps matching his, until they'd run the entire length of the path and back, exiting near her apartment.

"Do you want to get something to eat?" she asked as they weaved their way through traffic and pedestrians on the busy street.

"No." He gripped her arm and fairly dragged her the short distance to her building. After the conversation he'd done little more than watch her tits and ass bounce, and he wanted nothing so much as to lose himself in her for a little while. "Just open the door, okay? Let's go upstairs."

She read his intention easily, discomfort flashing across her face. "Are you okay? Maybe—"

He took the keys from her hand and opened the green door, nudging her into the stairwell. "I'm fine, Olivia. I've wanted to fuck you since you bent over that dolly this morning, and I don't want to wait anymore."

"Jarek, I…" She glanced around the stairwell, as though anyone lingering would be able to understand what he was saying.

"Tell me to go if you don't want to." He stopped on the second floor landing, watching her hesitate a few steps up.

"This is just really abrupt. I didn't know—"

He took a deep breath and let it out slowly. "Is it because of what I said?"

"What?"

"About my father? You think I'm an asshole because he was one?"

"No. I just thought you were sad, so—"

"Olivia. I'm not sad. I've got a fucking hard-on and I want your help with it. If you don't want to, then say so, but don't look at me like that."

"Like what?"

"Like you're sorry for me."

She scoffed. "I am the furthest thing from sorry for you."

"Then what's it going to be? You going to let me in?"

Her fingers gripped the rail for support, and he could see her hard nipples through the thin fabric of her shirt. "What are you going to do?" she asked.

Jarek climbed the stairs slowly, advancing as she retreated. "I'm going to bend you over the table right inside the door and fuck you," he said softly. "Is that what you want to hear? I've been doing a lot of talking tonight."

"I know you have."

"So let's take a break and do something else, okay?"

They reached the fourth floor, breathing hard. He could tell she was nervous, and didn't bother telling her she had nothing to fear from him. Almost all the people who had been afraid of him had good reason, but she didn't need to worry. He didn't say so, however. Just waited as she twisted the key in both locks, followed her inside, slammed the doors, bent her over the table, and pulled her shorts down to her knees. Her skin was damp with sweat and warm from exertion, and he freed his straining cock and slipped on a condom in record time. He kept her legs together and fit himself to her pink folds, pushing in and finding her slick but not wet, making the process excruciatingly slow.

She gripped the table over her head, knuckles white, relaxing only when he was buried to the hilt. He gave her a moment to adjust, then squeezed her ass to get her attention. "How does the song go, Olivia?" he asked mildly. "*I put my dick in.*" He pulled out and drove forward again. "*I take my dick out.*" He withdrew. "*I put my dick in and I shake it all about.*"

She trembled with a sudden laugh, smothering the sound with her forearm. He could see the tension easing from her shoulders as she correctly gauged his lighter mood. "Stop," she begged as he continued. "I have to sing this song for two more weeks."

He trailed a finger down her back, skimming between her ass cheeks, stopping at the tiny hole he'd never penetrated. "*I put my finger in…*" he murmured, pressing at the resisting ring of muscle.

She went completely still. "*Jarek.*"

"What? Have you ever done this?"

She wasn't stopping him, so he pushed until half his finger disappeared, the tight muscles clenching desperately. Her hesitation spoke volumes. "You've tried it?" he asked again.

"Once," she mumbled into her arm. "Chris…"

"And?"

"I made him stop."

He dragged his finger in and out, shallow, slow thrusts. "Why?"

"It felt…"

"Bad?"

She shook her head. "It was too much."

He prodded her with a second finger, but she was too tight. And he gave up trying altogether when she reached back to grip his wrist. She'd never really stopped him before, sexually. He was sure he'd done things to her Chris hadn't tried, but she'd gone along with him, participating equally. Now he let her still his hand, finger lodged inside, not moving.

"Am I hurting you?"

"I don't want you to…"

He leaned over her, brushing her blond hair to the side and kissing the nape of her neck. "You don't want me to fuck your ass?"

She shuddered. "No."

"You sure?"

Now she turned her head, looking at him out the corner of her eye. "Positive."

He grinned. Anal wasn't really his thing, but he liked this part. Thought she might like it, too. "Okay. I won't. Want me to take my finger out?" Her cheeks flamed as he wiggled the offending digit. "No? You like it? Want another one?"

"No."

"You can tell me if you do."

"I don't."

"Okay. Put your hand back over your head. You're blocking my view."

She met his gaze for a second and must have decided to believe whatever she saw there, because she returned her hand to the table and pressed her face into the crook of her elbow, granting him access. She was so wet, his cock slid in and out easily, and he groaned at the grip of her pussy, eyes locked on the finger buried in her back passage. He demanded so much honesty from people, but trust was another thing altogether. The people who broke down and told him the truth hadn't done it because they'd trusted him, they'd done it to get him to stop. Olivia allowed him to continue because she trusted him, because she saw something in him that didn't make her want to run screaming.

"I want to feel you come, Olivia." He whispered it into her hair, his voice rough.

"I'm close."

He slipped a hand over her hip, finding her swollen clit, grazing it with his fingertip. "Will this help?"

She shook. "Yes."

"Harder?" He circled her sensitive flesh, pressing more firmly when he got the reaction he was looking for.

"Yes, yes, yes…" Her cries were muffled by the table as she clamped down and writhed against him, pulling him deeper, drawing him in. He tormented her with the finger in her ass, tormented himself with the realization that when it came to Olivia he'd never feel like he had enough.

He curled over her, moving his hands to squeeze her slim shoulders as he pounded inside, pouring out his release with a groan, burying his forehead in her neck. When their breathing slowed, she lifted a hand to stroke his hair, soothing him, as though she somehow knew he needed it. Letting him know without words that he could trust her, too.

Olivia's eyes flew open and fixed on the alarm clock on the night-stand: six ten. It was six ten in the morning and something hard was pressing into the back of her thigh. Something that wasn't supposed to be in her warm, safe—

"Morning."

She almost toppled out of the bed when a broad arm wrapped around her waist and Jarek planted a kiss on her shoulder. She grabbed his wrist for balance and tried not to make a fool out of herself. He'd spent the night. For the first time. Ever. It was coming back to her now. Sex on the table. A quick run across the street for dinner. A movie (*27 Dresses*, to his extreme displeasure and her joy), more sex, this time slower and sweeter, and then…he'd just stayed there. She'd lain in bed, waiting for him to tense up the way he always did, the way he thought she didn't notice. He was physically uncomfortable with the idea of sleeping over, as well as emotionally pained by it. And yet Jarek had remained, lying on his back, eyes on the ceiling, not moving. She'd dozed off, expecting to be woken any moment by the bed shifting as he crawled out and went home, and it hadn't happened. At all, apparently. He hadn't left.

"You're here?" she mumbled.

"Yeah." The hand on her waist shifted up to squeeze her breast, and she turned her head and smiled into the pillow. He was spooned up against her—Jarek McLean, spooning—and enjoying it, if his erection were any indication.

"Did you sleep all right?"

"Fine. You?" He'd slept naked and she wore panties and a T-shirt, the former of which he worked down her thighs so she could kick them off. He insinuated a knee between hers, and cupped the soft folds between her legs.

"This is a surprise," she said in response.

He chuckled into her hair and fit his cock to her, nudging his way inside. "I know."

"What changed?" She bit her lip as he circled her clit with two slick fingers. She wasn't complaining; he'd been a diligent student since they'd started sleeping together. Initially his motivation had been simply to make her orgasms better. Once he'd figured out the key to her pleasure, he'd set himself the task of making them more frequent and intense. His talented fingers knew just what to do now, and she was soon breathing hard and thrusting back against him.

"Nothing," he said. "Everything."

"I see."

Suddenly he swore and pushed her hips away, pulling out and clambering over her and out of bed. He was buck naked, his protruding cock slick and shiny, and she stared at him, confused and trying not to laugh. "What's wrong?" she managed.

"This!" He gestured to his erection and cursed some more as he hunted for his pants and snatched them up.

Olivia sat up straight, alarmed and annoyed. He'd never left her unsatisfied before—not on purpose. "Would you please tell me—" She cut off when he held up a condom, wielding it like a weapon.

"I fucking forgot, Olivia. I fucking—Oh my God. I've never forgotten. Never. I don't—"

"Shh." She climbed out of bed and took the condom from his fingers. He hadn't opened it yet, and she still wanted him. Not without a condom, however. They were both clean, but she wasn't on birth control anymore—no need, for the past year—and she wasn't about to visit a doctor here if she didn't have to. "I just finished my period," she said, stroking his arm. "I won't get pregnant. Are you okay? Do you just want to…?" She let the phrase trail off, leaving the options open.

He took the condom from her hand, rolled it on, and backed her into the bed. She sank down and wordlessly he followed, propping her legs wide open and sliding inside.

"Are you okay?" she asked again.

"Yeah. Sorry about that." He hid his face in her neck and thrust gently.

"I was hoping your first time sleeping over would alleviate your fear of spending the night when you realized nothing terrible would happen."

His laugh was pained, muffled by her skin. "It's the opposite of terrible, Liv. You feel so fucking good. All over. You're the best thing I've ever felt."

She ran her fingers through his curls, letting them tangle. "You're sappy in the morning. Is that why you avoid staying over?"

"Guilty." He rocked against her, his pubic bone hitting her clit and sending her over the edge. He followed, lips fastened to her neck, hard enough that she knew she'd have her first hickey in years.

A while later Olivia went to take a shower while Jarek dressed and made the bed. When she came out she dressed for work and combed out her wet hair, then found him standing in the kitchen with a glass of orange juice and a banana, watching the bustling street below.

He poured her a drink and she accepted, watching him over the rim. "What?" he asked, looking suspicious.

"I think we should talk about starting a family," she said, straight-faced.

He spit his mouthful of orange juice back into his cup. "What did you just say?"

Olivia ticked up three fingers as she spoke. "Bed. Breakfast. Babies. That's the order." She tapped the third finger. "We're on point number three."

"Oh my God." He poured the remaining juice down the drain and rinsed out his cup. "You're fucking demented." He reached over and covered her fingers with his own, removing all three "points."

"I'm a woman, Jarek. This is how we do things. If someone spends the night and then eats breakfast, they have to marry you. It's the rule." She made a finger gun and shot his banana.

"You have a warped sense of humor, Olivia. I almost had a heart attack."

She laughed. "I would have saved you."

"Don't. Let me die if those are my options."

She winked and returned to the bathroom to dry her hair. He appeared in the doorway a few minutes later, watching. "What's up?" she asked.

"What's this?" *This* was the tourism information from Beijing she'd collected from one of the local travel agencies and arranged on her desk.

"I'm going to Beijing!" she shouted over the roar of the dryer.

"When?"

"Maybe in two weeks. I'll make it a long weekend. I want to see the Great Wall." She tapped the matching picture on the brochure and finished her hair. "Have you ever been?"

"No. Are you going with somebody?"

Olivia squeezed past him to sit at the table and put on her shoes. "I was going to ask you," she said, which was true. "And then if you said no, maybe I'd go by myself, or maybe someone else would want to come."

"Who?"

"I don't know. I haven't thought that far ahead. But I'm not going to be here much longer, and I wasted the first few months being so nervous about how new everything was that I kind of have to jam it all in. I'm going to Thailand, too."

"Thai — When?"

"First week of June. You're not invited, no offense. It's for my birthday. I booked it months ago. Apparently it's much easier to get around Thailand than China, so I think it'll be okay. I have to start figuring out how to be on my own, you know? Plus it looks really beautiful." She was talking too much, but the look on his face was making her antsy. He was so mistrusting, no matter how honest she was. Never mind that she'd never lied to him about anything before.

"You're going alone?"

"Yeah." She finished lacing up her shoes and scooped up her keys. "I have to go to work. You can think about Beijing if you want. I'm going, either way."

He set the pamphlets on the table and followed her out, down the treacherous stairwell to the street. The morning sun was bright, scooters and taxis zipped past, and the now-familiar city smells filled the air. The construction site and her school were in opposite directions, so they stopped on the sidewalk. Jarek had his hands in his pockets — something he always did when he was thinking — and studied the scene around them.

She pasted on a smile and stepped away. "Have a good day at work."

He nodded and examined his shoes, nodding to himself. "Okay."

"Okay, bye." She didn't take this stuff personally anymore. The mood swings. The man who opened up about his mother, then fucked her bent over a table. The man who told her he wasn't what she needed, then came over with a first aid kit. She didn't dwell on it. She'd had consistency before. Steady, reliable Chris. And look how that had turned out.

"I mean, okay, Beijing," he said, stopping her.

She turned. "Okay, you'll come?"

"Yeah. If you want."

She lifted a shoulder. "Whatever."

He cracked a smile. "*Those* are the three B's: bed, breakfast, Beijing."

"Is that it? I could have sworn it was babies."

"It's definitely Beijing."

"I suppose I could have misread it."

He was smiling again. She liked him when he was broody and dark, but she liked seeing him smile, too. She liked that it was a challenge and that she was up for it.

"Beijing," he said. "In two weeks."

"Two weeks," she echoed. "It's a date."

They'd never gone on an actual date, she mused as she sat at her desk and prepared for the day's lessons. Sure, they'd gone places together, but never anything special. More often than not they stopped somewhere for fried rice or noodles or plates of fried bok choy and shredded pork, still dressed in their running gear. Jarek had never called and asked her out, brought her flowers, held her hand. Sometimes she had to remind herself that she didn't care. This wasn't a typical relationship. Plus, she'd already had typical, and it had been a pretty epic failure.

"Good morning, Olivia."

She glanced up to spot Honor entering the classroom, Alan in tow. The Spiderman costume was nowhere to be seen today, instead he was dressed casually in jeans and a sweater. And for once he didn't look mutinous.

"Good morning, Honor. Good morning, Alan."

He shuffled his feet and his gaze shifted around the room. Honor squeezed his hand and said something in Mandarin and he mumbled a greeting that may or may not have been in English.

"What are you doing here so early?" Olivia asked, standing to meet them in the middle of the room. "There're still twenty minutes before the bell."

"Alan wants to show you something," Honor said. She spoke to Alan in Mandarin and he nodded, eyes fixed on the floor.

Olivia thought about what Jarek said, how Alan just wanted her to like him. How she just had to keep trying. "Okay," she said, smiling. "Let's see it."

Honor nudged Alan and he shrugged out of his backpack and dumped it on the floor. Olivia expected him to take something out of the bag, but instead he crouched low on the floor, one hand extended in front of him, face set in a serious scowl. She looked uncertainly at Honor, who was trying not to laugh, and then Alan started to…dance. Well, *dance* may not have been the best word. It was part interpretive dance, part made up martial art, and part spinning in circles. The whole thing appeared to have been carefully choreographed, lasted two minutes, and ended with Alan jumping in the air, karate chopping an invisible foe, and shrieking at the top of his lungs.

Olivia stared, wide-eyed, and made herself clap and smile when what she really wanted to do was gape at the kid. "Very good, Alan. That was so great!" She sounded about as sincere as Jarek had when he'd told her she was hilarious that morning, and felt just as shocked.

Alan dusted himself off, looking pleased, and brought his backpack to the desk, sitting down and taking out a workbook.

"What was that?" Olivia whispered.

Honor covered her mouth so she didn't laugh. "He wants to perform this dance as part of your play."

"He wants to be Spiderman and dance?"

"Yes."

"I…"

"At least you have many trees," Honor offered.

Olivia ran a hand through her hair. "That's true."

"Your boyfriend is very nice. The teachers think he is handsome."

"Oh yeah?" It was on the tip of her tongue to say that Jarek wasn't her boyfriend, then she remembered that he, in fact, was.

"Yes. Very tall. It's good."

"How about Ritchie?" Olivia asked. "Do you like him?"

Honor blushed. "Yes," she said. "I like him. But maybe…he does not like me. Not today."

Olivia frowned. "He likes you. He told me."

"Another day, yes. But now…maybe not."

"Why? What happened?"

"I have another boyfriend. Three other boyfriends."

Olivia's jaw dropped. "What?"

Honor waved a hand dismissively. "Not real boyfriends. I'm old now, and my parents want me to find a husband. So they call their friends and they send their sons to see me, and say they are my boyfriend. So I must agree."

"I — How old are you?"

"Twenty-three years old."

"That is *not* old."

"In China, maybe it is old. Almost old. Enough time to get married."

"Is that what you want?"

"Maybe. If I find the right husband."

"And these boyfriends…?"

"They are nothing. Not really."

"And Ritchie?"

A shrug. Honor looked uncomfortable. "He is different. But he does not want to be my boyfriend if I have another three boyfriends."

"Well…That's fair."

Two of the older Chinese teachers approached, neither of whom spoke English. They chatted with Honor, who translated, telling Olivia that they thought her hair was not shiny enough today, but that she had a handsome boyfriend. What was it with everybody and the need for brutal honesty?

"Thanks," Olivia said. "I'll tell him."

More chatter. "Do you love him?" Honor asked.

Her brows shot up. "I — no. He's just — It's — I — No." She looked around the courtyard in case he had somehow managed to sneak in. After the "she's not my girlfriend" debacle, she didn't want to have the tables turned, even if it was true. She didn't love him. She might, if they had more time, which they didn't.

There was more rapid fire conversation, of which she understood nothing. "They say he loves you," Honor informed her. "He made so many trees for you."

"That was just scrap wood."

"What? Wood? Yes, I know." The awkwardness was interrupted — or exacerbated — by the arrival of Zhang Laoshi, the school principal. Zhang Laoshi (Teacher Zhang, though she didn't actually teach any classes) was a small, middle-aged woman with a perpetual smile. She beamed at Olivia then said something to Honor in Mandarin, and the other girl's demeanor shifted slightly. Olivia had a moment of panic as she wondered if she was in trouble for having allowed four strange men onto the school grounds, but that was not the case. "Olivia," Honor began, somewhat formally. "Zhang Laoshi says that you have a nice boyfriend."

"Oh. Ah, thank you," Olivia said. She repeated the thanks in Mandarin, and everyone tittered as though she had made a polite joke. She wondered briefly if Jarek would find it funny or horrifying.

More chatter, then another translation. "Do you like teaching at this school?" Honor inquired.

"Yes." Olivia nodded, in case the answer wasn't clear.

"And do you know that your contract will finish at the end of June?"

"Ah, yes."

"And do you think you would like to stay for longer? Maybe to… how to say…December?"

Olivia hesitated, both surprised and on the spot. She knew it was difficult to find foreign teachers, particularly in the more rural areas, yet for some reason the concept of extending her contract had never really occurred to her. At the moment there was no reason for her to return to the States in late June as she had planned, but something made her hold back. The construction job would be done in mid-July, and Jarek and the other workers would leave, putting her back in the same friendless position she had started in.

"Can I think about it?" she asked.

Honor relayed the message to Zhang Laoshi, whose smile faltered slightly, then returned in full force. She nodded vigorously.

"Of course," Honor translated.

"Okay, thank you."

Zhang Laoshi waved good-bye as the bell rang to signal the start of the day. Olivia started for her classroom, but one of the Chinese teachers stopped her and said something to Honor.

"They invite you to come to the room and play mah-jongg at lunch."

Olivia looked at them, pleased. "Really?" Maybe she could stay here, after all. She could continue to make friends and—

"Oh, sorry, no. Not *play* mah-jongg. But watch others play mah-jongg. Maybe you can make that paper bird, what's the name?"

She tried not to show her disappointment. "A crane."

"Yes. You are not good, but you can try again."

Jarek ate lunch with Ritchie, Dale, and Brant. They sat in folding chairs and ate McDonald's, since it was the easiest place to order from when you didn't speak Mandarin and didn't feel like miming. Plus Dale wasn't a big fan of Chinese food, it turned out. "I'm telling you," he said, not for the first time. "A big fucking steak, a baked potato, a pile of onion rings…I'd swim home to just to eat a proper meal with a fork and knife."

"Stop," Brant groaned. "I just ate and you're making me hungry again."

"Another couple months," Ritchie pointed out. "Then you'll be back home."

Jarek watched something shift in Dale's expression, something dark and sad drifting across his eyes. His shoulders slumped a little and he crumpled the takeout bag in one hand then sent it soaring toward an overflowing trash can, where it bounced off the rim. Jarek forced himself to focus on his meal and not ask what the problem was. He wasn't in the business of learning people's secrets anymore, and these guys gossiped like old women, anyway. Surely Brant or Ritchie would follow up on it.

No such luck.

"What's Olivia up to today?" Brant asked, stuffing the remainder of his burger into his mouth.

Jarek kept his eyes on his meal. "She's working."

"And later?"

"Beats me. We don't hang out every day."

"What does she do instead?"

He shrugged. "I don't know."

"What do you do?"

Another shrug. "Whatever."

Dale snickered. "He jerks off and thinks about her tits."

The guys laughed but Jarek didn't. "Don't talk about her, Dale."

"Why not?"

"Because."

"Because she's his girlfriend," Brant piped up. "And he *loves* her."

Jarek finished his fries and stuck the container in the paper bag they'd come in. He wasn't talking about this. He didn't know when he'd gone from being the guy people avoided to the one they teased. "I'm getting back to work."

Dale rolled his eyes. "Oh, don't go. We can talk about something else. Like how this guy's making out with *his* girlfriend." He jerked a thumb toward Ritchie. "What is it with you two and teachers?"

Jarek looked at Ritchie speculatively. The younger man's cheeks were pink and the corners of his mouth turned down. "To take a page out of Jarek's book, she's not my girlfriend," Ritchie said, nodding at him. "She's already got a boyfriend. Three, in fact."

Dale and Brant sat up straighter. "What? Really?"

"Yeah. Her parents want her married off, and I guess they're all better than me. Actually, they don't know I exist. They're better than the idea of me, apparently."

"Think it's because you're white?" Dale asked, cutting, as always, to the chase.

"I don't know. Maybe."

Jarek couldn't help himself. "I thought you saw her all the time."

"I did. And then she told me she had three boyfriends."

"What'd you do?" Brant asked.

"What do you think I did? I left. I can't compete with guys her parents handpicked."

Dale slapped his knee. "You just gave up?"

"What am I supposed to do?"

"Take her out, man! Show her a good time. Impress her. Take her to karaoke. It's cliché, but it fucking works, especially here. People here love karaoke."

"I'm not going to karaoke. I don't know any Chinese songs."

"Jarek'll go with you. You can double date. Two teachers, the two of you. It's perfect."

"No," Jarek interjected. "No double dates. No karaoke."

But Ritchie was looking at him hopefully.

"No," he repeated. "Don't look at me." When had he gotten so fucking weak? Olivia looked at him from under her lashes and he caved. Ritchie peered at him from behind his glasses and he ended up singing songs in public? Absolutely not.

"I can't believe you're here," Olivia whispered. She was pressed up close against him, crammed as they all were into a small private room in one of Lazhou's extremely popular karaoke bars on Friday night. The room was dim and lined on three sides with a red velvet bench packed shoulder-to-shoulder with Olivia, Jarek, Ritchie, Honor, and a dozen teachers from her school.

The fourth wall housed a large TV that showed an Asian woman singing an extremely high-pitched song as Chinese characters scrolled across the bottom of the screen. One of the older teachers was singing along as the others clapped, and Jarek sipped his beer and tried not to kill himself.

Ritchie had looked so downtrodden after his lunchtime confession that Jarek found himself giving advice on how to win Honor's heart, as though he had any real experience. But Ritchie seemed to think he was some type of Don Juan and ate up the information like it might actually help. Jarek didn't point out that he'd never so much as called Olivia on the phone or brought her flowers. That the first time they'd kissed he'd walked away terrified, that the second time had been after he'd bullied his way into her apartment and fingered her to a mediocre orgasm. He didn't know fuck all about romance, but every time he looked at Ritchie and Honor, they seemed happy.

He couldn't say the same for Olivia. On several occasions he'd caught her studying the other couple, Honor sniffing the flowers Ritchie had bought her, noting how he held her hand and told her she was pretty. He'd given the advice, but Lord knew he didn't know how to follow it. He'd feel like such a fucking idiot telling her she had soft hair and a nice smile, even if it were true. And he couldn't just show up with flowers for no reason, could he? Who did that? He'd look like a lunatic.

A server came in to see if they wanted more drinks, and Jarek ordered another two bottles of beer.

"I've had enough!" Olivia had to shout to be heard over the deafening music, and he turned to press his lips to her ear.

"They're both mine. Just hold one for me."

She smiled, showing too many teeth, and he leaned in again and told her she was pretty.

"What?" She covered one ear and squinted at him.

"I said—" The music reached a crescendo, then, making them both rock back, startled by the shrieking volume.

Olivia laughed and he shook his head and finished the drink he had in his hand.

"What did you say?" she asked when it got a tiny bit quieter.

"Nothing. I forget."

She studied him for a second, then grinned at something over his shoulder. He followed her gaze to see the microphone coming his way, and he froze. No. Absolutely not.

"Jarek," Honor said formally. "Will you please sing a song?"

They were all looking at him. A dozen eager faces on one side, Olivia squeezing his knee on the other.

"Say yes," she whispered in his ear. He felt her breath on his skin and goose bumps sprung up on his arms, though that could have been pure terror as the torture device was pressed into his hand. He'd been scared before. He'd certainly been in far worse situations than this. He just couldn't think of any right now.

"I don't sing," he said. The microphone picked up the words and his voice boomed through the room, though absolutely everyone ignored him.

Honor translated for the teacher punching buttons on the karaoke machine. "It's an English song," she assured him. "Very easy."

"No, I—" He turned. "Olivia, tell them."

She was accepting the drinks from the server, and returned with a bottle in each hand. "I'd love to hear you sing."

"I don't fucking sing," he hissed. "You should know that."

"Not even a very English song?"

"No."

"He doesn't want to sing," she informed the group, shooting him an exaggerated look of disappointment.

They bemoaned his reluctance and he tried to pass off the microphone, but no one would take it. Then the opening strains of "Unchained Melody" began to play.

"Are you fucking kidding me?" he muttered. He shot Olivia a warning glare, as though she had selected the song or forced him to come tonight, even though the whole thing had been his idea. He had made a huge mistake helping Ritchie. This was why he didn't get involved in other people's lives. This was why he preferred to be alone. He didn't make himself do terrible, stupid things.

The room was dim enough that when Olivia slid her hand up his thigh and he tensed, no one noticed. She nipped his earlobe. "Sing, and I'll do anything you want later."

He shot her a warning look. "You don't want to know the shit I'd make you do."

She arched a brow and began to sing. She had a terrible voice, it turned out. It sounded like whale calls, but if she cared, it didn't show. Maybe umpteen rounds of children's songs erased all shame in a person.

Ritchie chimed in. Jarek elbowed him in the side but he wouldn't be deterred. The guy actually could sing, it turned out. Though perhaps next to Olivia, everyone sounded good. Behind Ritchie Jarek could see Honor grinning, hands clasped together proudly as she mouthed the words. In fact, everyone was mouthing the words, or something that looked like the words and sort of sounded like them, and he was the only one who wasn't participating.

He regarded Olivia, drinking one of the beers she'd said she didn't want, and singing along with that knowing look on her face, the one that said she knew she drove him crazy and didn't give a damn. He took the beer, lowered the microphone, and sang a few lines, leaning in so close that her eyes lost focus and she tipped back against the cushions. "Anything I want," he murmured against her lips.

She blinked, then smiled slowly. "Me first."

Much later, ears still ringing from the music and later the loud chatter as they'd sat around an enormous table eating copious amounts of fried food for two hours, Jarek herded Olivia into his apartment. She stumbled in her high heels, long legs scrambling to keep her upright. It was tempting to let her fall and see her splayed out on his floor, short skirt hiked up over her hips, but he didn't have the heart. Not even after her idea of "me first" meant three more English songs and one Chinese pop song. Jarek gripped her arm to steady her, then tugged her into the bathroom and started the shower.

"What's going on?" Olivia demanded, hands on her hips. Her cheeks were red, eyes glassy, and she was *drunk*. He'd never seen her this way, figuring maybe she'd gotten it out of her system in college, partying with her equally blond friends, making frat boys drool. But the more he thought about it, as he'd watched her tonight, laughing and singing and dancing, he realized it was more likely she just hadn't had anyone to do it with in a very long time.

"Get undressed," he ordered, helping her out of her jacket.

"I don't want to take a shower."

"Okay. Hold on to me and step out of your shoes."

She gripped his wrist for balance and sighed as her feet met the cool floor. She flexed her toes and rested her forehead against his shoulder. "I danced a lot."

"I know you did."

He tugged the sparkling tank top over her head and allowed himself one meager, lustful fantasy when her lace-covered breasts came into view.

"This is your apartment," Olivia said.

"That's right."

"I've been here before."

"You have."

"Ritchie said he's never been invited. Dale either. He lives across the hall."

He unzipped her skirt and let it pool around her ankles. Her back was to the mirror and he swallowed painfully as he saw the tiny black thong disappear between her ass cheeks. She swayed against him, breasts bumping his chest, and his hardening cock jumped to attention.

"C'mon," he murmured, unfastening her bra and setting it on the counter. "Take your panties off."

"What do you want to do?"

"I want you to take a shower."

"And then?"

And then she was probably going to pass out. "And then we'll see."

"I don't want to take a shower."

"Take your panties off."

She heaved an aggrieved sigh and did her best to glare at him as she hooked her thumbs under the lacy scrap of fabric and worked it down her tan thighs. He suspected her slow progress and artless shimmy had more to do with trying to keep her balance than trying to seduce him, but either way, it was having a very unfortunate effect on his dick.

"Good," he said, taking her hand. "Now get in the shower."

"I don't want to get my hair wet."

"That's a byproduct of standing in the water." He gripped her waist and guided her in. He didn't have a tub, just a tile-enclosed shower with a heavy glass door. He leaned against the open door and watched her wince as the lukewarm water hit her head. She shivered, eyes closed, and wrapped her arms around herself, but didn't move.

"Why am I in here?" she asked after a moment.

He ran a hand over his mouth and tried not to smile. "Because you smell bad."

Her eyes flew open. "I do not!" She sniffed her armpit. "I do?"

"It's not your fault. Wash your hair." He reached in to pick up the bottle of shampoo, then opened it and squeezed some into her palm.

"What kind of shampoo is this?"

He looked at the bottle. It was written in Chinese. "I don't know."

"It's going to make my hair dry."

Jarek had no idea what that might mean. "Just use it." Watching her lather up that long blond hair, tits thrust out, nipples hard in the cool water, was almost his undoing. He'd told her he'd make her do anything if he sang in the bar, and it turned out "anything" was take a shower. Solo. While he watched, unable to do anything about his raging hard-on. What. The. Fuck.

She rinsed out the shampoo, bubbles coursing down her body and circling the drain.

"Now soap up." He put the bar of soap in her hand and she stared at it in disgust.

"Do you have any shower gel?"

"No. I don't know what that is."

"You have to know what it is. It's important." She lurched forward and he reached in to catch her, soaking his button-up shirt in the process.

"Hold on to the wall and wash up. Why is it important to know about shower gel?"

She used one hand to rub the soap over herself haphazardly, and ticked up fingers on the hand resting against the tiled wall. "It smells good. It makes your skin soft. You can use a loofah."

She started to tilt and he caught her again. "Pay attention to what you're doing," he ordered.

"I am." She swatted at him and he sighed and stepped into the shower, fully clothed, his socks acting like sponges.

"Just hold the wall." He lathered his hands and soaped her slippery body, avoiding her upper thighs, her ass, her tits. This was the worst night of his life. Pure temptation under his hands, permission to do anything he wanted, and she was drunk off her ass. The restaurant had been filled with smoke, drinks had been spilled, and someone had thrown up. She smelled like all of it, and her lower legs were splattered with something he'd rather not think about.

He scrubbed her calves and resisted the urge to press his lips to the lean expanse of thigh an inch away from his face. He'd done a lot of things to people who didn't want them, but he wouldn't do a damn thing to Olivia tonight. He didn't want to dwell on the thought. Didn't want to know when he'd become a decent man.

"I'm really sleepy." She put her hands on his shoulders for balance, and jerked. "You're wearing your shirt!"

"Yeah. Turn around." He finished with the soap, then rose and unhooked the showerhead, spraying her down.

"That tickles!" She stumbled back and he wrapped an arm around her stomach, her breasts resting on his forearm.

"Try to stand up."

"You try to stand up." But the words were soft and slurred as she started to drift off.

"Don't fall asleep yet."

"You don't fall asleep…"

"Okay. Shut up. Let's get out." Jarek shut off the water and propped her up, toweling her off as best he could, wringing a shocking amount of water out of her long hair and still not making a dent.

She slumped against him and he sighed and scooped her up, feeling the long muscles in her thighs under his fingers, her shuddering breath on his damp shirt. He carried her into the bedroom, peeled back the covers, and lay her in his bed, keeping his eyes averted as he hastily covered her up. He wasn't sure how long this gentlemanly behavior could be maintained, and he wasn't going to press his luck.

Olivia flopped onto her stomach, mouth slightly open. He pushed the wet hair back from her face and went into the bathroom to strip, leaving his soaked clothes on the shower floor before pulling on dry boxers and willing his dick to behave. It felt weird to think about masturbating in the bathroom with her passed out in his bed, so he went into the kitchen for a glass of water, thinking about anything he could to avoid thinking about her. All that came to mind, however, were myriad filthy thoughts about the "anything" he didn't get to do tonight, and in the end he crawled into bed and stayed on the far side of the mattress with the pillow over his face and tried to forget she was there.

Chapter Twelve

Jarek leaned back in his chair and sipped his beer, listening to the chatter around him. It was the night before he and Olivia would head to Beijing, and they were having dinner with Brant, Dale, and Ritchie at a small restaurant near the construction site. The round table was covered with plates of sliced meat and vegetables, steamed rice, and buns served with condensed milk for dipping.

Olivia had left to find a bathroom, so he collected an assortment of food for her before the guys could eat it all, plucking out the green peppers and adding them to his own bowl.

"What are you doing?" Brant demanded.

Jarek looked up from his task. "Are you talking to me?"

"Yeah. Leave the girl's food alone."

"I'm saving her some," he snapped. "At the rate you guys eat, there'll be nothing left when she gets back."

Dale squinted at him. "Dude. You're *eating* her food."

"She hates green peppers. I was going to get them anyway." The men exchanged looks and Jarek felt something inside him clench instinctively. Nothing good could come of his friends teaming up. "What?"

"Nothing." Brant shrugged, way too casual, and polished off his beer. He slanted a look at Dale, who was also the picture of innocence. Even Ritchie, who was supposed to be on his side, was trying not to smile.

Jarek knew he shouldn't ask, but couldn't help himself. "What?" he demanded again.

"You're in love with her," Brant answered promptly.

Everything that was clenched unclenched in a loose wave of nausea. Everything, that is, except his fist, which gripped the bottle so tightly his knuckles turned white. "Shut the fuck up," he uttered, voice low. "I'm not—" Jarek glanced around to make sure Olivia wasn't within earshot. He wasn't about to have a repeat of the "she's not my girlfriend" debacle. "We're not in love."

"You're eating her green peppers, man. That's love." Dale's nod was absolute.

"It's called not wasting food."

"There's nothing wrong with it," Ritchie offered helpfully. "Olivia's beautiful. And she's smart and good with kids. Why wouldn't you love her?"

"I don't—" Another wary look over his shoulder. "I don't love her. Stop using that word."

Brant frowned. "Which word? Love?"

"Pepper?" Dale guessed. "Which is synonymous with love?"

Jarek closed his eyes and willed himself to calm down. His heart was racing. He didn't want Olivia to overhear this stupid conversation. It was the last thing he needed. Then he'd have to tell her the guys were joking, he didn't love her, and hurt her feelings. He liked her, sure. Loved things about her, yeah, absolutely. She had fantastic breasts. He really loved those. And her legs went on for miles, long and lean and perfect. So he loved those, too. And her hair, the softest thing he'd ever felt, was nice. And so what if her smile, the one that showed too many teeth, had somehow become the thing he looked forward to seeing most after a long day—

Oh *shit*.

"What'd I miss?"

Jarek jolted when Olivia dropped into the seat next to him and picked up her chopsticks. "Thanks for saving me some food," she said, digging in.

The guys were careful to avoid each other's eyes and spare themselves his wrath. Good, Jarek thought. He still had it. At least there was a tiny bit of testosterone left in his body. What had he been thinking, eating her peppers for her? It wasn't as though he loved green peppers and didn't have enough of his own. If she didn't want to eat them, let her pick them out of the bowl and set them aside, where they'd sit in a useless pile, getting cold and—dammit.

Brant and Dale started talking about a tennis tournament they'd been following on TV, and Jarek felt Olivia's hand on his knee. "What's wrong?" she asked, voice low so the other men wouldn't hear.

He shot her a forced smile. "Nothing."

"Are you nervous about Beijing?"

"No. Why would I be?"

"Because you said you didn't like traveling, and didn't want to deal with all the people."

Ah, right. The Shanghai trip. The one she'd gone on with Marcus. He didn't particularly want to go to Beijing, even if he would get to visit the Great Wall, but more than anything, he just didn't want her to find a replacement travel partner. "I'm not nervous. Just tired. It's been a long week." It was Friday, and it *had* been a long week. The exterior of the building was finished and he'd had a lot of work to do, installing doorframes and trim, and taking measurements for the custom furniture the company requested. He was tired, but that wasn't the problem.

Olivia nodded. "I hear you. You can sleep on the train. All fourteen hours, if you like. I'll wake you up when we get there. Or let you carry on to Mongolia."

"That's sweet. Thanks."

She winked at him and flagged down a server to ask for another drink. With her attention diverted, Dale and Brant stuck out their tongues and batted their eyes, doing their best to look like lovesick fools, frantically searching for green peppers on their plates so they might find what he had.

He definitely didn't love her, Jarek thought the next night. He tossed his bag on the end of the ancient bed and it fell on the floor. Typical of the entire fucking day. They'd tried and failed to get tickets for the overnight train and so had been stuck leaving at seven thirty in the morning, meaning they'd been wide awake for the bulk of the fourteen-hour trip. They had hard sleeper tickets, forcing them into a cramped space with six beds, three stacked one on top of the other like triple bunk beds, arm's reach from the opposing three. They shared the room with a couple with twins, and Jarek finally understood the one-child-per-family policy. The boys couldn't have been more than eight years old, with the boundless energy of rabid puppies. They shrieked and hollered the entire time, and their parents' scoldings were equally shrill and piercing. He tried to cover his head with the thin pillow that came with the rock hard bed, but it was approximately half an inch thick, smelled like onions, and proved useless.

Olivia tried cheering him up for the first couple of hours, chatting brightly until he snapped at her to leave him alone for the sleep she'd promised. She was offended but returned to her bottom bunk and did not speak again until lunchtime, when they bought instant noodles from the vendor who wheeled a creaky cart up and down the hall once an hour. Jarek burned his hand with the boiling water, cursing furiously and telling Olivia to shut up when she asked him to watch his language for the sake of the kids. Kids who *didn't speak English.*

She switched then from hurt to pissed, and things didn't improve over the next ten hours. She disappeared from time to time to "stretch her legs," and no, he didn't want to walk with her. He didn't like this kind of travel, he preferred airplanes, but she'd deemed it too expensive. Plus, she'd argued, they'd have to take the train to Shanghai anyway, so they may as well take it all the way to Beijing. There were a few other foreigners on the train, at least he'd seen them at the station before they'd boarded, yet they still garnered more than a few curious looks from people who strolled past the doorless doorway more often than he deemed necessary.

Olivia loaned him her mp3 player, which was, unfortunately, loaded with the unbearable music she listened to when running. The lyrics were trite and stupid, and it only got worse when his legs started twitching as though he wanted to run, when there was nowhere to escape to. And there were still eight hours left.

By the time they got to Beijing, Olivia was barely speaking to him. She'd befriended the two boys and taught them to play Go Fish, keeping them occupied for the last hours to their parents' relief and amusement. Jarek should have been relieved as well, but he was too fucking wound up to be grateful. He wanted off the train, away from all people, wanted to be alone for the first time in what felt like forever.

There was a reason he didn't do this shit, he reminded himself. Travel. Girlfriends. It was too much. It was a headache he just didn't need.

Now Olivia went into the bathroom and closed the door. After a moment he heard the water run as she brushed her teeth and washed her face. Jarek took a deep breath, rolled out his shoulders, and looked around the tiny room. Olivia had booked the place online, a "short distance" from the train station, which was actually two buses and then a cab when the bus route turned out to be completely incorrect. The hotel was on the small side, just six floors, each older and more decrepit than the last. The elevator wasn't working so they'd had to take the stairs to the fifth floor, and halfway up the light had gone out, leaving them with just the faint green glow of the emergency exits to lead the way. She'd joked that this was a breeze since they regularly navigated the dark stairwell in her apartment building, but he hadn't laughed and she hadn't tried again.

The room had a queen size bed, a wooden dresser, and a low table with a tube TV sitting on top. An enormous remote control rested on a thin guide book—in Chinese, of course—and the thin curtains on the window did nothing to block the light from the busy street below. Even now, ten minutes past midnight, the street was packed with cars and motorbikes and bicycles, the din of horns and bells filtering in through the open window.

Jarek's stomach growled, reminding him that he hadn't eaten anything since the package of vegetable chips Olivia had tossed at him around six o'clock. He glanced at the bathroom door, feeling a tiny bit guilty. She was probably hungry, too. And tired, having tried to compensate for his bad attitude all day. He peered out the window at the shops below, belly rumbling when he saw familiar golden arches.

He strode to the bathroom door, hand raised to knock, and Olivia flinched when she pulled the door open and found his fist an inch from her face. Something went off in the back of his skull, clanging like an alarm bell, though he couldn't tell if it was warning him off or signaling the start of something. It had been a long time since he'd hit somebody, not for lack of wanting. But he'd never hit a woman and he didn't intend to. He dropped his hand. "I was going to ask if you were hungry." His gaze roved over her face, hair pulled back in a bun, damp at the edges.

"Starving."

"Want to go out? Or I could grab something and bring it back."

She walked past him to the bag she'd set on the chair and pulled out some money. "You go."

"I don't want your money. Burgers okay?"

"Yes. Fine."

He looked at her and sighed. She didn't look back, tucking the bills into her wallet and digging around in her purse until she found lip gloss. She walked to the window as she applied it, looking out. Jarek wanted to say something but knew he'd make things worse, so he picked up the room key and went back down the dark stairwell and out into the warm night air.

The first thing he noticed was that there were many more white people in Beijing; the second was that many of them were Russian and didn't speak English. The restaurant was just half a block away but even though he was hungry, he took his time, willing the darkness to absorb his irritation, letting tight muscles loosen. He pointed at the picture menu and ordered burgers and fries and an apple pie for Olivia, then two bottles of water so they'd have something in the morning. He walked back faster than he'd walked over, wondering how the hell Jonah managed to make a marriage work. He'd been with Katrine for fifteen years—how did people do that? He'd failed to be a good boyfriend for fourteen *hours*, and was trying to make up for it with grease and corn syrup.

He trudged back up the stairs and let himself into the room. Olivia sat cross legged on the edge of the bed, watching TV as the Canadian man explained how to ask directions around a college campus. She'd changed into shorts and a T-shirt, and she was braless. Probably not a good time to ask for sex, so he set the bag on the bed beside her and kicked off his shoes, stripping off his jeans so he was in boxers and a T-shirt, then joined her on top of the covers. "Learn anything?" he asked.

"*Donde esta la biblioteca?*" she replied, unfolding the paper bag and inhaling deeply.

"You're a natural."

Olivia didn't answer, pulling out a handful of fries and sticking two in her mouth as she opened the box containing the hamburger. "Thanks," she said eventually.

"Yeah? For what?"

"The burger."

He waited until she looked at him, then held her gaze. "I'm sorry about today. Too many people. Too much noise."

She raised an eyebrow and ate another fry. "The city's supposed to be vacant tomorrow, so that should be better."

Jarek winced at the sarcasm and took a bite of his burger. "We'll see, I guess." It was Saturday night—well, Sunday morning—and they were scheduled to return to Lazhou on Tuesday night, giving them three full days to explore the city. Olivia had booked a trip to the Great Wall for Monday, and he had no idea what they'd do on the other days. On his previous travels he'd stuck close to the base or wherever he'd been working; he'd never really played the tourist. The only reason he'd come to Beijing was because she was here, and now he'd ruined it.

"I got you a pie."

"I'll save it for breakfast." Her eyes were trained on the television, but he knew she wasn't studying.

"Want me to say something else?"

"Like what?"

"I don't know. Just tell me."

She shrugged and finished the burger, licking special sauce off her fingers before wiping them on a napkin. "You don't have to say anything. If you want to stay in the room tomorrow, that's fine."

"I'm not going to stay in the room."

"I don't want to hang out with you if you're going to be like this. I'm pretty sure we'll encounter people tomorrow, Jarek."

"It'll be fine."

"You didn't even last an hour this morning."

"Those kids were fucking irritating, Olivia. You had to be annoyed."

"I deal with kids every day. Obviously we deal with it differently."

"Obviously."

She stuck her trash in the bag, then got up and stalked to the garbage can to toss it in. "Do you want to watch any more TV?" she asked.

"No."

She pressed the button at the base of the massive appliance and the screen went dark. He watched her ass as she moved around the bed, tugged back the covers, and slid under. Lamps on either side of the bed were on, so she turned hers off and rolled onto her side, giving him her back. "Good night."

Jarek finished his food and threw out the packaging, then went in the bathroom to brush his teeth and splash cold water on his face. It was completely irrational—and out of the realm of possibility—but he really wanted to fuck her right now. He decided to take a shower instead, but the "shower" was just a showerhead sticking out of the wall, no tub, no curtain, nothing to keep the water from spraying all over the room. They had a western toilet, at least, but it was a struggle to avoid soaking everything as he took a brief shower, jerking off and hoping it would help ease the tension.

Olivia was asleep—or pretending to be—when he climbed under the covers behind her. Despite her awful, tiny bed, they spent more nights at her place than his, and he'd gotten in the habit of sleeping curled up behind her, one hand splayed across her stomach. He did that now, ignoring her stiff posture—she was definitely awake—and breathing in the clean smell of her hair. He felt the smooth skin of her thighs on his, and wondered not for the first time how anyone could do this forever—and how they ever managed to stop.

The bright morning sun woke them up. He felt her shift, then her hand lifted to shield her eyes from the glare. The flimsy curtains were drawn but provided no cover, and by eight o'clock they could no longer pretend to be asleep.

Still curled on her side, Olivia stretched, arching as she did so, prying her hips away from the erection he inevitably woke up with when she was next to him. "Sleep well?" he asked. He hadn't, and not just because he felt bad about fighting with her, but also because the bed was extraordinarily uncomfortable.

"No," she answered. Without elaboration.

He pressed a kiss to the back of her neck. "You still mad?"

"Not really."

He nudged her with his cock. "Any chance you could help me out with this?"

She laughed, the sound muffled by the pillow. "Jarek."

"Come on. I'll convince you." He pulled her onto her back and shuffled under the covers, tugging her shorts and panties down her legs. She didn't fight as he shouldered her thighs apart, licking his way up the soft, sensitive skin until he found what he was looking for. He ate her out, slowly and thoroughly, until she knotted her fingers in his hair and writhed around, pleading with him to hurry.

"Are we still in a fight?" he murmured, tongue plunging inside.

"Gah…No. No. No — *Yes…*"

He circled her clit with his lips, tugging insistently, getting the answer he was looking for. Once she'd settled, he urged her onto her stomach and slid into her from behind the way he'd dreamed about all night. She was wet and welcoming and he felt so fucking relieved he almost didn't want to come, wanted to preserve this moment of forgiveness and acceptance so he could remember what it felt like. He was pretty sure none of the other people he'd hurt had forgiven him, and he'd certainly never tried to atone.

She came again and he came with her, then lay beside her as their breathing slowed. "Well," Olivia said. "I've never made up with someone like that before."

"No?"

"No."

"How many someones are we talking about?"

He watched her face, profile backlit by the sun, for telltale signs of lying, but all he saw was a faintly uncomfortable flush before she said, "Just one."

"Chris? That's the only person you've been with?"

"Yeah. First and only. Until you."

"Huh."

"How about you?"

It was his turn to feel uncomfortable. Why the hell had he started this conversation? He'd already known the answer, for fuck's sake. It didn't take a rocket scientist to deduce that she'd only ever been with Chris. And now that she'd turned the tables he couldn't very well not answer, not so soon after making up. He didn't want to spend the rest of the trip walking on eggshells.

Olivia broke the silence. "I really hope you're not counting."

"Shh. Hang on. One hundred and six…"

She laughed, but he wasn't fooled. She was still waiting. Then she sighed. "You don't have to tell me if you don't want to."

"I don't know how many, exactly."

"You don't know?"

"I didn't keep count. A few. More than…five."

"More than a hundred?"

Now he laughed. "No, Olivia."

"How many of them were serious?"

"Relationships?"

"Yeah."

He hesitated, not wanting to tell her the truth, but unwilling to lie. "None."

"Not one woman out of a hundred and six?"

"Nope." A hundred and six was a huge exaggeration, but he really didn't know the number. He'd never thought much about it, until now.

She was silent for a moment, then, "Why not?"

He resisted the impulse to sigh, knowing it would only make things worse. "I didn't want to. After Stacey—the first one—I enlisted, started working, traveling, and…I didn't have the urge."

"You didn't have the *urge*?" She didn't try to hide her disbelief.

"I like to fuck, Olivia. I didn't have the urge to see them again, that's all." He was crude on purpose; he wanted the conversation to end, but didn't want to be the one to do it so she couldn't hold it against him.

But she pressed on, undeterred. "So what changed?"

"With you? I don't know. You live nearby."

"*Jarek.*"

Uh-oh. The teacher voice. "What do you want me to say? I'm an asshole. I wanted to know what happened to your engagement ring. Then I was pissed that you called that first night 'fine.' Then I wanted to do better."

"Huh."

"And you live nearby."

She elbowed him in the gut. "Jerk."

"And you smell good."

"That's better."

"And I can't take my eyes off your ass."

She refused to be distracted. "Did things with Stacey end badly?"

He shook his head. "No. It just ended. I went away, we grew apart. Nothing dramatic. Just an ending."

"Do you keep in touch with her?"

"No. She married a golf pro and lives in Texas or something."

"A golf pro?"

He smiled. "Yeah."

"Do you golf?"

"No."

"Play any sports?"

"Hockey, sometimes. Not really."

"Do you think you'll go back to it?"

"Hockey? I don't know. It wasn't really a hobby."

"I meant the no relationships. When we're…done."

He pulled away and rolled onto his back. "I don't know what's going to happen when we leave here." And he really didn't want to think about it. He couldn't say that he wouldn't pick up women in bars, could he? That he'd never be horny and take care of that need the only way he'd known how until he'd met her? He certainly couldn't promise to call them afterward. "What about you? Are you going to see Chris when you go back?"

She shrugged, eyes on the ceiling. "Probably. It's a small town."

"And he lives with your parents."

A thin smile. "He moved out last month. I guess he finally realized it was strange for him to be living there."

"It was really fucking strange." A pause. "But that's not what I meant. Do you keep in touch? Are you going to get back together with him?"

A longer pause. "We don't keep in touch. But I've thought about it."

Something inside him pulled painfully tight, and he clenched his fists, then forced the muscles to relax. When he spoke, his voice came out remarkably level. "What do you mean?"

"I mean, I don't know what's going to happen when we leave here."

Ouch. His own words, used against him. "You're too good for him."

"Ha."

"What?"

"Am I too good for you?"

He ran a hand across his mouth. "What do you think?"

"You already know what I think. What do you think?"

"Yes, you're too good."

"Then why am I with you?"

"Because you're lonely."

She stretched again. "I was lonely. I'm not now. Why am I still doing this?"

He couldn't talk about it. He didn't have the answer. He didn't want to tell her he wasn't good and decent, the way she thought he was, so instead he rolled over and buried his face in her neck. "Because you wanted to split the cost of the trip," he mumbled.

She dragged her nails up his back, making him moan. "Am I that transparent?"

He laughed then, and didn't reply. He, Jarek McLean, the man who'd made a living getting answers, had none when it came to her.

They eventually got hungry and left the hotel around noon. Their hotel, it turned out, was even more rundown and unappealing in the daylight. The immediate vicinity was crowded and noisy, a strange combination of old and new as tiny hole-in-the-wall shops competed with the gaudy neon signs of newer constructions. It was a hot day, and Jarek wore board shorts and a T-shirt while Olivia opted for jeans and a tank top. Even though there were more foreigners here, her bright hair still drew stares.

Olivia was torn between the desire to take it all in and the urge to shrink away. She'd been in China for nearly five months, but it still somehow managed to seem so…foreign. So intimidating. She knew something was truly frightening when it made Jarek feel like the safest option. But her tall, cranky boyfriend seemed to recognize her anxiety because he held her hand, which he never did, and he was using the patient voice she used on her students when they were driving her crazy.

A few blocks later she spotted a noodle shop like the one near her apartment and suggested they eat there, since she knew the chain and what to order. The restaurant was small and cramped and very warm. Jarek spotted an empty table and went to claim it, and Olivia approached the counter nervously, suddenly anxious about speaking. She meant it last night when she told Jarek she'd rather tour the city alone than be with him if he was going to snap at her, but now that she was outside the cocoon of their dingy little hotel room, she was glad he was here. She'd crossed the ocean in a fit of foolish bravery, and become afraid the second she'd landed. Each week had been a little easier, but she wasn't the intrepid explorer she'd imagined she would be. She still needed someone to lean on, even though she was an adult who should be able to stand on her own two feet.

The older man at the cash register stared at her expectantly. He asked what she wanted in Mandarin, the words so fast she only caught them because she'd heard the question so many times before. Olivia straightened her spine and asked for her normal order, noodles with vegetables and two cans of Sprite.

His brow furrowed and he asked her to say it again.

She repeated the order three more times before he nodded, muttering to himself and punching keys on the register. He told her the price, using his hands to illustrate the numbers.

With the first obstacle overcome, she picked her way past children playing on the floor and pulled two drinks from the refrigerator, tempted to linger in its chill. Upon arriving in China she'd promptly learned that you had to specify you'd like your drink to be cold, otherwise you'd receive something lukewarm or boiling hot by default. She couldn't fathom drinking hot tea on a day like today, but half the occupied tables seemed to be doing just that.

She joined Jarek and sat down, sliding his can across the table and taking a deep breath as she looked out the window at the familiar, buzzing scene outside. She should be used to this by now. She'd been an outsider for so long, but couldn't seem to embrace it. She wanted things to be easy again, but it seemed they were only getting harder.

Jarek nudged her knee under the tiny table. "What's wrong?"

She smiled in spite of herself. She knew he loved asking questions, but he didn't like personal questions, didn't want people to dump their problems in his lap. He didn't want to help people, didn't want to be relied upon, didn't think he was that guy. But he was. He was that guy to her and she knew the guys at the site depended on him, too.

"I'm just hungry," she lied, cracking open the drink and taking a long swallow.

He sat across from her, still and observant. "Liar."

She watched him across the can, then trailed her tongue across her lower lip, catching the droplets that clung there. "Am not."

He nodded, then sat back in his chair. "Suit yourself."

This was better, she thought. She could be herself in this small bubble, just the two of them and food she knew and liked. China was her first foray outside of the United States. They'd always gone on family vacations within the country, popular destinations like Disney World and the Grand Canyon. She knew a handful of Spanish, but had never really needed to speak a foreign language before. She'd always, always been in her element, and things had never really been hard, until, of course, they were. She'd tried to be patient and wait for it to get better, but it hadn't, and then she'd fled. She'd come to China — China! — expecting things to be easier. They weren't. They were different. And they were hard. Because life was hard, and she was two weeks away from her twenty-eighth birthday and somehow she was only just now learning that lesson.

A server appeared with their food, and Olivia was relieved to see two plates of the familiar hand cut noodles slathered in tomato sauce, vegetables, sliced meat and egg. She picked out chopsticks from the basket on the table, pried them apart and dug in. Jarek reached across to steal an offensive green pepper from the top of the pile and she smiled at him. "I just feel like I'll never be able to be on my own," she said, eyes skittering away from his knowing stare. "I'm realizing that I've never been by myself, and I don't know how."

"You want me to abandon you some point during the day? Give you a feel for it?" He kept a straight face as he said it, but she saw the telltale twitch at the corner of his eye, the one that told her he was trying not to laugh.

"That day will come soon enough," she said, pointing at him with a chopstick. "Don't go anywhere."

Now it was his eyes that left hers, focusing on his food, even as she saw the tiniest smile break through his stern features. "Okay," he said. "I won't."

They walked for hours, first strolling through Tiananmen Square, then entering the Forbidden City, an enormous complex that had served as the Chinese imperial palace for five hundred years. Olivia insisted on paying for the audio tour, and though they were two people of hundreds doing the same thing, Jarek still felt like an idiot walking around with headphones, trying to stay on track so he was looking at the right item as it was being described.

He wasn't much for this sort of thing, but he had to admit that the scope and grandeur was impressive. For something built in the fourteen hundreds, it had held up well, and the carpenter in him couldn't help but admire the detailed workmanship. Olivia was taken with the painted scrolls and vases, ornate furniture and carvings, snapping the occasional photo. She hated doing it but needed something to send to her parents.

"Here," she said at one point, standing in front of an intricately carved doorway. "Take a picture of me."

"You want to remember this door for some reason?"

"I need to show them I'm surviving. Proof of life."

He shook his head but took the photo, handing back her camera and turning down the volume on his tour. "Are they worried about you being over here?"

She shrugged. "I don't think so. They're more concerned about Thailand, for whatever reason."

"What about it?"

"That I'm going by myself. A single woman traveling alone, all that."

"Are you worried about it?"

Another shrug. "A little. It'll be fine. I have to start sometime, right?"

He wasn't going to dwell on it. "Sure. Are you about done here?"

She looked surprised at the abrupt change of subject. "No. We have a million more things to see."

"We've been here for hours."

"But the tour's not over."

"All right. You keep walking, I'm going to Starbucks."

"What?" She followed his gaze to the eponymous coffee chain stationed in the Forbidden City, protested that it was blasphemous, then trailed him into the store and got some frozen chocolate concoction that she took with her as she left to continue the tour for another hour.

Jarek watched until she was out of sight, then bought an American newspaper and sat down to read. It was hard to concentrate. He hadn't slept well in the lumpy bed, and they'd been on their feet for seven hours. He was tired, and Olivia's enthusiasm made him feel old. What he really wanted to do was find a bar, order a cold beer, and relax for a while. Then he wanted to take Olivia back to their crappy hotel and ask for that "anything" she'd promised him on karaoke night, but had passed out before delivering. He'd intended to ask for it the next time he saw her, but she'd been on her period and had threatened to claw his eyes out if he so much as looked at her with any sort of lewd intentions, and he hadn't found the nerve again after that.

"Anything interesting happening?"

He glanced up from the paper—he'd read all of four pages—and blinked at Olivia in surprise. "What are you doing back so soon?"

"It's been an hour." She tried to stifle a yawn, but failed.

Jarek checked his watch. It had indeed been an hour. He'd just spent sixty minutes thinking about one woman and the things he'd like to do to her, and it appeared she was ready for bed, not a round of raunchy sex. "Let's get you some coffee," he said, standing.

She gave him an odd look. "No, thanks. I'm ready to go. Is there anything else you want to see?"

Yes, but he couldn't very well say so in polite company. "No. Let's go." He tucked the paper under one arm and held her hand in the other—when had he started doing that?—guiding them back to the street to flag a cab. Olivia dozed against his shoulder on the ride home, waking only long enough to make the trip up the stairs to their awful hotel room before collapsing on top of the covers and starting to snore. Jarek rolled his eyes and took off her sneakers and jeans. Her cheeks were flushed pink from the sun, and her arms were now a shade darker than her mile-long legs. He sighed and went to take a shower in the tiny, still-damp bathroom. It looked like "anything" would have to wait.

Chapter Thirteen

The bus trip to the Great Wall left at seven o'clock the next morning. Jarek grunted answers to Olivia's eager questions about what, exactly, his thoughts on the Great Wall were, and ignored her scowl when he didn't share her enthusiasm. Unlike Olivia, he had not slept peacefully for ten hours. He'd lain beside her, hoping she'd wake up, "accidentally" nudging her a few times to see if he could get her to open her eyes and help alleviate the tension in his groin. But she'd been dead to the world, coming to life at six thirty this morning, hopping in the shower and dressing in record time, then peppering him with questions.

"You're not bringing a camera?" she asked again as they hurried down the stairs to the cramped lobby.

"No."

"Okay. I'll send you some of mine."

"Fantastic."

She halted so suddenly that he ran into her and they barely avoided falling to the ground like idiots.

"Fuck, Olivia! Why did you stop?"

"Is it people that bother you, or transportation?" She looked at him suspiciously.

"What? People. People who stop without warning." He straightened his shirt and tried not to glower. There were already a dozen people in the lobby, all equipped with backpacks and water bottles, cameras slung around their necks. He had opted once again for board shorts and a T-shirt, and Olivia wore cut-offs and a loose tank top. They did not look prepared to hike the ten kilometer stretch of the Great Wall for which Olivia had signed them up.

"We have a three-hour bus ride," she said, a warning note in her voice. "I'm not interested in a repeat of our train trip."

"Relax. I'm going to sleep. Wake me when we get there."

A slender Chinese woman with a faint accent approached with a clipboard. "You are going to see the Great Wall of China?" she confirmed.

Olivia turned her back on him. "Yes. Olivia Clarke and Jarek McLean." She initialed the list next to their names and the woman handed her two tickets.

"You must keep these for the bus, to go and to come back. I am Sally, I will be the translator on the bus, but I do not go on the Wall, okay?"

"Sure."

Sally went off to find the remaining guests and Olivia handed him his ticket. "Ready, Sunshine?"

"Yeah." They filed after the other members of the group, climbing on a large, modern tour bus with comfortable seats and air conditioning, a blessing since the sun was already up and there were no clouds in the sky. They found two seats near the back and Jarek gestured for Olivia to take the window seat before sitting beside her, sliding on his sunglasses and closing his eyes.

A few minutes later the bus started up and they pulled away from the curb, engine rumbling. "Did you sleep last night?" Olivia asked.

"Yeah."

"Then what's wrong?"

"Nothing. Just wake me up when we get there. It'll be fine."

"Did I do something?"

"No."

"Do I talk in my sleep? I've heard that I do. Did I say something really insulting?"

"No."

"Nothing like, *Jarek McLean loves cotton candy and kittens and butterfly kisses?*"

He tried not to smile. "What is wrong with you?"

"That's what I dream about, Jarek."

"You dream about me?"

"Oh, God yes. Even when I'm awake."

He laughed, but didn't open his eyes. "Please shut up."

"What's wrong?"

"You don't want to know."

"Are you sick?"

Jarek inhaled deeply, praying for patience. This was like hanging out with Dale, who nagged him incessantly. "I'm not sick. I'm tired."

"But you said you slept."

"Are you trying to annoy me on purpose?"

"Kind of. I'm wide awake and I want you to entertain me until we get there."

His mouth twitched, and he reached over and cupped her head, bringing her ear to his lips. "I wanted to fuck you last night."

"I—What?"

"And *all* night. And this morning. And now we've got a bus ride and a hike and another bus ride until we're alone again. I'm really uncomfortable and this bus is too crowded to ask you to lean over here and suck me off, so please let me sleep."

She turned her head and they were close enough that their lips touched. "Was this the problem on the train, too?" Her gaze was guileless and blue, and he knew she could see right through him, but he couldn't look away.

"No. I hated those kids. You going to let me sleep before my problem becomes everyone else's business?"

He saw her eyes flicker past him, taking in the two eager young backpackers on the other side of the aisle. He already knew there was no way for her to get him off without being noticed, and he didn't really expect it. He'd fucked women in bathrooms and alleys, places that meant nothing when he should have known better. Olivia was different. He wanted more for her. Better than him, no question. But until she wised up to her situation, he'd take what he could get.

"OhmyGodJarekwakeup."

He jolted upright at the urgent note in Olivia's voice, twisting his neck painfully. "What?" he mumbled, massaging the aching muscle. "What is it?"

"We're here."

He peered at her over his sunglasses. "What's so fucking urgent?"

"Look."

The bus ground to a halt and the other passengers gathered their belongings with excited murmurs. Outside he could see the small parking lot, and beyond that, green. And some rock. But mostly green. "What am I looking at?"

Olivia raised her eyebrows and indicated that he should look higher. Jarek sighed and leaned over her, feeling her breasts against his shoulder as he craned his sore neck to look out the window — and up. And up. Until finally, at the top of a small mountain, he saw something that may or may not have resembled the guide book picture of the Great Wall.

Olivia pointed out the obvious: "We have to climb a mountain to get to the Wall. It's not part of the hike."

"You're kidding me." He winced as a ray of sunlight beamed into his eye, then pulled back, rolling his shoulders.

"No. I hope you're well-rested."

Sally gave the group instructions, basically, follow the marked path up the mountain, and hike east until they spotted the next parking lot. There were two small restaurants there for people who finished early; the bus left at four o'clock sharp, and if they weren't on it, they weren't going back to Beijing today. And have fun!

Jarek shot Olivia a meaningful look and she shrugged, then they filed off the bus, stretching cramped muscles when they got outside. It was hot. Unseasonably hot for late May, the sun bright and merciless, the Wall looming high above. Theirs was the only bus in the parking lot, and there were no more than thirty people heading up the mountain. The group quickly filtered apart so Jarek and Olivia were walking behind an older German couple whose brisk pace put them both to shame.

Thanks to the trees the hike to the top was in shade, and Jarek took a moment to appreciate that he hadn't seen this much nature and so few people since he'd arrived in China. It was only thirty minutes to the peak, then they were on the Wall, a surprisingly massive construction Olivia informed him was more than five thousand miles long. For some reason he'd imagined it to be waist-high, built on flat sand and stretching into the distance, but he couldn't have been more wrong. It careened along the mountain ridge, was high enough that he'd break an ankle — and probably more — if he tried to jump off, and was several yards across at most points.

They'd had three options when choosing to visit the Wall, the first being the most popular and repaired section, the second being this unkempt ten kilometer stretch, the third being a reportedly crumbling and dangerous section intended for serious visitors only. At the moment there were just half a dozen or so people from their group at the top, peering around at the never-ending sea of green forest and rolling mountains that stretched into the horizon. A cool breeze unstuck Jarek's shirt from his back, and for the first time in a long time, it was quiet. Peaceful. He felt…calm.

He looked down at Olivia when she squeezed his hand. She'd pulled her ponytail through the back of a baseball cap and squinted up at him. "You ready?"

"Yeah."

"Take a picture of me, please."

"Proof of life?"

"For now, anyway."

She leaned against the wall, Inner Mongolia somewhere in the distance, and smiled as he took the photo. He cupped his hand over the display to check the image, resisting the urge to grin at her too-big smile, the way the sun glinted off her hair and exposed shoulders, the way she managed to look so happy for no reason at all. It had been a long time since he'd felt that way, and this was the closest he'd come in as long as he could remember. Light. Unburdened.

They set off east as instructed, climbing and descending as the mountain ridge dictated. There were guard towers and parapets, tiny openings from which arrows could have been launched, and entire sections that had crumbled away, forcing them to jump over two foot gaps or risk falling down the mountain. Every once in a while they passed an elderly person from a nearby village selling marked up water and soft drinks, and Olivia bought them each a bottle since they'd long ago finished the ones they came with. They didn't talk a lot, and he lingered behind when they approached the steeply eroded staircases, ready to catch her if she fell…and watching her ass and thighs and calves and feet…everything, really. He was hot and sweaty and perverted.

At the halfway mark they encountered the German couple. They had stopped to take in the views and catch their breath, and Olivia made polite small talk while Jarek used her camera to take pictures of scenery that hadn't changed for the past hour. He watched the couple pose for a photo, Olivia giving them the three-count cue to smile, which they did eagerly. He thought of Jonah and Katrine, their mysterious happiness, and now this couple, in their sixties at least, still going strong. It was possible, he supposed, that love wasn't the worst thing to happen to a person.

"Can we return the favor?" the German man asked, gesturing to the camera Jarek held. "It's a nice place for a picture."

Olivia looked at him awkwardly. He'd rebuffed her offers to take his photo at several points along the Wall, and she'd stopped asking. He hadn't seen the point; it wasn't like he'd forget he'd been here, and if he wanted a proper photograph he'd buy a postcard in town. But suddenly he did want one. Just one picture with Olivia next to him, because he would forget this. In five weeks she would leave and his memory of her would dim and he'd go back to having nothing and preferring it that way.

She blinked in surprise when he agreed, handed over the camera and lifted an arm for her to stand beneath. She peered at him as she approached but he just nodded for her to hurry up and take her place, then draped his arm around her shoulders. After a second he felt her arm wrap around his waist, the soft, familiar squeeze of her fingers on his hip, the brush of her hair on his bicep. Jarek took a deep breath and smiled when ordered, reluctant to release Olivia when she went to retrieve the camera and study the picture. "Looks good," she said to the man. "Thank you."

"You're welcome."

The couple packed up their things and carried on with the hike. The next closest group was gathered on the Wall two hills behind them, and they were once again alone. "You're such a ham," Olivia accused, breaking the silence.

"I didn't want to hurt the guy's feelings."

"A ham and a softie. This hike is changing you, Jarek."

She started walking and he stared after her, knowing the hike had nothing to do with the changes, but not sure how to feel about it. About her. Aw, fuck. He knew how he felt about her, what he didn't know was what to do about it. How to stop it, since the feelings came with an expiration date that was going to be really damn painful. Jarek knew pain. He'd administered and received it, though not in equal measures, and he had the sneaking, terrifying suspicion that the scales were about to become even.

They hiked again in silence, and Jarek bought more overpriced-but-worth-every-penny water from a villager, pausing next to Olivia in a covered archway, enjoying the brief reprieve from the overbearing sun. If he squinted he could see what might possibly be the two small structures that marked the end of their trip, probably two or three kilometers away. There was a small river in the distance, lined on either side by towering green trees, and he would have given anything to dive in and cool off.

The next incline was very steep, the steps so eroded as to barely exist, and Olivia was using her hands to help climb when she slipped. He was about fifteen feet behind when he heard her surprised yelp, looking up just in time to see her skid down several steps. She didn't fall far, just a few feet, but enough to scrape up one of her knees and draw blood.

"You okay?" he asked, carefully jogging up to her.

"Ugh. Yeah. Fine." She stood and dusted herself off and he saw that the inside of her right arm was scratched, long pink lines with tiny dots of bright blood beading intermittently. He looked her over but there was really nothing he could do apart from pour his remaining water on her skinned knee and flick out the tiny rocks clinging to her flesh. She batted at his hands. "Ow. Stop."

"Hang on. You all right to walk?" He fumbled in his pocket and found a crumpled tissue, mopping up the watery trails of blood that trickled down her shin. The injuries were nothing more serious than the ones he'd sustained falling off his bike as a kid, and she flexed her knee and declared herself okay to continue.

Another kilometer later they were definitely approaching the parking lot, the bus already parked and waiting though they still had a good hour and a half left before they were due to depart. Olivia was walking stiffly, laughing off his offers to give her a piggy back or whip off his shirt to bandage her knee, but he could tell she was hurting. At the top of the final steep incline she was breathing hard and determinedly keeping her back to him, pretending to take in a view that was the same as all the others.

"Hey." He put a hand on her shoulder, surprised when she turned suddenly and buried her face in his chest. "You okay?"

"Fine. I'm being stupid," she mumbled. "It just hurts. Thanks for helping me."

"Of course I'd help you," he said, stroking her ponytail. "I love y—" He broke off abruptly, shock coloring his features, and clasped Olivia tightly against him so she couldn't pull back and look at his face. She heard him, no question; she'd gone rigid with surprise at the near-declaration. He cleared his throat awkwardly. "You'll be okay."

She tried to pull away but he kept her pinned against him, delaying the inevitable. He couldn't handle it if she looked at him with pity or hope, couldn't bear the thought of disappointing her. He'd carry her all the way back to the start of the hike if he could just make those almost-three little words never have almost happened.

"You can say it," she said, voice muffled against his chest. He could feel her lips move through his T-shirt, her hands gently stroking the small of his back as though she knew he was now the one who needed tending.

He tugged her ponytail lightly. "Don't."

She sighed then, and struggled slightly to get away, though he only released her when he heard her muttered "okay." She stepped back and adjusted her clothing, then glanced down and frowned. "I got blood on your leg."

He followed her gaze to the tiny red smudge on his calf. "I'll live." A bloodstain he could survive. That was about all he had the stomach for right now. "Go ahead," he said, when she lingered uncomfortably. "I'll be right there." Jarek avoided her stare, and after a second she blew out a breath and turned and continued, the end now in sight.

Alone again for the first time in a very long while, Jarek braced his hands on the crumbling edge of the wall and squeezed until the rocks dug painfully into his palms. The irony of the location for his slip up didn't elude him. He'd spent a lifetime erecting a wall around himself, very determinedly keeping people at a distance. And now here he stood, on a five thousand mile long wall that had taken centuries to build, cost hundreds of thousands of people their lives, and was rumored to be visible from fucking *outer space*, and the damn thing had never kept anybody out.

She knew he was faking it. Olivia glanced at Jarek out the corner of her eye as the bus bounced along on the way back to Beijing. After finishing the hike they'd cleaned up her leg, bought icy cold drinks at one of the restaurants, and waited for the bus to depart at four o'clock. He'd retreated into his shell, grunting the occasional answer, waving her off when she said she was going to walk around and take pictures, putting as much distance between them as possible. Now, an hour into the trip back to town, he had his eyes closed, sunglasses on, and was doing a terrible job of pretending to be asleep. Almost as terrible a job as they were doing pretending he hadn't almost said the L-word.

Olivia sighed and turned to look out the window. She wasn't really surprised to hear that Jarek cared about her; what had surprised them both was that he'd almost admitted it. But the near-admission didn't change anything, she thought. Their relationship had a time limit and one little word wouldn't make a difference. Not that he'd let her say anything. Whenever she looked at him with any kind of meaning he glared at her in warning and studied something in his lap or behind her or any place he didn't have to meet her eyes.

He feigned sleep all the way to Beijing. By the time they stepped off the bus shortly after seven that evening, the only conclusion Olivia had come to was that she wouldn't bring it up. He knew, she sort of knew, neither of them were admitting it, and who cared, really? She'd loved Chris for ten years and he'd turned on her in a heartbeat. Love was a feeling, not a guarantee, and she wasn't willing to open her heart to someone who couldn't—wouldn't—open his. Even if he might have already cracked open a door she thought she'd slammed shut a year ago.

It was obvious Jarek wasn't eager to return to the hotel room, no doubt expecting her to barricade the door and demand he utter the entire offensive syllable. *Love*. For a guy who thought he was some sort of reincarnation of the devil, who could cow bigger men with a stare, he was awfully afraid of this. Of her. A kindergarten teacher.

They sat in a brightly lit fast food restaurant and ate burgers and fries for dinner, again making minimal conversation. Olivia wanted to rehash the excitement of the hike and her thrill at having visited the Great Wall, but knew that any attempt to speak of the site of his not-quite-an-emotional-moment would be met with a firmly erected wall of his own. She chattered instead about her class's preparation for the play and the kids' excitement, Alan's choreography, Davy's art design, Rose's sound direction. The thing was a disaster, but she preferred to think of it as a Jackson Pollock painting: upon first glance it might be a hot mess, but true connoisseurs would recognize its heart. Its talent. Its meaning. Even if she hadn't completely finished the third act, where Little Red Riding Hood and the Spidermans and a few other random friends encountered the not-at-all-scary wolf who had definitely not eaten grandma.

Jarek delayed leaving the restaurant, even though she could tell he was tired. The sun and the exertion had taken its toll, and she felt the same, but being alone with her was obviously outside of his comfort zone. When they finally exited the restaurant she pointed to the glowing image of a colorful foot indicating a reflexology studio and suggested they go inside. On several occasions Jarek had referred to the practice as "voodoo" but now he agreed, and Olivia knew his ready acquiescence had more to do with his cowardly approach to dealing with his feelings than sore feet. But her feet *were* aching, so they went inside and took comfortable seats and plunged their feet into wooden buckets of hot, scented water and bit their lips to hide groans of pleasure.

"Voodoo, hmm?" she murmured.

"Witchcraft," he mumbled. "Dark arts."

"You love it."

He stiffened slightly at her unintentional use of the offensive word, but relaxed when the reflexologist removed his feet from the bucket, wrapped them in a warm white towel, and got to work. The same was happening for Olivia, so she let her eyes drift shut and gave into the lure of the massage, willing herself to stay awake so she could enjoy the experience and avoid waking up with drool on her chin.

"Ow ow ow," Jarek hissed at one point.

Olivia cracked open an eye to look at him. "What?"

He snatched up the laminated chart that indicated which part of the foot was connected to which other body part, and located the painful pressure point. "Apparently my esophagus is particularly sensitive."

Olivia's laugh was cut short by her own jolting pain. "Mother of God!" she gasped. The reflexologists, tiny Chinese women whose hands knew the strength of ten men, exchanged a look and laughed, muttering between themselves. They didn't need a translator to know what was being said, but the pressure eased up and the massage resumed its relaxing cadence.

"That was pretty amazing," Olivia remarked an hour later as they shuffled out of the shop. "My feet feel like clouds."

Jarek looked at her doubtfully. "Maybe they slipped something in your tea."

"Did I imagine that part where a woman came in and offered to continue the massage in our hotel room?"

"No, that happened."

She shuddered. Jarek had fielded the question with a polite but firm denial, and she'd been grateful for his interception. "I'm sleepy." She slouched against him tiredly, and to her relief he wrapped an arm around her shoulders to keep her upright and resumed walking.

"You and me both," he admitted, sounding grateful for the subject change. "It's nine thirty and it feels like two o'clock in the morning."

"Too much sun."

They entered the dingy hotel and waved hello to Sally, who was manning the tiny information booth. In the stairwell they stared in despair at the ascending stairs, unwilling to take another step. "Go on," Jarek urged. "Get up there."

"You go."

"Ladies first."

"I don't want your chivalry."

"Well, you're getting it."

Her lips curved in a tired smile and they reluctantly trekked up to the fifth floor, Jarek cursing the whole way. "We're getting a new room tomorrow."

"On the ground floor?" she asked, entering ahead of him.

"No. In a new hotel. A real hotel. With an actual shower."

"Oh God, a shower. I need one so badly."

He looked ready to say something, then bit the inside of his cheek. "You're lucky I'm still feeling chivalrous. It's all yours."

"I should go first, I only take five minutes. You're the one with a beauty regime and fancy conditioner."

"That was a gift from Katrine, I only use it to be nice."

"And because it makes your hair soft."

"Get in the bathroom, Olivia." He bent down and kissed her temple briefly, then shoved her into the tiny space. She went because she desperately wanted a shower, and also because she didn't want to risk saying anything that might ruin his tentative foray into civil conversation. He was a grown up, but sometimes she swore she had to treat him like one of her students, being encouraging, nurturing, and patient when all she really wanted to do was scream, "Why don't you get this? It's *easy!*"

But then, she knew, if she did that, he would never learn.

He was gone when she woke up. After taking in the empty space where Jarek should have been, Olivia rolled onto her side and squinted at the glowing red display on the alarm clock: 8:02. The room was uncharacteristically dim. The skies outside had opened up and begun pouring down rain, pelting the glass with a rhythmic patter. Olivia watched the shadowy rivulets through the thin curtains and tried to ignore the ache in her chest. She listened carefully for noise from the bathroom but it was quiet, and after a minute she sat up and looked around for his bag or a note or something, anything, to tell her he hadn't left. But there was nothing. His shoes were gone, and she was alone.

She flopped onto her back and opened her eyes as wide as she could, ignoring the stinging in her sinuses and trying to convince herself she didn't want to cry. She didn't need him. She didn't. She was perfectly capable of spending the day by herself—Lord only knew she'd done that a lot lately—and she had a train ticket and a job she loved and coworkers who liked—well, tolerated—her, and she would be fine.

But she was still crying. Hot, salty tears snaked down her cheeks and pooled in her ears until she shook her head. He'd hurt her feelings, that asshole. And she hadn't done anything wrong. In fact, she thought she'd done everything right. He'd almost said the L-word, asked her not to pursue it, and she hadn't. She'd pretended she thought he was sleeping on the bus ride, had hurried through her shower so there was still hot water left for his, and had been passed out in bed before he'd finished so he could continue to avoid talking about his dastardly feelings.

Olivia sat up abruptly, swiped the tears from her cheeks, and stalked into the bathroom to splash cold water on her face before her eyes got puffy. She wouldn't be able to haggle with the market vendors with any kind of authority if she looked like she'd spent the morning bawling her head off. She brushed her teeth and combed her hair until she was somewhat presentable, then counted her money and took a deep breath before putting on her shoes. She could do this. She could be alone in Beijing. She could be alone, period. People did it all the time.

She almost fainted when the door opened and Jarek stepped through, water dripping off his damp curls and trickling through his eyebrow. He looked surprised to see her as he wiped his face. "What are you doing up?"

It was hard to speak. Her chest and her throat were so tight—anger, relief, confusion—every emotion she could name was rising up so swift and painful she didn't know how to respond.

"Liv? You okay?" Jarek frowned and stepped out of his wet shoes, dropping his pack on the ground and approaching to peer at her with concern. "Are you sick?"

She snapped out of it and shoved him away, hard enough that he stumbled back several steps. "Where *were* you?" Her voice came out a little too shrill and desperate, and she bit her tongue to suppress the onslaught of frantic questions trying to burst out.

He cocked his head and reached into his pocket, pulling out a flat white key card. "Getting a new room at that hotel down the street. A real one, with an elevator and a big shower."

"Wha—? Why?"

"I told you this last night."

The previous evening came back to her, and he had indeed said those things. "I thought you were joking," she accused. "We only have one day left."

"I know. That's why I went out first thing to get it. You want to come with me or continue with this shrill harpy act?"

"I beg your pardon?" She didn't feel sad anymore. She felt angry and self-righteous. And offended. And, okay, relieved.

He took in her attire and frowned. "Where were you going?"

"To get breakfast. To see the city."

"In the rain?"

"People do it all the time, Jarek. Shit." She turned her back to him and covered her face, letting her cool fingers soothe her flaming cheeks. Now she just felt like an idiot. He'd been missing for what, ten minutes, and she'd *cried?*

She heard him sigh behind her. "Olivia. I was gone for half an hour. I didn't want to wake you. What do you want me to say?"

She dragged in a breath and willed herself to be mature about this. "How would you feel if you woke up and I was gone? And my bag was gone?"

He put a hand on her shoulder and turned her to face him. "Look, I'm sorry if you were upset, okay? My money, my passport, it's all in my bag, and I didn't want to sort through it and wake you up. Let's just get out of this palace and go to real hotel, okay?"

Olivia blinked and looked away, then nodded. A new hotel sounded nice. An elevator sounded really nice. "Fine."

He groaned. "Stop using 'fine' to describe things."

"Even when they are?" She gathered up her few belongings and added them to her backpack, then double-checked the room before following Jarek into the hall and down the stairs to the lobby to check out.

The streets were slightly less busy thanks to the rain, but it was still a challenge to find an available cab. Finally Olivia suggested they walk and look for a spot to eat breakfast along the way. They found a restaurant whose English signboard boasted the city's best steamed buns and went inside to order from the picture menu.

"What floor is the room on?" Olivia asked some time later. They had each eaten a bun filled with a mysterious red-brown paste that wasn't half bad, and had one left to share. Jarek pulled it apart with chopsticks, making a mess of everything, and she laughed as he gestured between two equally unappealing halves.

"Take your pick."

"Hmm. Choices." She selected one mangled piece and he took the other.

"Eight," he said.

"What?"

"Eighth floor," he clarified. "That's where the room is."

"And the elevators are working?"

"Yeah. I checked. Bathroom's nice, shower's enormous."

Her brows pulled together. "What's with your obsession with the shower?"

Jarek's expression turned pensive as he looked at her over the rim of his teacup. After a moment he answered. "Do you remember karaoke night?"

"Yes." There had only been one, and she hadn't been that drunk in a long time.

"How much?"

"Um…" Olivia winced, guilty. "Maybe half?"

"Do you remember me singing?"

She snorted. "Absolutely not."

"No? 'Unchained Melody' doesn't ring a bell?"

She narrowed her eyes. "I know the song. I don't recall you singing it."

"Well, I did."

"I don't believe you. Why would you do that?"

"Because you promised me something."

Her heart kicked up a notch. Something hazy was floating in the back of her mind, but she couldn't pull it into focus. "I did?"

"Yeah." His face was so serious, so sharp and handsome. She didn't doubt she'd have promised him something to get him to soften up, just for a night.

"What did I promise you?"

He glanced around to make sure no one was listening, then lowered his voice. "Anything."

"What? Anything?"

"Yes. You promised you'd do anything I wanted." He lifted a brow meaningfully.

"That doesn't sound like me."

"Yeah, well, it doesn't sound like you to get back to my place and pass out in a drunken heap, but you did that, too."

Erm. She couldn't argue with him there. She also couldn't deny the tiny thrill of arousal and excitement that pulsed through her at the tone of his voice and the intensity of his gaze. "Jog my memory," she said. Maybe a bit breathlessly. The remaining piece of steamed bun sat forgotten on her plate.

"You asked me to sing, I said hell no, you said you'd do anything, and I sang."

She couldn't help but laugh at his simplicity. "I meant, sing a few lines. See if I remember."

Now he laughed. "Forget it. You haven't paid up for the first time. Yet."

Olivia bit her lip. She was pretty sure she'd do whatever her wanted. He took her out of her comfort zone sometimes, but she always liked it in the end. And while she was turned on — and getting even more turned on the longer the conversation lasted — she was nervous, too. "And this has something to do with the shower?"

His cheeks pinkened slightly. "Yeah." His voice was hoarse. "You don't remember getting back to my place?"

"Not really. Just waking up."

"Well, you needed a shower, desperately, and could barely stand up, so I…helped you."

"Uh-huh." She was growing a bit leery.

"Relax. I didn't take advantage of you, even though I wanted to. Watching you in the shower, buck naked, water and bubbles everywhere, I'd have hooked you up to a homemade IV if I thought it'd sober you up enough to where I wouldn't feel guilty for fucking you."

She couldn't breathe. She could barely swallow the now-lukewarm tea. "You want to watch me take a shower?"

"For starters. What do you say?"

It was nine thirty in the morning and she was seriously aroused. Before coming to China she'd been sick of the stares. Since coming to China she'd gotten used to them and learned to tune them out. But now she wanted this. She wanted to feel his eyes on her and know that he wanted her so badly he was willing to wait for it. Willing to walk through the rain to find a place that had the shower that would fit his fantasies. It was oddly specific and she didn't know all the details, but she was ready to find out.

She stood. "Let's go."

Olivia gasped as her back hit the wall of the elevator with a thud. Jarek swallowed the sound, covering her lips with his, kissing her like he hadn't in days. The past two nights she'd been so tired she'd done nothing more than say good night and fall asleep, but now she was more than awake. She was wired. She tangled her fingers in his wet hair and pulled him impossibly closer, meeting his tongue with hers and grinning when she wrested a growl from him. It was normally so hard to get a reaction from him that it was especially rewarding when she did.

They were breathing hard as they exited onto the eighth floor, and Jarek fairly dragged her down the hall behind him. He whipped out the key card, pushed her inside, and pinned her against the wall, kissing her again, hard and thorough, the way she liked it. They dropped their packs on the ground and kicked off their shoes, and Olivia cracked open an eye to try to get a look at the room. She didn't realize Jarek had noticed until he laughed and pressed his lips to her forehead. "Go look around," he said, smacking her ass. "Make it quick."

She shot him a guilty smile and hurried into the sprawling space, meticulously clean with white walls and linens, offset only by ebony furniture and a single blooming orchid. She didn't think she'd ever been in a room as nice as this one; it must have cost a fortune. The hiss of the shower distracted her and she made her way to the open bathroom door to see Jarek stepping back from an enormous shower stall. It was enclosed in glass with a massive showerhead centered on the ceiling, water pouring down like a localized rain storm.

"What do you think?" he asked, not turning around.

She stood behind him and rose onto her tiptoes to press her chin to his shoulder. "It's beautiful."

He glanced back. "Yeah?"

"Yeah."

"Take off your clothes."

A tiny tremor rippled through her as she met his gaze, then dropped back on her heels to unbutton her jeans. The zipper followed and she stepped out of the wet denim, kicking it into the corner. It was silly but she felt underdressed for a room this nice, her plain clothes not fit for the fine finishes.

Jarek turned to watch her, his erection already tenting the front of his pants. His folded arms added to the already stern countenance, and though she felt shy, Olivia stripped out of her T-shirt, bra and panties and let him back her into the door, kissing her mouth as his hands explored her body. The room was warm and filling with steam, but his fingers elicited goose bumps everywhere he touched. She moaned against his lips and he squeezed her ass as he reluctantly released her.

"Get in the shower." It was a relief to hear the hoarse rasp in his voice; she felt the same way. Strained. Impatient. Achy.

Olivia crossed the room and pulled open the heavy glass door, stepping inside the enclosure and coming to a halt when she couldn't get the door to close. She turned to see Jarek holding it open, one shoulder propped against the frame. "Just like this," he said. "Face me and wash your hair."

She couldn't help but smile. "This is kinky, Jarek. Clean and dirty at the same time."

He failed to hide the tick in his jaw that said he was trying not to laugh. "Make lots of bubbles."

"I thought this fetish was unique to Japanese businessmen." She picked up the tiny bottle of complimentary shampoo, put too much in her palm, and stepped out of the heavy spray to lather up her long hair. She tipped her head and bit back a startled gasp when she felt Jarek's hands on her breasts, pinching her nipples lightly, then harder.

"Keep going." His voice was harsh, and after a second one hand tangled in the tuft of hair at the top of her thighs and tugged.

"Ah ah ah," she hissed, leaping back out of reach. His hands released her and she ducked under the spray of hot water to rinse her hair, feeling the suds make slippery tracks over her chest and stomach. Jarek made a pained sound, and when she opened her eyes, his shirt was gone and he was kicking off his pants and boxers. He stepped inside and closed the door, then kissed her greedily, water filling their mouths until they broke apart, chests heaving.

"You're beautiful, Olivia," he said suddenly, eyes raking over her. She felt the urge to cover herself but fisted her hands at her sides instead. He'd seen it all before, but he'd never studied her so openly, like he was committing her to memory. He picked up the bottle of conditioner, filled his palm, and reached up to adjust the showerhead so the spray was aimed at the far corner. She watched, blood thrumming, as he used his free hand to collect the towel he'd hung over the door and dropped it at his feet. "Your knee okay?" he asked, glancing at her leg. Her knee was fine. It was everything else that was on fire.

"Yes," she answered.

"Good. Kneel."

Olivia took a deep breath and knelt on the thick white towel, her face level with his throbbing erection. They'd done this lots of times, but never quite this way. Not with him giving orders. Never while he wrung out her hair in one hand and massaged in conditioner with the other.

"Suck," he whispered, nudging her lips with his cock, breaking her out of her trance. She wrapped one hand around the base and her lips around the head, doing all the things she knew he liked. She combed her nails over his ass, feeling him tense and hearing his sharp intake of breath. She could feel the tension in his thighs, the control he employed to resist thrusting forward too fast, even though he'd been teaching her to take him deeper than she ever would have guessed she could. Chris had never really pushed her; he liked sex, but he'd been happy with the way things were. So had she. Until Jarek.

She swallowed when he bumped the back of her throat, humming a little at the pleasure of him massaging her scalp with his big, rough hands. She sucked and jerked him harder as she felt him getting ready to come, and didn't panic when he held her head in place and began to pump his hips, fucking her mouth. He came with a long, painful growl, one hand braced on the shower wall, the other caught in her slippery hair as his thrusts slowed and he pulled away.

Olivia whimpered as the ache between her thighs intensified, a clenching urge she had never known to be quite this…desperate. Jarek readjusted the water so she could rinse her hair, helping her to her feet and steadying her when her knees threatened to give way. He picked up the wet towel and leaned against the wall, eyes scouring every inch of her body before lingering between her thighs. Olivia spread her legs a little bit, inviting him to do something about the need throbbing there, but instead he lowered a hand and found his cock, stroking it gently, rousing himself again.

Eventually he shut off the water and toweled her down before leading her out to the bed and lying her across the pristine white covers. The king size bed was firm, the linens soft, and every inch of her skin was on fire. "Jarek, please," she mumbled, watching him crawl over her closed legs, his fingertips tracing her shoulders, her arms, her wrists.

"Shh." He lowered himself, pressing them together from head to toe, and kissed her again, holding her hands over her head, controlling everything. She swore he'd never kissed her this much before, and it was driving her fucking crazy.

She twisted her face away. "Do something."

He chuckled into her neck, biting a little too hard. "I am."

"*Jarek.*"

"Uh-huh?" He trailed his tongue over her collarbone and fastened his lips around her straining nipple.

She squeezed her eyes shut tight. "You're killing me."

If he cared, it didn't show. He continued his painfully slow assault until his tongue had touched her everywhere but where she wanted it most. She'd tried opening her legs several times, but when he let her it was to lick a path up the inside of one thigh and back down the other, never touching the throbbing bundle of nerves at the top of her sex.

She squirmed and complained and he ignored her, pressing into the soles of her feet with his mean, awful fingers, dragging them up her calves, finding muscles she didn't know she had. "Please," she gasped when she was about to combust. "Stop. But don't stop. Please."

Her eyes flew open when he sat beside her, back resting against the padded headboard. He dragged her onto his lap so she straddled his muscled thighs, and she waited, quaking, as he rolled on a condom. She suspected he was suffering as much as she was, but it wasn't confirmed until he held her hips and guided his cock inside her that he cursed furiously and pressed his head back as though in agony.

Olivia wiggled her hips and felt the deliciously slippery stretch as she accepted him, loving the sensation of fullness, of being so close to someone that she could feel his heart beating. She wanted to prolong the moment of closeness but couldn't possibly do so without expiring from unfulfilled arousal, so she ground herself against him and cried out at the unbearable spasms that shook her.

"Fuck me, Olivia." His fingers dug painfully into her sides but she didn't care, rising onto her knees and sinking back down, again and again, thighs burning. She lost her rhythm and stopped moving altogether when he pushed two fingers between her ass cheeks and into her tight opening.

"Jarek," she gasped, avoiding his piercing stare.

He used his other hand to turn her head back, making her look at him as he moved his fingers, slippery with the juices he had gathered from farther below, in deeper. He'd been doing this more and more often, progressing from one finger to two, stretching her until she didn't think she could take anymore. Apart from one failed attempt with Chris, she had never thought about doing this with anyone, but now…maybe. In the distant future. With someone she trusted as much as she trusted him. Someone that wasn't Jarek, because he wouldn't be there.

"Keep moving," he ordered softly, thrusting his fingers for emphasis.

Olivia bit her lip and whimpered as she rocked back and forth, dragging a rough moan from her implacable boyfriend. He kissed her again and this time she didn't mind, wrapping her arms around his neck and her tongue around his, feeling him in every part of her, just like he wanted. Like she wanted.

When neither of them could take it anymore, he gripped her hip and surged into her, again and again, deep and hard. She pressed her forehead to his shoulder and didn't try to stifle her cries, feeling Jarek's coarse whispers against her hair. He opened his hand and reached for her clit with his thumb, rasping over the shrieking bundle of nerves until she exploded. She came harder than she'd ever come, nails digging into his back, teeth buried in his shoulder. He jerked viciously as his orgasm followed, then went still.

"That was something," she mumbled several long moments later, feeling him laugh beneath her, tasting the salt from his skin on her lips.

"That was *anything*," he corrected.

She smiled. "I think I need another shower."

"Don't go yet." He still had his fingers in her ass and he squeezed gently, keeping her in place as he kissed the corner of her swollen mouth. "Don't go anywhere."

Chapter Fourteen

She'd let it go, just as he'd asked. It had been one week since he'd almost—mostly—told Olivia he loved her, and as per his one-word request, she hadn't brought it up again. And try as he might to think about anything but, he couldn't stop wondering just what she would have said if he'd finished the thought and allowed her to respond. Would she have balked, looking appalled and uneasy? Or stiffened, standing frozen like a deer in the headlights? Or, worse yet, might she have said it back—*I love you, Jarek?* He couldn't bear the thought of her uttering the words, knowing he'd doubt every one of them. How could *she* love him? How could she *love* him? How could she love *him?*

He resumed taking out his frustration on the punching bag that hung in the corner of the gym trailer. It thudded against the wall with a soothing, familiar knock that shouldn't have relaxed him, but did. Just because he'd stopped hitting people didn't mean he didn't miss it. And just because he hadn't finished telling Olivia he loved her, didn't mean he didn't. Fuck. He hit the bag harder, feeling his shoulders burn.

"Dude. Would you *stop?*"

It took four more punches before the words filtered in. Jarek turned, sweat dripping from his brow and landing in a shiny puddle at his feet.

Dale lay on the weight bench, hands gripping the bar above him, clearly reluctant to hoist two hundred pounds over his head while the trailer shook.

Jarek wiped his chin. "Twenty more minutes."

"You've been at it for thirty!"

"So? I've got energy."

"You've got rage, idiot. What'd your brother say?"

Jesus Christ. He'd never known gossips like these men. Olivia had e-mailed him some of the pictures from Beijing and he'd forwarded them on to his brother, who had promptly replied with a picture of their father, wasting away in a hospital bed. He hadn't seen the guy in years, and he looked nothing like the man he remembered.

Aidan McLean had been a stocky, imposing figure, now shriveled to a hundred and twenty pounds of skin and bones, with gray, sagging skin and sunken eyes. Tubes ran in and out of his body and machines glowed in the background, their countless lights just blurry halos in the photograph. Jarek hadn't responded to the e-mail—not that there had been an actual message included, just a subject line altered to read "a matter of days," so Jonah had started calling. And calling. Just that morning Jarek had fielded a call that had gone the same as all the others: *He's dying. He doesn't remember much, but he asks about you. Come home. Say good-bye.* The only person Jarek had said good-bye to was his brother, when he'd hung up and turned off his phone. So the asshole had taken to calling Brant, asking him to apply pressure to the black sheep of the small family. And Brant had told Dale. Of fucking course.

"Same as usual," he grunted, snatching up his towel and mopping his forehead. "I'm done here. Go ahead." He dropped the towel on the floor and used it to wipe up the pool of sweat, surprised at the amount. Maybe he'd been working harder than he realized. Or maybe he'd gotten soft.

"You think you're going to go back?"

"No."

"Why not?"

"What difference would it make?"

"I don't know. Seems like you should."

"You didn't go back for your daughter's birthday."

"I sent a gift."

"You think I should send a fruit basket?"

"I think you should be less of an asshole."

"You first," he said, tossing the wet towel at Dale's head. The corner caught his cheek before it fell to the floor, and the other man grimaced.

"You're disgusting."

Jarek snatched up his bag and strode across the site and down the street to his apartment building. It was seven o'clock at night and pleasantly warm, but his skin felt prickly and hot. Agitated, much as he'd been since Jonah had started nagging him in earnest. He entered his dim apartment and climbed in the shower, keeping the water cool and holding his head under the spray, trying to drown out the persistent worry clawing at the back of his skull. What if he ended up that man, alone and withered in a hospital bed? There were certainly plenty of people who would love to see that picture, the man who had tortured them dying his own slow death, richly deserved. But what he really couldn't shake was the look in his father's eyes as he'd stared at the camera. The thin, unfamiliar face and unhealthy pallor belied the awareness that shone from the same blue eyes he faced in the mirror every day. In the split second the photo had been taken, Aidan McLean knew. He knew regret and shame and loss, the same feelings Jarek stubbornly refused to acknowledge or forgive.

He allowed himself the quick fantasy of taking the coward's way out, telling his brother that not only was he not going home to say good-bye, he wasn't coming home in July, period. If Olivia extended her contract, he could stay here with her until December, and pretend this was his real life. He'd said his good-bye to Aidan a long time ago, but he couldn't envision saying good-bye to her. Not yet.

He had keys to her apartment now. Olivia was the only woman to ever give him keys. *The only ones he'd ever even considered accepting*, he thought as he let himself in. She'd pretty much forced them on him, saying she didn't want to wait for him in the mornings when she had to go to work, and if he was that uncomfortable with the idea he could toss them back through the metal door once he'd locked it. Then she'd given him that look that said she thought he was a colossal idiot and an immature man child and he'd better not actually do it. So he'd put the keys in his pocket and now he shut the doors behind him and tilted his head to see her sitting in bed, watching something on her laptop.

"That better not be *Parenthood*," he warned, stepping out of his shoes.

The sound cut off. "It's definitely not."

"Olivia. We're only supposed to watch on Wednesdays."

"Yeah. Well. I didn't know you were coming over." They'd gone for their normal Monday run earlier, then he'd bailed on their dinner plans to go to the site and smack around the punching bag. It was a much less formidable opponent than his girlfriend.

Jarek got a carton of chocolate milk from the fridge and climbed onto the bed beside her. The last rays of sunlight filtered through the closed curtains on the window, and an ancient ceiling fan spun in the center of the room. It was nice in here. Calm. Safe.

"How many episodes have you watched?"

"Just the beginning of this one. I was making sure it was good quality."

"Uh-huh." It was hard to believe, but sometimes the counterfeit DVDs they bought were not perfect.

She peeked up at him. "So…"

"Well, start over if you already watched it."

"Just five minutes."

He reached over and hit the back arrow, then play. "If you say so." Jarek put an arm around her shoulders and pulled her close. He fiddled with her hair elastic so the sloppy bun came loose and her hair spilled down, brushing over his fevered skin. He leaned back to watch the show, unable to believe how ridiculously invested he was in the tangled lives of the Braverman family. Growing up they'd only had one television and Aidan was normally stationed in front of it, angry at the news or the basketball game or whatever happened to be on. They'd stayed out of his way, and as a result never got into the habit of sitting down to stare at the thing. But now here he was, watching TV like a normal person, with a girl next to him who thought he was okay, too.

The show ended and he yawned, stretching as he got up to throw away the empty milk carton. When he returned to the bedroom

Olivia was sitting on the edge of the bed looking nervous. He stopped at the door. "What's wrong?"

"I heard from Willa today."

"That's your teacher friend, right? The one in Boston?"

"Outside of Boston, yeah."

"She all right?"

"She's pregnant."

His heartbeat ground to a halt. They'd been careful, except for that one morning when he'd slipped up and been inside her for seconds — *seconds* — without a condom. How long ago had that been now? She couldn't be —

Olivia rolled her eyes. "I'm not trying to tell you I'm pregnant, Jarek."

He tried to swallow, his mouth suddenly painfully dry. "I didn't think you were."

She made a face that said she didn't believe him. "Anyway," she said with emphasis.

"Anyway…" He took a few tentative steps forward. Some distant part of him told him to man up and stop wondering about Willa, the friend whose intimate life details Olivia had shared some time ago, the one who'd lost a baby and was indirectly responsible for sending Olivia to China. He'd never met Willa, but he liked her.

"She's going to take maternity leave early, as a precaution, and the school still wants to hire me, if I'm available. Starting with summer school in July."

His damn heart stopped again. Somehow this news was worse than the possibility that she was having his baby. At least then they'd be together. "Are you? Available?"

She shrugged, looking up at him. "I haven't signed the new contract yet."

He sat down beside her. "When did you hear this?"

"I went to check my e-mail after our run. I was just watching *Parenthood* to try to distract myself from thinking about it."

"Don't make excuses. You were watching *Parenthood* because you're dishonest."

She smiled and relaxed a little. Jarek tried to do the same, but couldn't. It wasn't too long ago that she'd asked him about the work he did in Virginia and he told her he worked off and on for Brant, then kicked around aimlessly between jobs. He'd made Katrine a rocking chair when she was pregnant and she'd gushed about it to every woman she knew—which was approximately a million—and he'd taken random gigs making furniture for people when he felt like it. He wasn't rich but he had plenty of money saved; he could have easily stayed in China until the end of the year, job or no job. But he wouldn't stay without Olivia. Of course he hadn't told her any of this when she'd brought up the possibility of extending her contract. As far as she knew he was only staying two weeks past her original end date, and she'd be on her own for the rest of the year. Why the hell hadn't he said something?

He fingered the ends of her hair. "You going to take it?"

"I don't know."

"But you want to."

"It's a good opportunity."

"It sounds like it."

"And if I stayed here, it would only mean two extra weeks, right? Before you went back?"

He studied his scraped knuckles. "Yeah." Yeah. Right. It wasn't like he'd been contemplating moving his whole life here for her or anything.

"Is Jonah still calling about your dad?"

"Talking to anyone who'll listen."

"Do you—"

"Enough talk, okay?" Jarek resorted to doing what he did best with Olivia, since getting the answers he wanted never seemed to work with her. He placed her laptop on the floor and yanked his shirt over his head.

"Alan, come sit up here, please."

The classroom chatter ceased as everyone turned to look at Alan, sitting stick straight in his seat near the back. He looked at Olivia, confused and alarmed, and she smiled to calm him. "You're not in trouble," she said. "Just come sit at my desk. I need you to help me with something."

"Help" was a word the kids knew, and at once they were all eager to assist. Tiny hands shot into the air and a chorus of "I want to helps" filled the air. "Thank you, thank you for offering," Olivia interrupted over the din. "But I only need one person to help me right now, and that person is Alan. Take your bag, too."

Alan cautiously shuffled up to the front and climbed into Olivia's vacated seat. She tried not to smile as she waited. He was a conflicted kid, that one. At once loathe to be the center of attention, yet craving it intensely. She'd figured out that part of his disdain for her had come from the fact that he found the material too easy, but the contempt had been tempered by her continued enthusiasm and encouragement of his dance routines. In order to feel like a good teacher and not just a cheerleader, she'd started giving him smaller, more challenging assignments to keep him busy while she reviewed material he already knew too well.

Olivia handed Alan a stack of mixed up alphabet flashcards and asked him to help put them in order from A to Z. She tried to look embarrassed as she lied and said she'd dropped them, though the truth was she'd shuffled them up before class started just so she'd have something to keep him busy.

"I WANT TO HELP!" Rose trilled.

Olivia silenced her with a raised eyebrow. "I beg your pardon?"

Rose pouted and slumped in her chair. She was still thrilled to be in charge of the CD player, but she required a lot of attention sometimes, though perhaps not the kind Olivia cheerfully bestowed on her. "Stand up, please, Rose."

Rose's eyes widened. "No."

"Now."

Rose clapped a hand to her brow and stood up dramatically. The class was familiar with Olivia's hideous brand of torture, and Rose in particular had an abundance of experience with it. Though they had come a long way in their English education, no one appreciated being forced to stand up in front of the class and answer five English questions.

"How old are you?" Olivia inquired.

Rose sighed, pained. "I'm five years old."

"What's your favorite color?"

"Red."

"Full sentences."

Rose blew out a noisy breath, lips flapping. "My favorite color is red."

"Tell me something that is yellow."

"Bananas is yellow."

Close enough. "What animal eats bananas?"

"The monkey eats bananas."

"Hmm. Very good."

Rose tried to sit down.

"Stand up, Rose. That was only four."

Rose rolled her eyes and remained standing.

Olivia scratched her chin like she was trying to think of a really good question. The children giggled in anticipation; the final question was always the same. "Tell me, Rose…" she began slowly, "do you like me?"

Rose tried not to smile, hands clenched into tiny fists at her side. "Yes," she said through gritted teeth. "I like Olivia."

"I'm sorry, what? I couldn't hear you." This was their odd little routine.

Rose made a frustrated sound. "I like Olivia," she said, louder.

"Did anyone hear that?"

"YES!"

"You did? What did Rose say?"

"I LIKE OLIVIA!" they cried.

Olivia gaped at Rose in mock surprise. "You do? Oh, thank you, Rose. I like you too. You can sit down now."

Rose covered her face as she sat down, trying not to look delighted.

"And thank you, everybody," Olivia added. "I like you all."

"THANK YOU!"

Right on cue the lunch bell rang, and she ushered the kids out the door, admonishing them not to tackle one another in their eagerness to get to the cafeteria. She would miss them, she thought sadly. She'd had this thought for every class she'd taught over the years—though not every student—and knew it would pass, but this morning she'd informed the school that she would not be extending her contract and things felt final and official. It would all be over in just five weeks, one of which she wouldn't even be present for, with her seven-day trip to Thailand looming on the horizon.

Olivia tidied up the room, ate a cup of noodles at her desk, then hurried down the road to the closest Internet café, a dingy, cramped affair that was full at all hours of the day. She waited for a computer, paid for sixty minutes, and sat down, ignoring the stares of the largely male group. She'd booked her flight months ago, a non-refundable ticket to Bangkok that she'd hoped would make it impossible for her to chicken out of the trip. But even as she scrolled through the colorful tourism pages that promised pristine beaches, relaxing massages and pure bliss, she was anxious.

Technically she had come to China alone, but those first months had been awful, and it didn't really count, since she hadn't been remotely brave. She'd been pathetically lonely, actually, and it was only after meeting Jarek that she'd started to explore Lazhou. Then she'd gone to Shanghai with Marcus, and Beijing with Jarek, and though she knew it was time to strike out on her own, if only to know that she could, she wished he were coming with her. It was hard to picture Jarek lying on a beach, book in one hand, tropical drink in the other, but the image made her smile.

Olivia shook her head and focused on her task. Brant had been to Thailand several times and had given her the name of a hostel he liked in Bangkok, where she'd spend the first two days, then the name of a resort on one of the southern islands where she would spend the bulk of her trip. Her hand hovered over the mouse, fingers reluctant to click on the "confirm" button that would book her a room at each place, but she did it. Then, because they'd made her promise, she e-mailed her parents the accommodation information to reassure both them and herself that she wouldn't be sleeping in the street.

The day of Olivia's departure came much too quickly. It felt like she had returned from Beijing only to repack her bag and head out again. Her flight left at midafternoon, so she slept in as best as her nerves would let her, then added the final items to her pack and went to flag down a cab before she could talk herself out of it. Jarek had been roped into another supply run to Yangzhou so he couldn't come to the airport with her, not that she'd expect it given his contempt of everyone who dared take public transportation. Besides, she didn't need his help. She was going on vacation in a tropical paradise. She should be elated, not terrified.

Eight hours later, Olivia touched down in Bangkok. It was surprisingly easy to navigate her way through customs and out to a bus that took her into town. Her hostel was located on Khao San Road, a popular street for backpackers and travelers, and it was ten o'clock at night when she arrived in her tiny room, furnished much the same as her apartment with a twin bed, ceiling fan, and single nightstand.

Olivia sat on the bed with a thunk. The room was hot and night sounds drifted in through her open third-floor window. She was once again in a country where she knew no one and nothing, but it didn't feel nearly as overwhelming as her arrival in China. There had been at least a dozen tourists downstairs with accents ranging from American to British to Australian, and so many more crowding the street. She would have only one full day in Bangkok before catching a twelve-hour bus south, so she tried to think positive thoughts as she gathered her converted money and went back downstairs to explore the crowded street market.

It was hot and sticky outside, but she barely noticed. The sights and sounds of the market were a distraction, and it had been so long since she hadn't been the focus of stares and whispers that Olivia began to feel a weight lift from her shoulders. The vendors spoke English and she overpaid for a knee-length skirt woven through with silver thread, and bought a smoothie made with fruit she'd never seen before. There was tons of street food, including fried cockroaches and starfish, which she declined, but she did summon her courage and eat a scorpion, which wasn't as disgusting as she'd imagined, not that she'd ever feel the urge to eat another one.

The next day she toured the city, riding in a *tuk tuk*, visiting several enormous Thai Buddha statues and the stunning Grand Palace. She e-mailed photos to Jarek and her parents, telling them she'd arrived safely and was having a great time, which was true. The fact that she missed Jarek gnawed at her. She'd be twenty-eight in four days; it was past time she learned how to be alone.

The twelve-hour bus ride the next morning was long but uneventful, and the ferry to Koh Phangan was packed with fellow travelers. Olivia sat inside and tried to watch an old Tom Cruise movie, but soon gave in and weaved her way onto the deck to join the throngs pressed against the railing, watching the clear waters part beneath them as they approached the island.

She caught a taxi to the small beachfront resort, a series of cozy huts arranged on the sand facing the ocean. It was paradise, and she had four full days here. Just palm trees, sunshine, and warm ocean waters extending for miles. Her muscles were stiff and sore from the day of travel, so she dropped her pack on the queen size bed — a novelty — changed into a bikini, wrapped a towel around her hips, and stepped outside onto the warm white sand.

Her doubts about the trip faded the second she lay in the shade of a towering palm tree. Her parents had always said they needed to take two-week vacations: one week to get used to being on vacation, the second to actually be on vacation. But they had never been to Koh Phangan.

She let her mind drift like the faint white slivers of clouds in the sky, the random thoughts somehow always coalescing into something that reminded her of Jarek. When she heard her name, she thought she'd imagined it. The small stretch of beach was sparsely populated, and the closest people were at least twenty yards away. Then it came again.

"Olivia."

She sat up and looked around, but she was alone.

Then: "Olivia."

She wasn't crazy. He was behind her. She couldn't stop the smile from spreading across her face as she turned, ridiculously hopeful. And then she froze, because the man approaching wasn't at all the one she wanted to see.

Jarek couldn't seem to unclench his fists. Or his teeth. He felt like an angry, impotent superhero stuck in his regular body, straining to transform into his furious alter ego and failing over and over again. He'd been pacing the length of his apartment for the better part of an hour, waiting for Olivia to turn up. She said she'd come over at five, and it was closer to six. She was never late. But today she was. And, as far as he knew, she'd never lied to him. Until now.

He took a deep breath and forced himself to let it out, feeling half an ounce of tension leave his body before returning tenfold. He couldn't remember the last time he'd been this angry. This worked up. Or maybe he could. Maybe all he had to do was think back to last Friday, when he'd gone to the Internet café on his lunch break to e-mail her for her birthday. He hadn't heard from her since her first day in Bangkok, which should have been his first clue. Still, he'd sent her a fucking *e-card* and said he hoped she was enjoying her trip. And then he'd stared at the screen for twenty minutes, constantly refreshing before accepting that she wasn't going to magically write back on command.

The next day he'd returned to the café and logged into his account, ignoring five unread messages from Jonah to click on the only one he wanted to see. Her message was short and sweet, the predictable comments about how beautiful Thailand was, how warm and relaxing, how delicious the food. She'd attached seven photos and he'd given them a cursory glance and prepared to log out when something caught his eye. A reflection in a shop window, a bright blue smear. It wasn't a big deal, just the T-shirt of the person Olivia had asked to take a photo for her. But something had gone off in the back of his mind, some little warning signal he'd learned not to ignore. It had been years since he'd let this part of himself take over, but it had come back to him in a heartbeat. He'd enlarged the other pictures and scanned them carefully, finding the blue T-shirt reflected in two more shots, once in her sunglasses, the next in a water glass in a photo taken from across the table at a beachside restaurant.

It wasn't farfetched to think that Olivia might make friends on her trip, go sightseeing with them, stop for dinner. But he knew better than that. The reflection in the shop window was a tall man with pale legs, so probably not a local. The image reflected in her sunglasses was much clearer, highlighting the tilt of the guy's head as he'd peered down at the camera's display before photographing a bikini-clad Olivia drinking from a cracked coconut and making a silly face.

He'd sat back in his chair in the smoky café, feeling like his chest was collapsing in on itself, each rib puncturing an organ so everything inside him seeped together in a toxic, fatal mess. She hadn't made a new friend in Thailand. She'd gone with Chris. He'd never been so sure of anything in his life, and someone who made a living torturing the truth out of people was always sure.

So now here he was, pacing, cracking his knuckles the way his father had while he'd waited for his wife to come home from another night out with her "friends." And he was just as pathetic as Aidan, because he knew he wouldn't leave her. Wouldn't ignore her knock, whenever it came, wouldn't refuse to let her in. He'd pull open the door and step back so she could come inside and trample over his heart some more. But unlike his father, he wouldn't act like he didn't know what she'd been doing. He'd get answers, and let them sink in and hurt and fester so he learned his fucking lesson. And then, in case that wasn't enough, he had a backup plan. He may not be able to leave her, but he knew just how to make her leave him.

The tentative knock came at quarter to seven. Jarek had been nursing the same glass of scotch for forty-five minutes, and it hadn't done a damn thing to take the edge off. He strode to the door and pulled it open, and for a second they just stared at each other. He studied every inch of the most beautiful face he'd ever seen, waiting for the guilt to cloud her eyes, for her to confess. And then she smiled.

"Sorry I'm late," Olivia said. "I slept way longer than I expected."

He forced himself to swallow, keeping his voice neutral. "No problem. Come in."

"Thanks." She slipped past him with a small plastic bag in her hand and stopped at the kitchen counter where he'd rested his glass. "Are you celebrating something?" she asked, nodding at the scotch.

Ha. "No."

She looked him over as he approached, and then stood on her toes to kiss him. He struggled to not kiss her back, not to wrap his arms around her like he wanted, tried not to let her know this was the last time. It took everything he had, but he stood there stiffly until she dropped back onto her heels. Olivia frowned slightly, then shook it off and reached into the bag. "I got you something."

He looked at the item she held in her hand: a tiny box with a clear lid, segmented into nine squares, each holding a brightly colored candle in the shape of an exotic flower. "Candles?"

"For your bathroom. Since you like spa experiences so much."

"I don't know where you get your ideas."

"And this." When he didn't take the candles she set them on the counter and pulled out a carved wooden elephant. "This is sacred." The words were deadpan, and he knew she meant for him to smile, but he didn't. He couldn't.

"Thanks." He didn't accept the elephant, either, so she placed it next to the candles. He watched her other hand where it still gripped the bag, trembling slightly. She was nervous. As she should be.

"I brought some pictures, if you want to see them."

"Of course." He shifted his weight and she moved back, startled, then forced a smile and pulled out a small paper envelope of printed photos. He noticed then that she hadn't brought her camera; she'd probably removed all the pictures of Chris from the pile, bringing him the censored version of her trip. God, he fucking hated her right now. He tried to keep it from showing in his eyes, downing the last of his scotch in one burning swallow.

"Um…Do you want to sit down?"

"No. Here's fine." He took the photos, flipping through them casually. Busy streets, towering Buddhas, the Golden Palace, colorful fruits and flowers, fried insects for sale. Palm trees, beaches, the occasional shot of Olivia posing next to some random object, several glowing sunsets. At one point she tried to comment on the pictures, but he silenced her with a grunt and she subsided. If he hadn't already made up his mind, that would have sealed it. Olivia never tolerated his mood swings; she was only doing so because she felt bad. Which she should. Which she would.

"These are nice," he said, setting the pictures on the counter. "Where are the rest?"

She ran her thumb over the edge of the envelope, watching the paper flex. "Those were the best ones. That's all I brought."

It hadn't escaped his notice that of the three reflection photos, she'd only printed one, the one with the shop window. The one that wouldn't have meant anything without the other two to show the continued presence of the guy in the blue shirt. Of Chris.

"Yeah?" He looked down at her, waiting until she met his stare.

"Yeah."

"How was your trip?"

Her smile was strained. Her eyes creased at the corners, but they were a cloudy blue, desperate and sad. He didn't even want to think about what his own eyes looked like right now. "It was great," she said. "It was beautiful."

"Easy to get around?"

She rolled her eyes. "So easy. Way better than it is here. Everyone I met spoke English, signs were in English. And it was so cheap. I ate a scorpion."

He lifted a brow. "No kidding. And?"

"Not good, but not terrible."

"Anything else?"

"No, just the scorpion."

"I mean, is there anything else you want to tell me?" Maybe he could forgive her. Maybe he could let it go, wouldn't watch her walk out the door and begin the inevitable process of hating him. Maybe if she told him the truth right this instant, it wouldn't be so bad.

But she didn't. "No," she said.

His palm had been pressed flat against the cool surface of the counter, but now it closed into a fist, so tight his short nails cut into his skin. "No?"

She sucked in a breath and shook her head. This time her look was pleading. *Please don't ask me. Please don't ask me.*

"How's Chris?" he asked.

Olivia made a small sound, something like a sob she tried and failed to keep inside. Her lower lip trembled, and for the first time since he'd seen her, he didn't want to kiss her. He wanted to hurt her like he hurt.

"How did you know?"

His breath came out in a whoosh, as though she'd sucker punched him. He hadn't realized until just then that he'd been holding out hope he'd been wrong. That she'd stare at him guilelessly and ask what he was talking about. He never considered her answering his question with one of her own.

"Just tell me," he said.

"I didn't know he was going to be there."

"Bullshit."

She glared at him, though she had no right to. "I didn't," she insisted. "He showed up. My parents told him where I was staying, and he was waiting for me when I got there."

"Uh-huh."

"I didn't know," she repeated, a satisfyingly desperate note creeping into her voice.

"Were you going to tell me?"

For a second it looked like she might cry, then she pulled it together. "No."

Both his eyebrows raised. "No?"

"No. I wanted to avoid this."

"What? Breaking up?"

She straightened. "We're not breaking up."

He coughed out a laugh. "I don't think you get a say."

"Nothing happened, Jarek. There was nothing to tell you."

"So if I went on vacation with some other woman, you wouldn't want to know?"

Her nostrils flared. "I didn't go on vacation with him. He *showed up*."

"Right. Did you fuck him?"

Now her fists clenched as she tried to stay calm. "No."

"Share a room?"

"No."

"But you hung out together."

A pause. "Yes. He wanted to…make amends."

"Yeah? How?"

She scowled. "How you think, Jarek. But I said no. And he accepted that."

"Really? You said no? When two weeks ago you said you didn't know what you'd do when the two of you got together again?"

"That's right. Two weeks ago when you said you loved me and told me not to tell you that I lov—"

He covered her mouth with his hand and shoved her back into the refrigerator, hard enough that her head bounced. She winced, but he didn't let go. "Don't you fucking say it!" he roared.

She pushed at his chest but he didn't move, even when the tears that had been threatening to spill over finally made good on their promise, painting two shiny tracks down her cheeks. She clawed his hand away, chest rising and falling, hurt and angry. "You're a coward, Jarek. You only want the answers you feel like hearing. You don't want to hear that someone cares about you. You don't want to hear about my trip. How Chris showed up and I turned him down and then we hung out together because I've known him my entire life and he was the only person I knew in the whole country. What was I going to do, avoid him? He had the room next to mine."

"Shut up."

"Does that mean nothing to you? That I could have gone back to having everything the way it used to be, but I didn't?"

He gripped her chin and forced her to meet his gaze. "All I know is that you fucking lied to me, Olivia."

She wrenched her face from his grasp and gathered up the photos, her spine straight. "I'm leaving now. Find me when you grow up."

He didn't say a word as she walked out, though he knew she was expecting him to. He did follow her, however, taking the stairs to the ground level, emerging in the lobby in time to see her round the corner to the street where she'd soon pass the construction site. Where she'd learn what he had done.

Jarek kept a safe distance, halting when he saw Dale call to her from just inside the fence, beckoning her to the lounge trailer. She hesitated because she hated Dale, but she'd just fought with one of the few friends she had, so off she went, like a lamb to the slaughter. He waited until she climbed into the trailer, then jogged over to stand out of sight next to the open door. He heard Dale offer her a beer and inquire after her trip. The tear stains on her face had to be obvious, but his loyal companion didn't waver. He knew exactly what he was supposed to do, and thanks to Olivia's late arrival, he probably had three extra beers in his system to further fuel his mission.

There was a pause, then the shuffling of paper as Dale obediently looked over her photographs. "This one's nice," he said.

Jarek gritted his teeth and rested his head against the trailer. There had been men who'd wanted to do his old job, wanted to have the stomach for it, but just didn't. They'd waited outside the cramped rooms until he emerged with answers, laying witness to the devastation he'd left behind. He felt like those men now. He wanted to look but he didn't. He didn't have the stomach for it anymore, but he didn't move a muscle to stop it, either.

"Yeah," Olivia said reluctantly.

"This one, too."

"Okay. Thanks."

"You have nice tits, Olivia."

"Okay, Dale. Give me my pictures back, I'm going to leave."

There was the rustle of the plastic bag, then a muttered curse as Dale held onto the picture. "Let me keep this one," he said.

"No."

"Come on. At least I'll have something in front of me when I jerk off. Jarek's stories about you are hot and all, but I like a visual aid, you know?"

He could picture her freezing, all the color draining from her pretty face. And then she took the bait.

"What did you say?"

He imagined Dale shrugging, face ruddy from alcohol and indignation on behalf of his betrayed friend. The friend using him to break her heart the way he didn't have the balls to do himself.

"Relax," Dale said dismissively. "I knew you'd be up for anything. And I knew you two screwed in the carpentry trailer. I fucking knew it."

"You don't know anything." Her voice was like ice.

"No? I don't know how he watched that sappy movie so you'd let him finger you that first night? Why wouldn't you let me touch you, Olivia? I don't care if you banged your friend in Thailand. I'm not fussy."

"You're disgusting. Keep the photos." The words were cold, but her voice broke halfway through.

"Come on, just tell me what it was like swallowing his cock in the shower in Beijing."

"Fuck you, Dale."

"And how many fingers you let him shove up your ass."

Her breath caught on a sob and there was a thud as she threw the photos down and stormed from the trailer. She noticed Jarek at the last second, looking at him through watery blue eyes, her face composed apart from the tears.

"Olivia." He didn't know what the fuck else to say.

She strode through the site, out to the street, putting on sunglasses to hide her eyes. He followed her and she let him, didn't push him away when he walked right beside her, tugged her arm to move her out of the way of a careening bicycle. She didn't even fight when he wiped the tears dripping off her chin with the hem of his T-shirt, and that's when he knew it was worse than he thought.

The woman he knew made him work for every inch. Forced him to sit through a thousand awful movies, open himself up, spend fourteen hours on a train. That was the woman he'd *worked* for. The woman *letting* him made him nervous. This woman was someone else entirely, and he had no idea what she would do.

She let him into the building, and he followed her up four flights of stairs. She let him come into her apartment, then kiss her, then take off all her clothes and lay her on the bed while he stripped, too. He didn't know what she was doing, didn't even know what he was doing, just that he couldn't seem to stop. She barely moved beneath him, returning his kiss with a detached passion, parting her legs at his urging, but not wrapping them around his hips. He stroked her all over, fondling the breasts he'd told Dale about in great detail three nights ago when they'd gone out and gotten drunk because he didn't know what to do with himself. The night he'd told Dale everything, the one thing he'd promised Olivia he'd never do.

He teased her nipples until they were tight and her heart drummed against her ribs so hard he could feel it. All the while he buried a hand between her legs, pushing two and then three fingers inside, manipulating her the way he'd finally — finally — learned she liked, feeling her grow wetter and wetter. He rolled on a condom and fucked her, kissing her neck and the spot beneath her ear that usually made her moan, but today she bit her lip and stayed silent.

He moved gently inside her, then harder, and still nothing. He pulled out and slid down her body, pressing her legs open and covering the swollen pink flesh with his mouth, licking up everything and pushing his tongue inside. She failed to hide a moan behind her hand, so he kept going, inserting two fingers into her pussy, stroking the rough spot on her inner wall, feeling her clamp down unwillingly. He knew her now, and she knew him, like it or not. He would make her come no matter how long it took and she knew this too, which was maybe why she let it happen. He sucked her clit against his teeth and she came, bearing down on him, though the hands that usually fisted painfully tight in his hair were resting on the pillow beside her head. The foot that was normally pressed between his shoulder blades was planted firmly on the mattress. He was touching her, but she was not touching him.

Well, fuck that. When the contractions eased he rose over her and slammed his cock inside, too deep and too hard, making her wince. But she didn't cry out. She turned her head to the side and stared at the wall as he fucked her until he came, and she never made a sound.

He remembered her telling him once about the awful words they'd spray painted on her car, how she'd paid twice to have it repainted. And how she'd decided to leave it after the third time, because she couldn't keep affording to make the same mistakes. She'd never fought back, because Olivia didn't fight fire with fire. She doused it with icy water, then stood, staring pensively at the smoldering ashes as though trying to decide if she should sweep them up or let them blow away in the wind.

Jarek didn't know what he wanted her to do. He knew only that she had bested him at his own game, and she hadn't even been playing.

"Get out," she said.

"Okay, guys, are you ready?"

"READY!" the class whisper-screamed, the lowest volume setting they knew.

"You're going to be great. We've been practicing for a long time, and I know you can do this."

Their collective attention was promptly seized by Alan shuffling out from the tiny changing area. Instead of the expected Spiderman suit he now wore red tights, a red T-shirt, and a red cape. And red socks with a web pattern, the only sign of his former role. The little girl who had originally been cast as Red was sick with the flu, and they'd had only one hour's notice to replace her. Because Alan both secretly loved performing and had choreographed most of the dancing, he was the best choice for her replacement.

"Shh," Olivia warned the kids before they could laugh, pressing a finger to her lips. Then, "Thank you for your help, Alan."

"You're welcome," he responded automatically. She squeezed his hand and instead of folding his arms and rejecting her, he actually squeezed back. Her eyes stung and she blinked rapidly, telling herself not to be ridiculous. There were five days left in the school year; seven days until she left China for good. That's why she was emotional.

It had been fifteen days since the breakup. She hadn't seen or heard from Jarek. She hadn't visited the site or tried to call. And she wouldn't. They were over. After Dale's taunts she'd wanted nothing so much as to return to Jarek's apartment, find the biggest knife he had, and stab him through the heart. Instead she'd stormed out of the trailer and found him listening—*listening!*—right outside, like the coward he was. And then she'd gone numb. All the heat that had suffused her at Dale's words, the betrayal that burned in her blood, it had frozen solid. She couldn't feel a thing. So she let him follow her home and kiss her and fuck her, and afterward as he lay on top of her, their hearts pounding in sync, she reached the conclusion that had been too long in coming: if this was all he had to offer, she would rather be alone.

Part of her was furious with her parents for having a hand in Chris's "surprise," but deep down she knew they were just trying to make up for the past year. They thought she had no friends, so they sent her one. They sent her the best man they knew.

The moment she turned and saw Chris, her heart had stopped. For so long his had been the only face she'd wanted to see, the smile that warmed her, the anchor that kept her tethered to everything she knew and loved. But he wasn't that man anymore, and even though he apologized and took responsibility for everything that had happened, it didn't make a difference. Some small piece of her had always wondered if they could ever try again. They'd been so perfect once, surely one rough year over the span of a lifetime wasn't such a bad record? Then he'd taken her hand and asked for a second chance, and she'd said no. And she'd meant it.

He'd accepted the rejection with the same grace he applied to everything else, and then because he'd booked the hut next to hers for the rest of the week, they spent the trip together. What was she supposed to do, hide every time he came looking for her? She had already fled to the other side of the world, she wouldn't keep running.

So they'd toured the island, watched movies in the outdoor dining room, gone snorkeling and hiking and lain on the beach, and celebrated her birthday with banana pancakes and coconut ice cream. When the week was over they'd taken the twelve-hour bus back to Bangkok and said good-bye at the airport. She'd spent the entire flight back to Shanghai debating what, if anything, to tell Jarek, and in the end she decided to say nothing. His overreaction to her day trip with Marcus supported her choice, and Chris's surprise had nothing to do with him, anyway. Nothing had happened, and she didn't want to fight with him when they had so little time left together. Plus, if he didn't ask, it wasn't really lying, was it? And how could he know?

"O-liv-ya?"

She glanced down at Davy, dressed in his butterfly costume, glitter smeared across his smooth cheeks. "Yes, buddy?"

"I want to go to the bathroom."

"I want to go to the bathroom!" someone else piped up.

"I want to go—"

"Okay, okay!" she hissed. "The bathroom is down the hall. Two people can go at the same time. Davy, you are first. Sam, you can go, too." It was always this way; when one had to go, they all had to go, even when they didn't.

She checked her watch and blew out a nervous breath. It was eleven-oh-five; according to the program, they were scheduled to go on at ten after. They'd been seated in their assigned row until seven minutes ago when they'd filed backstage to make their final preparations. So far the other class performances had been a mixture of Chinese and English, songs and dances and things she hadn't understood but the parents had been delighted by. And there were a lot of people in the audience; over two hundred, she'd estimated.

"Olivia, you have three minutes!" Honor announced, hurrying in from the stage with her class. Her kids were beaming, thrilled at having had their moment in the spotlight, and Olivia warned her class to behave then ran onto the stage while the curtain was drawn to drag props into place.

She yanked the trees into position, rolled out the carefully painted roll of paper that denoted a winding river, and the garishly colored cardboard front of grandma's house. Before she'd left for Thailand, she still hadn't finished the final act of the play, the scene where Little Red Riding Hood (and several Spidermans and butterflies and other forest creatures) arrived at the cabin and found the not scary wolf who had not eaten grandma. It wasn't until she thought about Jarek in the aftermath of their breakup that she knew how it should end.

On the opposite side of the curtain she heard Zhang Laoshi introducing the performance, and scurried back to collect the kids and order them into position. Then the heavy curtains drew back and Rose pressed play and the show started.

Olivia stood at the edge of the stage, very nearly out of sight, to troubleshoot. But the kids knew their roles, and soon Alan — Red — was talking to "her" mother (and father, and brother, and sister, and pet monkey) about visiting grandma with a variety of gifts.

"Does the grandmother like cake?" the mother asked.

"Yes, the grandmother likes cake!" Red answered.

"Does the grandmother like shampoo?"

"Yes, the grandmother likes shampoo!"

And so it went until Red and her brother, sister, and pet monkey were ready to leave on their trip, trailed by live action cake, shampoo, two flowers, a carton of milk, and an ice cream cone. They skipped through the wooden forest while singing a song about trees and meeting three butterflies, three birds, and three Spidermans, who came in handy when it came time to cross the river that naturally did not have a bridge.

Olivia covered her mouth and smiled as the Spidermans spun a "web" across the water for the group to traverse. The audience tittered and applauded as appropriate, and the entire senseless thing suddenly made perfect sense. When they first encountered the Big Bad Wolf, Olivia risked a look at Zhang Laoshi in the front row; her perpetual smile wavered as she took in the angry snout and pointy ears and clawed hands worn by one of the boys in the class.

"Hello," the wolf said. "I am Wolf. Nice to meet you."

"Hello, I am Red," said Red. "Nice to meet you too."

They shook hands and Red introduced her gaggle of friends, and said she was en route to meet grandma at her orange house with a yellow door, the only paint colors they'd had enough of when it had come time to paint the cardboard. The wolf distracted Red and her friends, then darted into the forest, knocking over two trees and making five kids cry. Olivia hustled out to calm them and straighten the trees as the parents laughed.

"Very good!" she assured them. "Keep going! You're almost at grandma's house!"

The kids wove back and forth across the stage on an imaginary winding pathway through the forest, until they arrived at the house.

"Who is it?" called the wolf from behind the door.

"I am Red!" Alan cried. "May I come in?"

"Come in, please!"

The wolf pushed open the door and the whole crew fought to get inside, then Olivia rushed out to take the cardboard away and reveal the "interior" of the house, which consisted of two small chairs positioned facing each other, and a table. The wolf sat on one chair with his feet on the other, a blanket covering his lap. He now wore a sleeping cap to pretend to be grandma.

"Who are you?" Red demanded.

"I am grandmother!" the wolf replied.

"Hello, grandmother! I love you." At this point Red was supposed to kiss grandma, but Alan just shot Olivia a distasteful look and shook his head no.

She shrugged and waved for them to continue. One by one Red introduced all of the friends and items she had come with, the appropriate items then sat on or stood near the table, and the rest prepared to leave. Until grandma/the wolf jumped up to block them.

"I want to eat you!" he roared.

The kids screamed.

Zhang Laoshi covered her mouth and looked around in alarm.

"Stop!" Red commanded.

The wolf froze.

"You do not have big ears!" Red accused.

Slowly the wolf pulled off the big ears.

"You do not have big hands!" Davy the butterfly pointed out, twirling in a circle.

The wolf pulled off the big hands.

"You do not have a big nose!" the pet monkey exclaimed, jumping.

The wolf pulled off the big nose, so all that remained was a boy in a pair of sweatpants and a T-shirt with a dump truck on the front.

"You are not a wolf!" the kids shouted. "You are a boy!"

The wolf/boy hung his head in shame. "Yes," he admitted. "I am a boy."

Just then, grandma, played by Rose, strolled in, explained that she had been at the store, but was happy to see Red and her friends. Rose darted off stage to press play on the CD player, then hurried back to perform the final dance number, as arranged by Alan. Out in the audience Zhang Laoshi was still covering her mouth, but now she looked perplexed instead of alarmed, as did most of the parents. The other students were laughing hysterically. But her class didn't give a damn. They danced their hearts out, sang gibberish at the top of their lungs, and Olivia sang along and clapped her hands, long before the applause started.

"Okay. I guess…that's it." Olivia had enjoyed a lot of alone time these past weeks, and had taken to talking to herself on occasion. She dumped the final pile of debris from the dustpan into the trash and wiped her hands on her jeans, then checked her watch for the thousandth time. Her flight to Boston left at five o'clock in the evening, and she had to catch the train at noon. It was eleven ten. Still a little early to head to the station, but there was nothing else to do. She had given away the few household items she owned, shipped a box of souvenirs for Willa to hold for her, and the apartment was now as clean and bare as the day she'd arrived.

It felt like a lifetime ago. Lazhou had been cold and dark and mysterious, and somehow it had come to feel like home. Or some semblance of home, where not everyone was a friend and not everything was perfect, a lesson she had been a little late in learning. She'd made mistakes, no doubt. Everyone did. She'd learned from them. Even Dale, with his awful, ruddy face and lewd words had come by to apologize, lingering outside the school gates the day after the graduation performance to plead his case. She'd stared at him, equal parts surprised and pissed, as he told her how Jarek had gotten drunk and spilled his guts, his heartache, their secrets. How he'd asked him to say those things to her and how he'd agreed because he'd wanted to punish her for hurting his friend. How he understood now how stupid and cruel he had been. And then he'd really surprised her by somehow managing to champion Jarek, pointing out that the guy wasn't used to feeling anything and didn't know how to process his emotions. By the time he finished, Olivia had accepted his apology and told him he was forgiven, if only to get him to go away. It would take time for the exchange in the trailer to fade, but it would happen. Soon it would be just another dark memory, and like the others, she would learn to let it go.

She went to use the bathroom one more time before leaving, and when she came out she skidded to a halt. She'd left the wooden door open to let the air circulate, and now Jarek stood outside the metal door, backlit by the sun. His expression was hard to determine in the shadows, but his voice was not. "Olivia."

She kept her voice level. "Hi."

His head shifted slightly as he looked around at the empty walls, the bare mattress visible in the background. "Can I come in?" he asked.

Her lower lip trembled and she fought to remain composed. She really hadn't expected to see him again. She'd told him her departure date a long time ago, but didn't know if he was here because he'd remembered or if it was just an unfortunate coincidence. But instead of telling him to fuck off, she said, "It's not locked." She had never tried to keep him out, she realized. For all his effort at warning her away, his certainty that he was the mythical big bad wolf, she'd seen him as the boy dressed up in scowls and glares and intimidation, and never the villain he imagined himself to be. He'd spent so long trying not to be someone else that he failed to see who he was. Who he could be. She wasn't angry so much as she was disappointed. In him. For him.

Jarek entered and stopped just inside the threshold. Olivia was several feet away, near the wall where she'd stood the night he'd apologized after the bar. A wry smile touched his lips, as though he were picturing the same thing. "So this is it," he said eventually.

She nodded, not really sure if he was referring to the end of them or her time in China. "I'm on my way to the station."

"When's your train?"

"Twelve."

He pursed his lips. "Right." He studied her two medium-sized suitcases and backpack, waiting by the door. "You don't have much to take with you."

"I know."

"Are you flying to Detroit first?"

"No. Straight to Boston."

He pulled in a breath that was deep enough she could see his chest rise under his thin T-shirt. He was wearing board shorts and flip flops as though he planned to head to the non-existent beach after this. Whatever "this" was.

"Well," she said, when he didn't speak.

"I'm sorry," he said abruptly. "I'm—" He broke off and looked away, pushing an agitated hand through his hair. "I wanted to tell you I'm really fucking sorry."

Her eyes filled with tears she refused to shed. She'd cried all freaking week. Saying good-bye to her students, the teachers, Ritchie and Honor, alone in her apartment. She couldn't possibly have any tears left.

"Okay, Jarek."

"No, Olivia. It's not okay."

"It is what it is."

He pinched the bridge of his nose. "I watched the play."

Her eyebrows lifted in surprise. "I didn't see you there."

"I know. I just…wanted to. I wasn't there long. Ritchie told me what time, so I came and then I left right after."

"Huh."

"It was really weird."

She couldn't help it; she laughed. "I know."

"You looked beautiful."

She sucked in a wounded breath. "Please don't."

He crossed to her suddenly, and raised a hand to tilt her head so she looked up at him, even though she didn't want to. "You are," he said seriously. "You're perfect. I didn't deserve you. I'm sorry I hurt you. It wasn't Dale's fault. It was all me. It doesn't matter now, but I want you to know that I didn't say anything until that last week. I wasn't betraying you all along."

She wouldn't cry. She wouldn't. Perfect meant nothing. She had been perfect her whole life, and then she'd done one thing people hadn't liked and they'd turned on her. So had he. "Okay."

"Tell me you understand."

"I understand."

"Olivia."

"I have to go, Jarek."

His hand fell and when she risked a look at him, his eyes were closed. "Sure," he said. "I'll come with you to the train station."

"You don't have to do that."

But he was already picking up the suitcases and hefting them out the door. She didn't waste her breath arguing, not sure she even wanted to. So it hurt to breathe. She'd get over it. She'd keep putting one foot in front of the other until she got where she was supposed to be, wherever that was.

Olivia collected her backpack and purse, then locked the doors and followed Jarek downstairs to flag a cab. He loaded the bags in the trunk and gestured for her to get in first, then climbed in after. She asked to go to the train station, a seven or eight minute ride, and folded her hands in her lap. She knew Jarek was watching her but she didn't know what she was supposed to say. *I forgive you?* She would, some day, she was sure. But not right now. Not when he'd found the courage to show up and apologize three weeks too late, then failed to muster the nerve to say the thing that scared him most.

"You nervous?" he asked eventually. "About starting over?"

She shrugged. "It'll be okay. At least I speak the language." It was a weak joke, but he smiled anyway.

They got to the station and he paid the fare, even when she told him not to. He grabbed her bags from the trunk and carried them through the milling crowd to the boarding area. "You going to be all right with these?"

"They're not heavy." She looked at the large clock on the wall. Twenty minutes until her train departed. "I have to go."

"I know."

"Take care, Jarek."

A muscle in his neck twitched, then suddenly he pulled her against him, his arms like steel bands around her torso, holding her tight. She could barely breathe, barely manage to lift her arms to hug him back, her fingers brushing the soft fabric of his T-shirt.

"Olivia."

Her eyes sank shut. She was suddenly so, so tired. She didn't know if she was coming or going, beginning or ending. "Just say it," she said softly.

His grip tightened. "Don't say it back."

She didn't answer, just watched the narrow hand on the clock tick past ten agonizing seconds.

"I love you, Olivia," he murmured into her hair. That was all he said. Maybe all he could say. Five more seconds passed before he released her.

She stepped back and wiped her eyes. "Good-bye, Jarek." She gathered her bags and walked away, showing her ticket to the gate attendant and following the crowd to the platform. She didn't look over her shoulder to see if Jarek was watching, didn't want to extend their painful good-bye to epic proportions. She loved him, she hated him, she loved him. And if he didn't know by now, he never would.

Chapter Seventeen

The three weeks between breaking up and saying good-bye at the train station were the longest of his life. Jarek worked non-stop, willing time to speed up and his mind to stay empty, but neither happened. He thought about her constantly, as he had for months. Only now, instead of seeing smiling Olivia, or rather, naked, smiling Olivia, he saw her in profile. He saw her hair splayed on the pillow beneath her head, face twisted away as she uttered the only words he deserved: get out.

He'd listened. He'd gone home and gone to work and hadn't done much more than eat, drink, and sleep when he wasn't in the carpentry trailer. He made more furniture than he'd ever made in his life. Desks with intricate inlaid designs, chairs with backs carved to resemble the woodwork he saw on temples around town. He took precise measurements for built-in bookshelves, spending hours getting every cut just right. Everything was perfect. And it was all wrong.

No matter what he did he couldn't stop thinking about her. About it. What he'd done. And the worst part was, he'd done far worse shit in his life—a thousand times—and he'd never felt bad. A man didn't walk into those rooms and do the things he had done without being absolutely certain he was right. He'd never questioned his decisions or his tactics, and when he got the answers he was looking for, he didn't question those either. He followed his instincts and they had never led him astray. Until now. Now he couldn't stop asking the one question he had never allowed himself: what if he was wrong?

The answer wasn't reassuring. He knew, without a doubt, that he'd been wrong. Oh, she'd been in Thailand with Chris, all right. And yes, she'd lied about it. And yes, he'd been hurt and furious and right to feel that way—but none of that mattered. He'd been wrong, and he had so little experience with apologies—hell, most of that experience was with her—that he didn't know what to do to repair such a monumental fuck up. So he poured everything he had into the furniture, into making something good and lasting that he'd leave behind and have no opportunity to destroy. And it still wasn't enough.

He worked through the night again, collapsing in bed shortly after five a.m., as had become his routine. As sleep claimed him he knew it was the last time he'd wake up and know he could still try to fix this, that she was just twenty minutes away. Because try as he might to forget, he couldn't: Olivia was leaving today. And if there was any sort of merciful god looking down on him, they'd let him sleep for twelve hours, until she was out of reach and he finally had a decent excuse for not walking his ass down there and telling her what she needed to hear.

If there was anyone looking down that day, they showed him no mercy. Jarek woke up at nine a.m. and could not fall back asleep. He contemplated the bottle of scotch that still sat on the counter where he'd left it three weeks ago, but even his muddled brain knew it was too early. Or too late. He should have started drinking at midnight, when it was socially acceptable.

He lay in bed and tried to drift off, but he couldn't. He went to the gym trailer and punched the sandbag until he couldn't breathe. He took the longest shower of his life. He tried to read. Watch TV. Tried to sleep again. And somehow it was only eleven o'clock. He remembered that her flight was in the late afternoon, but had no idea when she'd leave for the train station, so he dressed slowly, forced down some food, and at eleven thirty started the painfully slow slog to her apartment.

Her inner door was open so he could see the bare expanse inside, suitcases packed and ready to go. Then she'd stepped out of the bathroom and everything he thought he wanted to say fled his mind and his heart stopped beating and the only thing he knew was he loved her and he was sorry and it couldn't be the end, even when it was.

He certainly hadn't planned on taking her to the train station, but she was already so distant that he felt the ridiculous urge to extend their technical closeness as long as he could. Then, when she told him to take care, he grabbed her without a second thought. He wanted to hold her there until the train left, until by pure osmosis she absorbed the fact that he loved her and was pathetically sorry, but she wasn't a science experiment or a mind reader. When she ordered him to "just say it," he didn't pretend not to know which words she was referring to. If he thought it took everything he had to utter the three most painful words of his life, he was wrong again. Letting her go and watching her leave almost brought him to his knees. He stayed in place, people ebbing and flowing around him, garnering more strange stares than normal, until the train left. And for ten minutes beyond that, until he knew she hadn't changed her mind and stayed on the platform as the train rolled away.

She was gone.

He turned and began the walk home, aimless. He could go to work, sure. There was still lots to do. And technically, he was supposed to be working. But that didn't seem important. Somehow his days had become structured around Olivia—when he would see her, what they would do, what she would say—and now that she was gone, he felt…free. In the most terrible way. For the first time in his life, he didn't want to be alone.

When the phone in his pocket rang, he fumbled for it frantically, almost falling off the curb. He yanked the phone loose, praying it was Olivia calling to say he was forgiven. That she'd come back. But it wasn't her name on the display, it was Jonah's. And even before he answered he knew what his brother would say. Olivia wasn't the only person he had lost today.

The ensuing conversation was even more predictable: No, Jarek wouldn't come home early. No, he wouldn't be there for the funeral. Yes, he would chip in for the costs. Yes, he was a terrible son and brother and human being. No, he didn't care. Yes, he did.

He wiled away the next two weeks with slightly less fervor. Jonah told Brant about Aidan's passing and the three friends he hadn't really wanted kept him company when he wasn't working or sleeping.

They didn't ask about Olivia, though Dale had no doubt relayed the whole miserable saga. Ritchie tentatively revealed that he planned to stay in Lazhou past the project deadline, just to see where things with Honor might go, and Jarek tried not to be jealous, another emotion he had never really known before coming to this godforsaken place. He was feeling a lot of things now, when he'd rather feel nothing, but that no longer seemed like an option.

They'd been back in Virginia for a week. Reverse culture shock and jet lag had worn off, and yet, for some reason, Dale lingered. Jarek, Brant, Jonah, and Dale sat in a booth in the corner of a local pub, eating a late lunch that consisted entirely of deep fried food and alcohol. Jarek thought he had given up the habit of asking questions that were none of his business, but the longer Dale's story about his daughter's piano recital wore on, the less he could take it. "Dude," he interrupted. "Why are you still here?"

Dale broke off and stared at him blankly. "I'm waiting on my refill."

"In *Virginia*. Why aren't you in South Carolina with your family?" The atmosphere at the table shifted, turning at once from relaxed and carefree to vaguely uncomfortable. It was one of the few occasions where Jarek was the one without answers, but even before Dale spoke, he knew.

"She kicked me out, man." His beefy, crude friend used a French fry to draw a circle in the ketchup on his plate. "Last year."

Jarek sighed. "Fuck. Sorry."

"You didn't know."

No, he hadn't known. If he'd spent a single second thinking about it, he might have come to the same conclusion. The way Dale spoke so reverently about his kids, the picture of his family that had prime placement in his wallet. The lewd stories about the mysterious women he banged in China, none of whom Jarek had ever actually seen, all just overcompensation for his own broken heart. The old Jarek would have kicked himself for not recognizing it sooner, but now he just felt…bad. He felt bad for his friend. And then he felt even worse when he realized he'd just admitted that Dale, of all people, was his friend. How had this happened?

"Is that why you're always prying into my life?"

Dale shrugged. "Maybe."

He eyeballed Brant. "What's your excuse?"

"Dale made me?"

"Ass." Dale jammed an elbow into his friend's gut, and though Brant was a big guy, he winced. Jarek was grateful he'd taken the seat next to his brother.

"Is this topic on the table then?" Jonah asked, sensing a moment of weakness. "Olivia?"

"No," Jarek interrupted, at the same moment Brant and Dale said, "Yes," much louder. "No," he repeated.

"Are you going to call her?" Dale inquired, ignoring his refusal.

Jarek gritted his teeth. "I don't have her number."

Brant scratched his jaw. "I do."

"What? Why would you have it?"

"She gave it to Ritchie, and he gave it to me. Just in case."

"In case what?"

"In case I decided to call her," Brant drawled, rolling his eyes. "In case you ever pulled your head out of your ass, idiot."

Jarek tried to take an extremely long time finishing his beer, but the other men just waited. They may be the only friends he had, but he didn't like them. "She hates me," he said finally.

"Yeah," Dale said.

Brant nodded.

"You should call her," Jonah suggested.

Jarek twisted in the booth to look at him. "Did you not hear what I just said?"

His brother couldn't have cared less. "No one said it was easy, man."

"What would you know? You've been married your whole life."

"That's exactly why I know, moron. You think I let Katrine walk away every time she gets mad? Or that she lets me?"

"You two don't fight."

"Everybody fights."

Jarek stared between the men at the table. They all nodded sagely. He wasn't overreacting to this. He wasn't. He'd done a terrible thing. She'd left him. Sure, she'd always been scheduled to leave on that day, but the timing wasn't a coincidence. Except, now that he thought about it…She hadn't looked at him with hate at the train station. There'd been something else in her eyes, too. Not love. Not sadness. But maybe…pity. Something he could work toward fixing.

He ran a hand through his too-long hair and blew out a breath. "What do I do?"

Brant slid a scrap of paper across the table, ten digits written in remarkably neat handwriting. "Call her," he said.

It wasn't easy to overcome a lifetime of avoidance. Though he had her number safely stowed in his wallet, it took Jarek four weeks to pick up the phone.

The week after the conversation in the bar, Jonah had convinced him to go to the cemetery where Aidan's ashes were buried, and Jarek had reluctantly agreed, if only to appease his brother. He stood looking down at the tiny, flat plaque in the grass, the predictable names and dates carved in block letters. He wasn't entirely sure what Jonah had wanted him to feel, but he was pretty sure he was supposed to feel *something*. Instead he felt nothing. None of the anger that had consumed him when he thought of his father. None of the resentment. Somehow that angry void in his life had filled itself up with friends he hadn't wanted, and a girlfriend he wasn't looking for. A hobby that had turned into genuine passion, and a brother who didn't give up on him, no matter how tempting he made it. He wasn't his father. He wasn't the result of an aptitude test. His faults were his own, but so were whatever positive qualities he happened to possess. The ones Olivia had seen.

Now he sat on the edge of his bed in the room above Jonah's garage. The bed was draped in a unicorn-patterned comforter, a hand-me-down from his nieces, and the small window was covered with pink blinds. Katrine's collection of mystery novels—including every Nancy Drew and Hardy Boys book ever written—gathered dust on a shelf lined with paper flowers. He had never stayed in Virginia long enough to warrant getting his own place, but he knew he couldn't stay here much longer. Jonah had failed to mention he'd joined a band and kept his drum kit in the garage, practicing daily. Katrine was lovely and gracious, but it was hard to look at her without feeling envious. Oh, there had been plenty of times in his life when he'd wished there was a woman around, but he'd never imagined them staying long term. And now he thought about nothing else.

There was a pounding on the door and he jumped. "Did you call yet?" Dale shouted through the wood.

Jarek took a deep breath. The three of them were on the other side, ears undoubtedly pressed to the door, trying to eavesdrop. They'd pleaded with him to let them be in the room while he made the call, but he'd flatly refused. He'd even lied and told them he'd already done it, but they hadn't believed him. Then he said he was going to do it tomorrow, and they'd looked him over doubtfully and declared him a liar, which he was. He was sick with nerves and had to get this over with. He felt like a fourteen-year-old boy calling the most popular girl in school and asking her on a date. Which, with the exception of their ages, summed things up pretty accurately.

His fingers were cold as he punched in the numbers, praying they were wrong. Or that the phone would ring and ring and she'd never pick up. And she didn't have voice mail.

"Hello?"

The phone slipped from his hand and bounced on the mattress, landing on a mane of rainbow-colored hair. He cursed under his breath and snatched it up.

"Hello?" she said again. The sound of her voice coursed through him, making his heart pound. The last time he heard it she had been saying good-bye.

"Olivia?" he managed. Now that she'd answered, he didn't want her to hang up. He also didn't want to be one of those creepy mouth breathers that called single women when they were home alone. At least he hoped she was alone.

The pause extended so long he thought she might have hung up. Or fainted. But then came a startled, "Jarek?"

"Yeah. Hi."

A shorter pause. "Hi."

His muscles turned to liquid and he lay down on the bed. He'd been in some truly terrifying situations over the course of his life. He could count on both hands the number of times he thought he wouldn't make it out of some scenario alive. But he couldn't remember ever being this scared. "How are you?" he forced himself to inquire.

"I'm…good," she answered. Purposely avoiding the F-word. "How are you?"

"I'm okay."

"Um…where are you?"

"Virginia. My brother's place."

"Oh."

Was he crazy, or was there a note of disappointment in her voice? Like maybe she was hoping he'd say he was standing on her front lawn with a thousand roses, the way Brant had suggested?

"How are you settling in?" he asked eventually.

"Good," she said. "It's nice here. Summer school keeps me busy."

"Right. Of course."

"What are you up to?"

"Not much. Avoiding Dale, mostly."

A thump on the door. "Hey!"

Olivia laughed, hearing the indignant cry. "Still unsuccessful."

Jarek smiled. The muscles around his mouth hurt, as though he hadn't used them in forever. "Yeah." He couldn't get a read on her. Couldn't tell if she was happy to hear from him or completely indifferent.

"Well," she said, when the silence stretched on. "I should probably go."

"What are you doing on Saturday?" he blurted out.

More silence. "Saturday?"

"Yeah. This Saturday. Do you want to go on a picnic?" The picnic had been Jonah's idea. Katrine had seconded it, and since she willingly chose life with a McLean brother, he'd gone with it, even if it sounded fucking stupid when he said it out loud.

"A picnic." She sounded baffled. "Where?"

Oh God. Of course she would ask that. They were five hundred miles apart, for Christ's sake. "I'll come to you," he said. "On Saturday."

She was going to say no. Who went on picnics anymore? She probably had a million better things to do. But she surprised him again when she asked, "What time?"

Relief had him sagging into the mattress. "One o'clock." The guys had told him what to say, but he'd forgotten everything but the most basic details. Picnic. Saturday. One.

"Okay," she said.

Olivia disconnected and stared at the phone in her hand as though it had magically materialized there. Had that just happened? Had Jarek McLean really just called and asked her on a date? And had she accepted?

She slumped into one of the mismatched chairs at her kitchen table and looked around the room, trying to decide if she was dreaming. Her tiny rented house looked normal. Tidy, cozy, a hodgepodge of furniture and finds she'd scoured from summer yard sales and secondhand stores.

She was starting over. Again. Exchanging one life for another, hoping for something better. Unlike the breakup with Chris, she hadn't kept her phone close by, hoping Jarek would call. He didn't have her new number, and even though he'd had the old one, he'd never used it. So it had come as the shock of her life when she picked up the phone ten minutes ago and heard his voice.

This time it was different. She'd been so alone when she met Jarek in Lazhou, desperate for company. But there was a difference, she knew now, between being lonely and being alone. When she saw him, it would be because she wanted to, not because he was better than the alternative. She had changed. She was stronger, less naïve. She had chosen not to carry the weight of her resentment with her, and she had forgiven Chris, and her parents, and even Dale.

It was too easy to cling to hurt feelings and bitter grudges, to let insecurity fester. Every day she urged her kids to be brave, to raise their hands and try again. She taught them not to hide from their mistakes but to grow from them, and now she would follow her own advice. On Saturday she would meet Jarek with no expectations. If she had learned anything over the past year and a half, it was that life wasn't easy, but it wasn't impossible, either. It was a work in progress, and she was ready.

It was nowhere near as easy as the movies made it look, Jarek thought, shuffling up her short driveway three days later. He had the ridiculous-looking picnic basket in one hand and flowers in the other. He'd watched those corny romantic comedies with her, scoffing at Richard Gere climbing the fire escape to woo Julia Roberts, and Colin Firth running through the streets of Portugal with his poorly translated speech, but he hadn't given them nearly enough credit. This shit was *hard*.

He stepped onto the front porch and set down the basket to ring the bell, wiping damp hands on his shorts. Jonah had tried to convince him to wear a suit and tie to show Olivia he was serious, but Katrine had intervened and told him to wear whatever he wanted. He wouldn't pretend to be someone he wasn't; if Olivia still loved him, it would be for who he was.

The door opened, and there she stood, three feet away and utterly perfect. He couldn't speak as he took her in, couldn't believe he'd lasted six weeks without her. And he thanked God he hadn't worn a fucking suit, as Jonah had suggested. She wore white shorts and a green tank top, her blond hair hanging loose and straight down her back. Her feet were bare and she wore no makeup or jewelry. She wasn't pretending either, but then again, she never had.

"Hey," he said.

"Hey."

He thrust the flowers at her. "These are for you."

She stared at the small bouquet, bemused. "Thank you." She took them from his iron grip, her fingers brushing his. "Come in. I'll put them in water."

He stepped into the doorway but went no farther, watching her mile-long legs stride down a short hall and round the corner. After a second he heard water running, then she returned empty-handed.

"This is it," she said, gesturing to the small living room. It was filled with poorly made furniture that made his fingers twitch. "Do you want a tour?"

Oh, yes, he wanted a tour. He wanted to come inside and lock the door and never come out again. But he couldn't do that; his friends had made him promise. No matter his desperate urges, this was a first date, and he had to keep his hands to himself. Be a gentleman, whatever the hell that meant.

"Another time," he said, without thinking. The surprised look on her face made him hear the words for what they were, the admitted hope that there would, in fact, be another time.

She stepped into a pair of Birkenstocks and tucked her hair behind her ears. "Are you ready to go? Should I bring anything?"

"No, I've got it." Actually, he wasn't sure what he had, because Brant and Dale and Katrine had gone shopping for this excursion, not trusting him not to screw it up. And he'd let them, because he didn't know what the hell people brought on picnics, because he'd never been on one. His assignment had been to look up Olivia's address online and find a nearby park. Now they strode down the street side-by-side, not touching. The sun was bright, but a light breeze kept it from being unpleasantly hot.

"Do you know where you're going?" she asked after a block.

"Yeah. There's a place up ahead on the right. Charleston Park. Do you know it?"

"I know it."

Another couple blocks.

"Did you get the job finished?" she inquired. "The travel office?"

"Oh. Yeah. They were happy with it. Glad to be done."

"That's good."

They reached the edge of the park and climbed the grassy hill, passing a small playground and several people laid out on towels, reading or sunbathing. Jarek chose a private spot under a tall oak tree, the leafy branches providing much-needed shade, and set down the basket, flexing his fingers. He prayed for mercy as he pulled back the lid, finding a blanket folded on top and spreading it on the grass.

Olivia sat down and he sat beside her, catching a whiff of apples when she pulled her hair over the opposite shoulder to keep it out of her face. "I have no idea what's in here," Jarek admitted, tugging cloth napkins from the basket. "I didn't pack it."

"No? Who did?"

"Dale. Brant. Katrine."

"You didn't look inside?"

"They told me I wouldn't be able to repack it properly if I did. So I might not know what everything is. And it might be disgusting." He pulled out a jar of red pepper jelly, which he'd never heard of, and a baguette wrapped in wax paper. Good. He knew what to do with bread. There was a wedge of brie, which he set between them, and a round of cheese that smelled rancid.

Olivia made a face.

"I think this might be expired," he said, tossing it over his shoulder where it hit the tree and rolled away.

She smiled. "Good call."

She helped him unpack the rest, chicken and fruit and warm iced tea. He tried to keep his eyes on the task, but it was impossible not to let his gaze skate down the exposed length of her tan legs, the tempting curve of her breasts in the fitted tank top.

"You look nice," he said.

She glanced at him. "Thank you."

"I was supposed to say that when you opened the door, but I forgot."

"Do you have a script?"

He smiled wryly. "I'm no good at remembering lines when you're around."

"Ah."

They made open-face sandwiches and ate without speaking.

"I was surprised to hear from you," Olivia said.

Something in his chest clenched. "I'm terrible on the phone."

"So you say. But here we are."

"You're my first date in a really long time."

She nodded but didn't say anything, and the tightness around his heart increased.

"Are you seeing someone?" he asked, fingers closing around the blanket as his old instincts kicked in.

She hesitated, then shook her head. "No."

"But?" He forced his hand to relax.

"But Willa set me up with her friend. A banker."

"You didn't go?"

"We went out twice."

"And he was an asshole?"

"Oh, he was wonderful. Tall, handsome, funny."

He rubbed his brow. "Jesus."

"But."

"But he was a thief?"

She laughed. "I guess I wasn't ready."

"Why not?"

She looked at him from under her lashes. "Why do you think?"

"Because you have too many scars from your last relationship?"

Her lips curved. "No scars."

"Then what?"

"You're asking too many questions, Jarek. Why don't you tell me what you've been up to since getting back?"

He would much rather continue the original line of questioning, but knew when to back off. He ate another piece of chicken before answering. "Not much. Hanging out with my brother's family. Brant and Dale. Nothing special."

"Uh-huh. Have you…met anybody?"

"Women?"

"Yes."

"No, Olivia."

"Why not?"

"You want me to say it?"

"If it's true."

He could say it. He'd been practicing in the car the whole way over. Nine hours of lame ass recitations. He could do this. "There hasn't been anyone else since I met you. I don't want any other women because I'm in love with you." He stared out over the park, the horizon visible from their perch on the hill.

"Huh," she said.

He shot her a look. "What?"

"Who are you talking to?"

"What?"

"I'm sitting right here, not off in the distance somewhere."

His lips twitched. "Well. That's true." This is what he'd wanted, wasn't it? For her to be sitting beside him. And yet for some reason it was so hard to look at her and tell her the truth. But he didn't want to be a coward anymore. She wasn't a bad person. She wouldn't have agreed to come on this picnic if she hated him. And she wouldn't be telling him to confess his feelings if she didn't want to hear them. She wasn't going to hurt him. He trusted her. Jarek looked her square in the face and she stared back, those blue eyes waiting patiently. She could wait forever, if she felt like it. He never should have dated a kindergarten teacher. "I love you, Olivia."

He saw the lines of her body relax; he hadn't realized how tense she was. That she'd truly doubted his ability to say the words. "And I'm still really sorry," he added. "For before." He couldn't look at her anymore, it was getting weird. He flicked a bread crumb off the blanket.

"I'm sorry I lied to you about Chris."

He glanced up in surprise. Of all the things she could have said, he'd never expected that. "Yeah," he said. "Well. I'm not exactly the easiest person to confess to. And it's nothing compared to what I did."

"It still wasn't good."

"It's forgiven."

"Really? Just like that?"

He shrugged. It was true. If she said nothing had happened in Thailand, then nothing had happened. "Just like that."

"Well," she said. "I forgive you too."

His heart stuttered. "You do?"

"Why else would I be here?"

"The free food?"

"Hmm. Speaking of which, I notice there are no green peppers in here."

He flushed, caught. "That was my one non-contribution to the basket."

"It's nice of you to remember."

He remembered everything about her. He couldn't—wouldn't—forget, no matter what happened between them.

"I love you, Jarek," she said quietly. "In case you didn't know."

He was watching her feet, the pink painted toes that had tempted him so painfully the first night he'd visited her apartment. The time he'd kissed her, so rock hard he thought he might die. He leaned over now and kissed her again, this time without warning or plea for forgiveness. He didn't hold her in place, either, keeping his hands braced on the blanket behind him, angling his body to press his lips against hers, feeling their perfect softness against his.

She was similarly positioned but he was taller, and her shoulder pressed into his chest, preventing him from getting the contact he craved. But this was their first date, he remembered belatedly, and Jonah had told him that first base was the furthest he could go. He hated his brother sometimes, but he pulled away.

"Where do you go after this?" she asked, watching his mouth, eyes glazed. He loved seeing that look on her face, loved being the one who put it there.

"Back to the hotel," he said promptly.

She blinked. "What?"

"I—" He cut himself off. "You didn't mean right after this date. You meant in general."

"Yeah." She smiled faintly. "In general."

"I've got to get my own place," he answered, chewing on a grape to discourage himself from kissing her again. "Jonah plays the drums now."

Olivia burst out laughing, holding her plastic cup of warm tea over the grass so it didn't spill on the blanket. "Wow."

"He's awful."

"Where?"

"Where…?"

"Where will this new place be? Close to Jonah?"

"Definitely not too close," he said firmly.

"Ah." She sipped her drink and he watched her carefully, trying to gauge her response.

"I could go anywhere," he said cautiously. "Get a place with a garage, build furniture. Hang around."

She looked at him from the corner of her eye. "Uh-huh."

"It could be…here."

She just waited.

"If that wouldn't freak you out."

She bit her lip. "I've got some pretty terrible furniture."

"The worst," he agreed.

She tried to hide a smile. "It wouldn't freak me out if you were here." She copied him and popped a grape into her mouth, and he saw that the white line on the base of her ring finger was no longer visible. Time had reclaimed the small reminder of her old life with a man she had chosen not to take back. Olivia was perfectly capable of making her own decisions, and here she was.

"Say it again," he said.

Her lips formed an O of surprise and she swallowed the grape. "You sure?"

"Yeah."

She looked him in the eye. "I love you, Jarek," she said. He held her gaze as long as he could, shuddering as the words sank in. They eased past the debris of the crumbling walls he'd built and landed at the only unbelievable, unquestionable conclusion: it was true.

Acknowledgments

There are so many people involved in the success of a book, and I'm truly thankful to everyone who plays a part in this journey. From acquiring, editing, designing, promoting, reading, and reviewing—I owe an enormous debt of gratitude to all those who give their time and energy to sharing this story.

To the wonderful women at Omnific whose vision make this possible—thank you! To Jennifer Haren and her endless positivity—thank you! To Milli Davis, my first Going the Distance cheerleader—thank you!

And to the staff and students at the Changzhou kindergarten I was so lucky to work at for a year and a half—xie xie. Thank you for reminding me every day that I have so much more to learn than I could ever teach. You inspire me still.

About the Author

Julianna Keyes is a Canadian writer who has lived on both coasts and several places in between. She's been skydiving, bungee jumping and white water rafting, but nothing thrills—or terrifies—her as much as the blank page. She loves Chinese food, foreign languages, baseball and television, though not necessarily in that order. She writes sizzling stories with strong characters, plenty of conflict, and lots of making up. This is her second novel.

New Adult Romance

Three Daves by Nicki Elson
Streamline by Jennifer Lane
The Shades series: *Shades of Atlantis* & *Shades of Avalon* by Carol Oates
The Heart series: *Beside Your Heart, Disclosure of the Heart* & *Forever Your Heart*
by Mary Whitney
Romancing the Bookworm by Kate Evangelista
Flirting with Chaos by Kenya Wright
The Vice, Virtue & Video series: *Revealed, Captured, Desired* & *Devoted*
by Bianca Giovanni
Granton University series: *Loving Lies* by Linda Kage

Paranormal Romance

The Light series: *Seers of Light, Whisper of Light* & *Circle of Light* by Jennifer DeLucy
The Hanaford Park series: *Eve of Samhain* & *Pleasures Untold* by Lisa Sanchez
Immortal Awakening by KC Randall
The Seraphim series: *Crushed Seraphim* & *Bittersweet Seraphim* by Debra Anastasia
The Guardian's Wild Child by Feather Stone
Grave Refrain by Sarah M. Glover
The Divinity series: *Divinity* & *Entity* by Patricia Leever
The Blood Vine series: *Blood Vine, Blood Entangled* & *Blood Reunited*
by Amber Belldene
Divine Temptation by Nicki Elson
The Dead Rapture series: *Love in the Time of the Dead* & *Love at the End of Days*
by Tera Shanley
The Hidden Races series: *Incandescent* (book 1) by M.V. Freeman
Something Wicked by Carol Oates

Romantic Suspense

Whirlwind by Robin DeJarnett
The CONduct series: *With Good Behavior, Bad Behavior* & *On Best Behavior*
by Jennifer Lane
Indivisible by Jessica McQuinn
Between the Lies by Alison Oburia
Blind Man's Bargain by Tracy Winegar

Erotic Romance

The Keyhole series: *Becoming sage* (book 1) by Kasi Alexander
The Keyhole series: *Saving sunni* (book 2) by Kasi & Reggie Alexander
The Winemaker's Dinner: *Appetizers* & *Entrée* by Dr. Ivan Rusilko & Everly Drummond
The Winemaker's Dinner: *Dessert* by Dr. Ivan Rusilko
Client Nº 5 by Joy Fulcher

Historical Romance

Cat O' Nine Tails by Patricia Leever
Burning Embers by Hannah Fielding
Seven for a Secret by Rumer Haven

Anthologies

A Valentine Anthology including short stories by
Alice Clayton ("With a Double Oven"),
Jennifer DeLucy ("Magnus of Pfelt, Conquering Viking Lord"),
Nicki Elson ("I Don't Do Valentine's Day"),
Jessica McQuinn ("Better Than One Dead Rose and a Monkey Card"),
Victoria Michaels ("Home to Jackson"), and
Alison Oburia ("The Bridge")

Taking Liberties including an introduction by Tiffany Reisz and short stories by
Mina Vaughn ("John Hancock-Blocked"),
Linda Cunningham ("A Boston Marriage"),
Joy Fulcher ("Tea for Two"),
KC Holly ("The British Are Coming!"),
Kimberly Jensen & Scott Stark ("E. Pluribus Threesome"), and
Vivian Rider ("M'Lady's Secret Service")

Sets

The Heart Series Box Set (*Beside Your Heart, Disclosure of the Heart* &
Forever Your Heart) by Mary Whitney
The CONduct Series Box Set (*With Good Behavior, Bad Behavior* &
On Best Behavior) by Jennifer Lane
The Light Series Box Set (*Seers of Light, Whisper of Light, Circle of Light* &
Glimpse of Light) by Jennifer DeLucy
The Blood Vine Series Box Set (*Blood Vine, Blood Entangled, Blood Reunited* &
Blood Eternal) by Amber Belldene

Singles, Novellas & Special Editions

It's Only Kinky the First Time (A Keyhole series single) by Kasi Alexander
Learning the Ropes (A Keyhole series single) by Kasi & Reggie Alexander
The Winemaker's Dinner: RSVP by Dr. Ivan Rusilko
The Winemaker's Dinner: No Reservations by Everly Drummond
Big Guns by Jessica McQuinn
Concessions by Robin DeJarnett
Starstruck by Lisa Sanchez
New Flame by BJ Thornton

Shackled by Debra Anastasia
Swim Recruit by Jennifer Lane
Sway by Nicki Elson
Full Speed Ahead by Susan Kaye Quinn
The Second Sunrise by Hannah Downing
The Summer Prince by Carol Oates
Whatever it Takes by Sarah M. Glover
Clarity (A *Divinity* prequel single) by Patricia Leever
A Christmas Wish (A *Cocktails & Dreams* single) by Autumn Markus
Late Night with Andres by Debra Anastasia
Poughkeepsie (enhanced iPad app collector's edition) by Debra Anastasia
Poughkeepsie (audio book edition) by Debra Anastasia
Blood Eternal (A Blood Vine series single, epilogue to series) by Amber Belldene
Carnaval de Amor (*The Winemaker's Dinner*, Spanish edition)
by Dr. Ivan Rusilko & Everly Drummond

coming soon from
OMNIFIC PUBLISHING

The Enclave series: *Closer and Closer* (book 1) by Jenna Barton
The Dead Rapture series: *Love Starts with Z* (book 3) by Tera Shanley
The Hidden Races series: *Illumination* (book 2) by M.V. Freeman
Missing Pieces by Meredith Tate